Her writing is sharp and exquisite.

— JULIA QUINN, AUTHOR OF THE
BRIDGERTON SERIES

An insatiable rake falls for an eccentric genius. Too bad she's his innocent bride, and he has vowed never to touch her.

Harriet "Harry" Lovelock lives a life of the mind, and she *knows* she can prove a theorem that has baffled male mathematicians for two centuries. But her stepmother wants her married and the swirl of the Season saps Harry's energy and distracts her from her work. She has to put an end to the tedium of balls. Now. Full stop.

Thomas Drake, the Earl Drake, devotes himself to the pleasures of the flesh, even as he wrestles with his own demons and intractable problems. He needs to marry wealth, but could he ever be satisfied by just one woman?

She can spend all her time on her proof. He can have any woman he wants, except her. **Their marriage of convenience could prove to be the perfect partnership—as long as love never enters the equation.**

Convergence of Desire is book one of the steamy Regency romance series *The Lovelocks of London* from author Felicity

Niven. However, it can be enjoyed as a stand-alone book. It has a happily-ever-after ending, a marriage of convenience, a slow burn, a neurodivergent heroine, and no cliffhanger.

Content warnings: steamy sexual material, coarse language, physical and sexual assault, consensual non-monogamy.

Convergence of Desire

Convergence of Desire

The Lovelocks of London

Book One

Felicity Niven

Publisher: Bletherskite Books, PO Box 450824, Atlanta, GA 31145

ISBN: 978-1-958917-01-5

Edited by Grace Bradley, gracebradleyediting.com

Cover Design by James, GoOnWrite.com

Dedicated to Sophie Germain,
1776–1831.

Contents

ONE

"Harry!"

In the room she called her own, the one she had begged her father for when he had built this house, the pale young woman muttered to herself and dipped her quill pen in the inkpot and bent over her paper. Much like the woman, the room was tall and narrow. And rather odd. It was wedged in among the extra bedchambers, with one door and one window. There was one key to the lock on the door, a key which she wore on a chain around her neck. No other people—not her sisters, not her stepmother, and certainly no maids—were ever allowed into the room. Years ago, when she was very young, from time to time her father would ask permission to enter *her room*. He would sit at the far end, in the one chair at the one table in front of the one window, and look at her scratchings on the papers.

"It's the calculus, Papa. Do you see how clever it is?"

He would sigh and rub his eyes behind his glasses and smile.

"I see how clever *you* are, my darling girl. It's far beyond the mind of this old banker. I have spent too much of my life

thinking in shillings and pounds to start now thinking in—
what did you call it?—the calculus."

And then he would stand and pat the top of her head
lightly and tell her to be sure to obey her stepmother and to be
a good, agreeable girl.

"Harry!"

The young woman muttered to herself more loudly,
dipping her pen with increasing ferocity into her inkpot, splat-
tering ink onto the wrist of her sleeve, filling her paper with
symbols. She had a new lemma, or sub-theorem, in mind to
send to Dean Haddington of Cambridge. It might be a fresh
start on the conjecture. The idea held a great deal of promise
—if she could just get it down on paper.

Then the banging on the door started.

"Harriet Lovelock, you come out of there this instant!"

Mrs. Catherine Lovelock, *née* Catherine Cooke of the London
stage, originally Kate Cooksey of the West Midlands, stood in
the hallway, fuming. She still dressed in the lavender of half
mourning, even though her beloved had died over four years
ago, and now one of her tiny lavender boots peeped out from
under her lavender skirt as she kicked the door while she
rapped with her knuckles.

She took a deep breath, filled her lungs, and used the voice
that had reached the back row of the Theatre-Royal, Drury
Lane.

"HARRIET-YOU-COME-OUT-THIS-INST—"

The door suddenly opened and Mrs. Lovelock, using all
the skills of balance and grace she could muster, kept herself
from falling forward despite having put a great deal of vigor
behind each of her raps and kicks on the door.

Her ungainly stepdaughter stood in the doorway, her
light-brown hair wild with tendrils, ink smudge on her face.

"I do my best but since an 'instant' is an infinitesimal amount of time, no matter how fast I go, I can't possibly come to the door in an 'instant.'" Harriet, or Harry, as she was better known to her family, frowned as she stepped out of the room and turned and locked the door behind her. "On the other hand, it *is* very satisfying to know that I disprove Zeno's paradox every time I cross *my room* to open the door." Harry put her chain with the key on it back around her neck.

Catherine looked up at her stepdaughter's hazel eyes, sure she must be making fun of her, but, as always, Harry was in dead earnest. Catherine's fury melted into anxiety. Oh, what was she going to do with this peculiar beanstalk of a girl? Catherine stood on her tiptoes and started scrubbing at the ink blotch on Harry's face with her lavender handkerchief.

"Harry, Harry, Harry," she scolded. "You have to get dressed for Lady Huxley's ball. Your hair is a fright, and your face has more ink on it than a newspaper. Didn't you notice the time?"

Harry took the handkerchief from her stepmother and took over scrubbing at her cheek with it with one hand, while absently patting her hair with the other. "I noticed it was getting darker, which made me think about the spinning of the globe and why we don't get flung off into space as the Earth turns. And when I couldn't see anymore, I lit a candle."

"Did you blow out the candle?"

"Yes," Harry scoffed. She looked down at the once delicately tinted handkerchief. "I'm afraid this is now quite ruined." She handed the ink-smeared handkerchief back to her stepmother. "No. I don't know. Let me—" She quickly opened the door with her key and darted into the room. "No, no, Mama Katie, I didn't snuff the candle in *my room*." She reappeared and locked the door again. "But now I have."

Catherine took her stepdaughter by the elbow—and what an exceedingly bony elbow it was, did the girl never eat?—and bustled Harry down the hallway and the winding staircase to her bedchamber, where Harry's lady's maid Smythe stood waiting. There would be time tomorrow for remonstrances about the dangers of using candles in *her room* where no one could check them. But now, time was short. She reminded herself that she mustn't mention *that* as time was one of Harry's hobbyhorses and could lead to a disquisition on the structure and meaning of time and, yes, there was no time for that.

"We shan't have ti—" Catherine caught herself and started again, more loudly and firmly. "We shan't have a bath. But we must get your face very clean since you won't wear powder. It is good that your hair curls on its own as the tongs have not been heated. And have you eaten anything today? I've had Smythe lay out your green gown but now that I see it, I am thinking it should be one of your white gowns? You've become much too sallow for the green. Arabella is in white, too, so you will be a pair. If only you would wear a bit of rouge . . . and I want to see you smile at this ball, Harry, and have fun."

Harriet violently kicked off her slippers and then turned toward her stepmother.

"I will smile," and she forced the corners of her lips up in an insincere and horrible rictus of a grin, "but I can't promise to have fun."

Two

Thirty miles away and thirty-seven hours earlier, Thomas Drake leaned over and whispered in the ear of his stallion Octavius, "Come on, boy, let's rampage." And with that, the horse, as if he hadn't been ridden hard by his master for the last hour, broke into a long-legged gallop across the meadow of wet wildflowers and sweet grass. The sun was now fully up.

Thomas kept his forward lean and held the reins loosely even as he gripped the horse's back with his knees. A visitor to these parts might have seen a tall rider with powerful shoulders and a shock of dark hair galloping full out on a chestnut stallion and thought the rider must be carrying word of an imminent invasion, so great was his reckless urgency. Any villager or farmer would have known that it was just the Earl Drake, out for his morning ride.

Thomas had saddled and led Octavius out of the stable before dawn, hoping to escape without notice. One of the very young grooms, really a glorified stableboy, had shown up in the dark stable yard, rubbing his eyes. He had politely insisted on both checking the buckling of the girth on the saddle and

giving Thomas a hand up. Thomas had not made a fuss. He
had drunk heavily the night before and he had not slept since
then. He was no longer drunk, but he *was* heartsick. And
heartsick, sleep-deprived men could make fatal errors.

"If anyone asks, I'll be back for breakfast," he had told the
groom once he was in the saddle.

"Yes, Lord Drake."

And he had ridden out.

Riding had always been the great solace of his life. He was
a man who sought many pleasures but had few comforts. He
had lived as dissolute a life as he could afford, but women and
alcohol could only briefly distract him and stay his restlessness.
However, he could ride Octavius for hours on end, over the
lands owned by his family for hundreds of years, until he had
memorized each inch of every forest and lea, the shape of every
tenant farmer's chimney, every footpath, every meandering
stream. He could lose himself in the land that surrounded
Sommerleigh and in the effort of his horse and in his own
sweat and pounding pulse. And then he could sleep. It was the
only time he could sleep more than an hour or two without
the benefit of drink or a whore.

His best friend and current guest, James Cavendish,
Marquess of Daventry and son and heir of the Duke of
Middlewich, thought that Thomas' love for Octavius was
unnatural.

"You haven't been pleasured by the right woman, Tom. If
you would just bed the new redheaded doxy at Madame
Flora's, you would give up that stallion for good," James had
said when he had arrived at Sommerleigh last night and found
Thomas currying Octavius in the stable.

Thomas *had*, of course, already bedded the redheaded
doxy. Many times. He had reveled in her abundant breasts and
in her lovely firm backside as he had lifted her hips up to
thrust between her legs. The release, as always, was sweet, but

fleeting, gone from his mind almost as soon as the woman had rolled away and he had buttoned the fall of his trousers.

No, the pleasure he found in riding Octavius was of an entirely different sort. It was physical, yes, but it was also a pleasure of the soul. He felt an unstinting glory in being alive as he rode until he and Octavius were both exhausted and covered in sweat.

And it had always been his particular thrill to ride after a violent storm, when the air had a new sharp cleanness to it and the grasses were wet and heavy. Last night, Thomas had sat in his library for hours, James long gone to bed. He had stared out the window at the raging storm, which matched the violence of his feelings. And as the storm had died, the tumult in his head had quieted and been replaced by a kind of grief. In the predawn stillness, he had gone to the stable to find Octavius.

He slowed Octavius now to a trot and turned him toward the grounds of the manse. His dark hair and his shirt were drenched with sweat, and he felt he had perspired the very last traces of the previous night's whisky out of his system. He straightened his broad shoulders and rubbed the stubble on his chin. His mind was clear on one thing.

Today, he would ask James what to do.

He had invited James down from town for this very conversation. Thomas was not the sort to unburden himself for the sake of unburdening, but he hoped his friend would give him advice that might miraculously change his fortunes.

James was the best sort of friend, Thomas thought. James, long and lean, with his sandy-brown hair that curled mischievously, his gray eyes that crinkled at the corners when he laughed—he was a man of joy. He was not completely undiscriminating, but he could always find a rose in a manure pile, if there were a rose to be found. He drank a little too much at times, lost a little too much at cards, but he had no demons Thomas knew of.

James had often come down to Sommerleigh, even before Thomas' father had died. James would say that he needed "a country respite," which meant he had overspent his allowance and had to wait until his father the duke had disbursed the next set of funds before he could resume his life as a rake-about-town. James could have always gone to the duchy of Middlewich, but he said his parents were too disapproving and his dear sisters were too overwhelming in number.

Thomas' father had always been a gloomy sort of man as long as Thomas could remember, but James' quips and clever conversation could make the old earl smile and even laugh. Looking back now, Thomas was glad that by bringing James to Sommerleigh, he had done at least *something* to ease the older man's worry.

And now he had inherited his father's burden.

After a day of procrastination on the part of Thomas, accompanied by hunting and a dinner of wild hare they had shot themselves, James and Thomas ensconced themselves in the library. James told a long, ribald tale he had heard from another rake about a racehorse jockey. Thomas laughed in the right places, he thought, but as the fire burned down, James quieted. He shucked off his boots and thrust his stockinged feet toward the dying flames.

"Tom, tell me what's wrong."

Thomas put his elbows on his knees and his head in his hands.

"It's all right, I can guess. It's money, isn't it?"

Thomas looked up, startled. James smiled.

"Well, I knew *you* wouldn't be silly for love, unless it's love for that old stallion, so that left illness or money. And you seem fit, so that left money. And I noticed you didn't have a gamekeeper come with us today for the shooting and I thought that a little odd. You didn't sack old Ransome, did you?"

Thomas sighed. "Mr. Dunbar—you know, the merchant who bought the next estate—asked if I knew where he might find a good gamekeeper. I spoke to Ransome and, after tiptoeing around the subject, I came to find that he was very amenable to becoming Mr. Dunbar's gamekeeper, especially since it meant a hefty increase in pay. In fact, Mr. Dunbar had already offered Ransome the job behind my back, but Ransome felt he couldn't leave his position since he and his father and his father's father had been with the family so long. So, it was a bit of a saving grace, because it meant I could lose one servant's salary without sacking anyone."

"I would think that having no gamekeeper would *not* save on expenses," James said thoughtfully. "Seems penny wise and pound foolish. You'll lose all your pheasants to poachers."

Thomas groaned and put his head in his hands again and pulled on his dark hair in frustration. "I must retrench but I suspect that the situation is so far gone that I could never retrench successfully."

James leaned back and raised his glass of claret up in front of the fire so that the crystal sparkled with reflected embers and the wine glowed like liquid rubies. "Now, now, Tom, have another glass of this fine claret from your cellars and tell Uncle Jamie all about it."

And so Thomas did.

He was facing a devastating, humiliating bankruptcy. The expense of running the Sommerleigh estate far outstripped the rents coming in from his farmers. And there were debts, enormous ones, that his father and his grandfather had accrued. As a young man, his father had made some unwise investments in the Americas that had become worthless after the War of Independence. Thousands had been lost. Thousands had been borrowed and spent. The old earl's way of dealing with the problem had been to spend at the same rate as always and to keep borrowing. And then he had died, and Thomas had blindly continued this pattern. And now Thomas might very well be the last Lord Drake to own these lands and this house. He was near ruin.

James listened and drank and listened more. He asked questions, pointed ones, and although he didn't gasp at the figures mentioned, his eyes widened once or twice when he realized the amount of money involved.

Thomas finished and there was silence.

"I'd give you the money if I had it, you know that," James said.

"I know you would, but I wouldn't take it because there is no way I could ever pay you back."

"You could marry my frightful sister Charlotte and remove her from my father's household. That would compensate me." James laughed.

And despite his anguish, Thomas also laughed until tears came. Charlotte was James' fourteen-year-old sister who delighted in finding toads in the garden and putting them in visitors' beds. Thomas had been the victim of this when he had visited the duchy of Middlewich last year.

He wiped his eyes. "Well, I can't wait for her to come of age. I need the money now."

James kept laughing. "And I think Father has already engaged her to the Marquess of Wentworth, to boot!" They both hooted. The Marquess of Wentworth was seven years old.

"But seriously, why *don't* you marry?" James said when he was finally done laughing. "It's a well-established way of injecting money into a family. And, as you must know, you're awfully good-looking. Some rich girl will quickly set her cap at you."

Thomas rubbed the stubble on his jaw. "I have thought of marrying," he said slowly.

"Well, why not? I don't think the stallion will get jealous. We'll find you a lovely daughter of a rich man who wants his grandchildren to be lords and ladies. We'll give your future father-in-law some of this claret, draw up some very generous articles of marriage, you'll hie yourself to the altar, and in a jiffy, the estate is saved. And you'll have some company when you're at Sommerleigh. It must be lonely, knocking about this big house all by yourself. What about that lovely girl, Mr. Dunbar's second daughter? The redheaded one. I think she has a bit of a fancy for you. And you for her, surely?"

"Maybe." Thomas stood, picked up a candle, and strode around the room.

He had never been as good with words as he would have liked, and he felt that it would be especially difficult to voice his thoughts on this subject. He stopped for a moment and looked at himself in the one mirror that hung in this room lined with dusty volumes of books he had never read.

He knew that women liked his looks. At least the women he had bedded had told him so, and he didn't think it was just because he had paid them. At balls and dinners among the *ton* in London, ladies often gazed at him. He held up the candle and tried to appraise himself from a neutral standpoint. His eyes were blue, even as his hair was so dark as to appear black. His brows were dark too and if he concentrated, he could even relax them enough not to appear menacing. His jaw was strong. His mouth was fine and his teeth quite good. His nose was straight and a bit too prominent for his own liking. But again, women had told him it was a well-proportioned nose.

"See?" James called out from the fire. "Devilishly handsome."

Thomas walked back to him. "It's not the handsome part I'm worried about."

"So, Tom, what is it? You must hurry as I am getting quite drunk and the quality of my counsel is quickly degrading."

"It's the devilish part."

There was a pause. Thomas looked at his friend. James smiled up at him, gray eyes crinkling. Oh, could James understand?

Thomas threw himself into his wing chair.

"I'm not an evil man."

"Of course, you're not!" James thumped the arm of his chair in agreement.

"But Jamie, I have appetites."

James chortled. "As do all men."

"But to tie myself to one . . . dish to eat, for the rest of my life."

James shook his head as if to clear it. "I am drunk so let's not speak in metaphors. You are worried about bedding one woman, your wife, for the rest of your life? Well, you won't. You will still whore with all the rest of us fellows, as you have always done."

"But you know that I have always needed more . . . companionship than all the rest of you."

"And now you will be able to afford it, Tom."

"But those girls you think I should pursue and marry, women like Hope Dunbar—"

"Think seriously about this Dunbar girl. She's exactly the right type for you. First, she's rich. Second, she's a redhead, and I know how you feel about redheads. Third, she's probably sharp as a needle about money since her father is in trade and she could get this place organized in a modern way. And lastly, she's amply endowed in other ways." James wriggled his eyebrows lasciviously.

Hope Dunbar was rich and quite beautiful, it was true. She *had* seemed taken with him the times they had met at country balls. And the lower necklines young ladies wore did show off her breasts to great advantage. Thomas had to admit that there were times, in his bedchamber, alone, that she had risen to the tops of his thoughts and stayed there, naked in his imagination, until he had spent.

But no. She wouldn't do. Thomas groaned again.

"I can't marry her."

"Why not?"

Thomas took a deep breath. "These girls, these young girls, they are so . . . please don't laugh, Jamie, please don't. They are quite perfect, aren't they? Pristine. And I am so . . . not."

James closed his eyes and lay back. "You think the men, the other men besides you, who marry these virgins are holy saints?"

"No," Thomas said abruptly. He knew they weren't.

He had known his distant cousin Mr. Hugh Drake was no saint. Thomas had taken against him immediately—the way Mr. Drake had looked at Thomas' sister Jane when he had come to see the old earl. Thomas was ten years of age and he did not know what those roving eyes meant exactly; it was as if Mr. Drake were hungry, and Jane were an iced cake.

Hugh Drake was next in line to inherit the title after Thomas. He had said the reason for his visit was to see Sommerleigh and "what I might get if the boy dies."

And then his father had sold Jane to Mr. Hugh Drake. Thomas used the word "sold" deliberately in all his thoughts on the subject. His father had taken money from Mr. Drake and then married Jane to the man when she was just sixteen. It had been an unusual arrangement. But now Thomas knew his father must have had no money for a dowry and the bride price Jane had brought had allowed the estate to stumble on for a few more years.

Jane had not even had the pleasure of a Season in town before she had married.

Thomas knew Jane must have been frightened. She had had no mother to prepare her for her marriage. Indeed, Jane had really been a mother herself to Thomas his whole life, ever since their mother had died giving birth to him. His nurse Turner maintained that Jane had insisted on carrying him everywhere when she was just six. "She was a mite and you were a big baby, my lord," she would say with a chuckle. "She gave me and the other nursemaids very little to do."

So Jane—delicate, sweet, lovely Jane—had gone to her wedding bed with the very coarse Hugh Drake. And when she had arisen the next morning, she was no longer Jane. Thomas knew no other way to describe it. She had disappeared. She had said nothing, she had not even met Thomas' eyes before her husband had bundled her into a coach and taken her away to Manchester.

He had only seen Jane once more before she died. He had finally secured an invitation to visit the couple. His nephew Phillip, whom he had never met, was two. He himself was thirteen now, full of himself as a young viscount, his courtesy title as his father's heir apparent. After a long journey, he had arrived at the Drakes' town house in Manchester.

Jane's physical change had been astonishing. Her pale-blue eyes had held pinpoint pupils that did not seem to see him. She had sat propped up on a sofa in a drawing room, wearing a stained dress—she who had been so careful with the few pretty things she had owned as a child. There had been a bottle of laudanum near at hand. She had smiled absently as he told her about his new colt Octavius and then she had fallen asleep, drooling.

He had asked Mr. Drake if Jane was sick, and Mr. Drake had assured Thomas that the best doctors were attending his sister. And then Mr. Drake had taken Thomas out for the evening and introduced him to, and paid for, his very first whore.

Thomas had stayed a week in Manchester. He had spent all his nights with whores chosen for him by Mr. Drake, and he had spent all his days walking the streets of the town, spending his allowance money on strumpets of his own choosing. Mr. Drake had schooled Thomas on the use of prophylactics or French Letters, so Thomas had spared some coin for those as well.

Thomas had lost himself that week in the pleasures of the flesh. In some ways, he felt he never found himself again. He had learned all parts of the female anatomy. He had been as Magellan and had discovered new worlds in breasts and thighs and buttocks and every orifice a woman had. He had felt the unfettered power of using female bodies to please his own. Several of the women had been amused enough by his age and his lordly ways to take him in hand and show him ways of pleasing them. He had liked that, too. It had aroused him. Not as much as fornicating had or the use of a whore's mouth on his cock. But he had quickly learned that a little teasing, a little attention, led to some extras that never appeared on his bill.

And he had learned he liked kissing. Wet mouths meeting, lips and tongues touching—kissing was intercourse writ small.

When he had returned to his brother-in-law's house for clothes and food and more money, he had also made time to amuse his nephew Phillip in the nursery. He had been a lively little fellow, inquisitive and affectionate. Thomas had been glad to see that the nursemaids were careful to keep Phillip away from Jane.

He had avoided his sister until the day of his departure.

Her eyes had been almost normal that morning, but she had been agitated, plucking at her own hands and her dress in a near frenzy. He had bent to kiss her cheek, and she had seen the unmistakable love bites on his neck. Perhaps she had even smelled the strong sea scent of last night's whore on his face. She had slapped him then. She had not really injured him, she was too weak for that, but his Jane had never raised a hand to him or any living creature when she had lived at Sommerleigh.

She had slapped him again. And then, she had howled. Like a beast who had been skewered in the gut. A maid had rushed in and pushed him out. As he had left the house, his cheek burning, her howl ringing in his ears, he had passed the boy from the apothecary going around the side of the house, carrying several bottles of laudanum.

"You're late," he had heard the housekeeper standing at the side door, scolding the boy.

Six months later, his father had received a curt note from Mr. Drake that Jane had died and been buried in Manchester.

Six years after that, a coach had come to Sommerleigh, carrying Phillip and a nursemaid. The nursemaid had carried a clipping from a Manchester newspaper that said Mr. Hugh Drake had been murderously stabbed in a brothel in Manchester. The paper had not directly said it was a brothel, but it was implied. Thomas had recognized the location mentioned in the paper. It was the very same den of vice where Mr. Drake had first schooled him in exchanging pleasure for money.

Unlike last night's violent storm, it was mizzling tonight at Sommerleigh.

Thomas got up and moved away from the fire to the windows. He couldn't see anything except the rain on the window panes. It was like Sommerleigh had already vanished.

"Eureka!"

Thomas turned around to see James, holding his glass, dancing a jig in front of the fire.

"Congratulations, Tom! You are acquainted with genius!" James crowed.

Thomas snorted. "Genius for drunken buffoonery, maybe."

"No, my Lord Drake! Just extraordinary, full-on genius. I have the solution to all your problems."

"Tell me."

James swept up the almost-empty decanter and brought it over to the window where Thomas was standing. He poured half the remainder of the wine in his glass, shoved it at Thomas, and then held up the decanter itself for a toast.

"The solution is to marry a very particular kind of rich woman."

Thomas lowered the glass. "I—"

"I know, I know." James interrupted. "You have some mistaken idea about the purity of women and that you will despoil them. I remember now that you will never take a virgin at the brothel. But it's all foolishness, I tell you. Girls are as randy as we. I know, I have sisters." He belched. "That came out wrong. Let genius have its moment, please. The solution is marry . . . a rich widow."

Thomas hunched his shoulders.

James went on, "Marry a mature, rich widow. There will be no illusions, no false promises, no deceptions. She will know exactly what she is getting in you. A handsome man on her arm, the title of the Countess Drake, the occasional poke."

"Marry an old woman?"

"An older woman, not an old woman. And one as rich as Croesus! I mean as rich as Croesus' widow!" James drained the decanter and took Thomas' glass and drank his. He then began to slur his words noticeably.

"You already have an heir in your nephew so she need not be fertile. She won't mind your whoring. She'll be happy to have you occupied so she can spend more time on gosship and

clothes. She'll probably have a very good cook in town. All the
besht widows do. She'll be no virgin that you can ruin. Her
flower would have been definitely, absolutely, shertainly,
already plucked. I think I drank more of thish claret than you.
I better go to bed. Will you ring for my valet? And now that I
think of it, I remember that Creeshushush wife committed
suicide before Creesh—whatitsname popped off, so maybe
I'm thinking of Midash."

Thomas laughed despite himself and put his shoulder
under his friend's arm just as James murmured, "Upsidaisy"
and slumped. Thomas got him to the sofa, and within
minutes, James' longtime valet had appeared and taken James
up to bed.

Despite last night's sleeplessness, a day full of exercise, far
too much claret, Thomas stayed awake late, musing over
James' idea.

THREE

Mrs. Catherine Lovelock sat in the carriage across from her two daughters. After some delay, which actually had more to do with getting Harry to eat than with getting her dressed, they were all on their way to Lady Huxley's ball.

Now, as she gazed at them, she could see it had been a mistake to have dressed them in the same color. The two girls, seven years apart in age, were so dissimilar. Harriet, so tall, so thin, so sallow as to have almost a green cast to her skin, hunched, lost in thought, rhythmically tapping her head against the side of the carriage and her fingers on her lap. And Arabella, just sixteen, newly out, fashioned so much in Catherine's own mold. Blonde and petite and pink and rounded where she should be.

Arabella was Catherine's only daughter by blood. Harry and her older sister Mary had been Edward's daughters by his first wife who had succumbed to consumption. Like many men in London, the banker Edward Lovelock had fallen in love with Catherine's portrayal of Ophelia in the bard's

Hamlet at the Theatre-Royal, Drury Lane. Only after her retirement from the stage and their wedding, had he learned the woman who played the mad would-be-bride of the Danish prince with such abandon was actually a firm and sensible manager. And then he had worshiped his Katie until the day he had died. She had taken his household in hand, swept Mary and Harriet under her wing, and given him what she felt every man wanted—a house of peace.

Harry had been the thorniest of twigs in Catherine's soft little nest. But, in time, she felt she had helped smooth Harry out. She had taught her to look people in the eyes and to smile and to sit with a minimum of fidgeting. Catherine herself had learned to quiet Harry's inexplicable rages that seemed to arise from nowhere. She had supported Edward's indulgence of Harriet's love for numbers and books. When he had built Catherine their large new house in Mayfair, she had looked the plans over, and resting her hand on the little bump that was becoming Arabella, had pointed out that there was plenty of space to give six-year-old Harry the room she had asked for, away from the nursery. She had persuaded and paid many bookish young men from Cambridge to spend a few hours with the adolescent Harry, as she herself sat in a drawing room with them, not understanding one syllable of what passed. Most of the young men had walked away from the house, shaking their heads, but the last one—the one she suspected of dangerous radicalism—had taken Catherine aside and told her to stop wasting her money.

"She outstrips us all," he had said grimly. "She should *teach* at Cambridge. But she never will."

Harriet's older sister Mary had been quite a bit easier. In fact, Mary was enchanting in every way. A graceful dancer, beautiful face and figure, impeccable manners, great skill at the pianoforte with a lovely voice to match. It was for Mary's sake four years ago that Catherine had first leveraged the Lovelock wealth into invitations to the balls of the *ton*'s Season. There had been many lords very interested in meeting the extremely wealthy and lovely Mary Lovelock. And within six weeks of the start of her first Season, Mary had become the Viscountess Tregaron and lived now quite happily in a castle with her husband in Wales.

Mary had given Catherine hope that Harry might one day turn into a butterfly. Not that Harry was a grub, that was a disloyal comparison, but she had become even more peculiar since her father's death. Her habits and speech more erratic. Her sleep and her presence at meals nonexistent.

Arabella grabbed Harry's gloved hand with hers and squeezed it. Harry looked down at their conjoined hands and seemed to recognize the signal and stilled her hands and stopped thumping her head against the carriage wall.

"I'm so excited." Arabella leaned forward toward Catherine. "My first Lady Huxley ball in my first Season, Mama. I can't believe that we will be with all the lords and ladies. Oh, Harry, do you think there will be many people there?"

"Yes, it will be crowded just like last year. And I will be able to give you the figure of the attendance afterward within a very small margin of error."

"And, Harry, this is your fourth Season, isn't it? Since Papa was not well," and here Arabella faltered for a moment, "I mean to say, you started later than I did. And Mary got married her first Season, didn't she? But she started even later. Do you think you will get married this Season?"

Harry snorted. "There is neither a man stupid enough nor clever enough to marry me."

Catherine frowned, but Arabella pealed with laughter. "Oh, Harry, you don't want to be alone all your life, do you? Just you and what's-his-name, that French mathematician? Fermat!"

. . .

Harry leaned back again but managed to refrain from resuming her head thumping.

Her fourth Season. That meant she had already wasted months of her life with balls. In her head, a number inscribed itself. Two thousand and fifty-nine hours. That is how long she had spent in dressing for and riding to and sitting at and riding from balls and then, blessedly, undressing and ridding herself of her unnecessary corset.

And then the hours spent in calls. Well, she hadn't had many of those herself, really only the most desperate types sought her out and then quickly turned tail. But she had been forced to sit through Mary's calls. She remembered one afternoon when she had very nearly screamed at the Viscount Tregaron, the man who had married Mary, "Just ask her! She'll say yes!" Catherine had looked at Harry just then and must have sensed the impending explosion because she had suddenly asked Harry to go look in on Arabella's lessons.

"How many more Seasons do I have, Mama Katie?" Harry's voice cut across Arabella's chatter in the carriage.

Catherine seemed startled.

"Well, Harry, you'll have Seasons until you get married, you know that."

"*You* didn't have Seasons."

Catherine looked down at her own gloved hands. Harry bit her lip. She had said something wrong as usual. She had forgotten that her stepmother didn't like to be reminded too often of her own girlhood.

But Catherine looked up quickly again and laughed lightly. "No, I had seasons on the stage, which suited me a great deal more. Especially when I got to play Viola in *Twelfth Night* and wear a sword and swagger about in breeches."

Harry couldn't imagine her feminine stepmother in breeches, but everyone, including her father, had always said that she had been quite brilliant and an extraordinary mimic.

Catherine herself had acknowledged that she had been gifted when she had spoken to nine-year-old Harry after a disastrous call on Harry's great-aunt. Great-Aunt Lucy Lovelock had declared that Harry was odd and perverse and should be locked away in Bedlam. Harry hadn't known what she had done to prompt Great-Aunt Lucy's reaction, but Catherine had sat with Harry afterward and held her hands.

"This is from Shakespeare, Harry. *All the world's a stage, And all the men and women merely players; They have their exits and their entrances; And one man in his time plays many parts.*"

"Was that one of your speeches, Mama Katie?"

"No, that is a man's part, but I mean to show you that you can be an actress, too, like me."

Harry had shaken her head. "I would be too frightened."

"No, not on stage, but in drawing rooms and dining rooms and in shops. You have your own room, do you not?" Harry had clutched the key she kept on a chain round her neck and nodded. Catherine had gone on, "You have your room and that is the place where you play no role. And in your father's heart and in my heart, you never need play a role. But in the rest of the world—oh, Harry, it would make your journey so much easier if you would act. Could you learn?"

"I don't think so."

"Harry, you are clever. You can learn anything. And, if I may be so bold to say, you would have a very talented actress for a teacher."

"Who?"

Laughter had erupted from Catherine then and she had taken out a handkerchief to dab at her eyes and then had wiped Harry's tear-stained face for good measure. "Me, dear Harry, me."

Harry knitted her brow in frustration as the carriage slowed outside Lady Huxley's house.

Two thousand and sixty hours wasted now. When any minute someone else could be on the brink of proving Fermat's conjecture after one hundred eighty-one years of failed proofs. When someone else could be about to win the prize offered by the *Académie des Sciences* in Paris for proving the conjecture. Now that was a prize worth going after. Not some fool of a husband she would never please anyway.

She was going to have to put a stop to this time-wasting, brain-shriveling, corset-requiring lost cause.

But how?

Perhaps she could write a letter and ask advice from her mentor Dean George Haddington at Cambridge.

No, she couldn't do that. She could consult him on any matter of difficulties with number theory, but she could not ask for help with the problem of balls. He did not know she was female, let alone a twenty-three-year-old heiress compelled to make the rounds of the Season's balls, on display for the marriage market.

No, Harry could not tell Dean Haddington she was a woman. No, not until she finished her proof of Fermat's conjecture. And then only because she would have to. Her sex would be evident when she went to claim her prize and to deliver the prize lecture at the *Académie des Sciences*. But then she would be crowned in glory. The mathematical elite would be forced to accept her, wouldn't they? Including Dean Haddington, the only person on the planet right now who had any inkling of what was in her mind. The only person who understood her. Of course, the dean might be angry to find that the young man he had corresponded with so generously was actually a girl. He might abandon her then. But it would be worth sacrificing their friendship in the end if she could prove the conjecture. Wouldn't it?

But she was never going to prove it if she had to keep

wasting her time this way. Unfortunately, her stepmother was an immovable object. Could she, Harry, summon the will to be an unstoppable force?

FOUR

When Thomas returned to the house from his foggy morning ride, coated in dew and sweat and rain, he found James tucking into eggs and smoked haddock and toast in the breakfast room.

"Well met!" James called out as Thomas came in one of the doors from the lawn.

"Met well!" Thomas answered.

James looked refreshed and none the worse for his excess of drink last night.

"You're quite muddy, Tom. You've already been out and about on that horse, eh?"

"Barely went to bed, Jamie."

Thomas sat down and asked for coffee. One of the younger footmen brought it to him.

"I've decided to take your advice."

"Splendid!" A pause, the clink of the fork on the plate. Then around a mouthful, "What advice is that?"

"To marry a rich widow," Thomas said. He had no other options at this point. He must have the money to save Sommerleigh, and he had no other way to get it. But he could not bring himself to marry an innocent girl and ruin her. As his sister had been ruined. He would not expose a virgin to his appetites. He would not be party to that. Ever. And James was right. A widow would not be shocked and would likely be happy to have her marital duties co-opted by Madame Flora's whores.

"Oh, yes, *my* very own Eureka!" James chewed and swallowed. "I'm just glad I didn't get the idea in the bath and run naked through the house. *That* would have scandalized the maids."

Thomas blew on his coffee. "Mrs. Dewey, my housekeeper, would have appreciated it though. She has a soft spot for you."

"Well." James wiped his mouth and put his napkin on the table. "I hope your valet Jackson has your evening clothes ready because Lady Huxley's ball is tonight."

"Tonight? Oh, no, Jamie, I'm not ready to go to any ball tonight. I must . . . I must lay my plans. I must strategize."

"Pfft." James dismissed him. "Lady Huxley's ball is *the* event. I personally know of several eligible and rich widows who will be there tonight. Lady Huxley herself, of course, although she is a bit of an old bat—"

One of the footmen stifled a giggle at that moment.

"—but the prize, and a slippery prize she would be, the widow Mrs. Catherine Lovelock might be there as well."

"Slippery?"

"It is rumored that several gentlemen have sought her favor since her husband Edward died, and they have all been roundly rejected."

"Her late husband was Edward Lovelock, the banker?"

"Surely a suitable stand-in for Croesus." James winked and grinned. "And Tom, I hear that Mrs. Lovelock is a beauty. She was on the stage for years before she married him. With her, you might never have reason to wander. And there will be dozens of other lovely widows there as well. As you know, despite childbirth, many women seem to have the knack of outliving their husbands."

So, James cajoled and persuaded until Thomas found himself cleaned up and in James' carriage, on the way to London for Lady Huxley's ball that night. Once his valet Jackson found Thomas some rooms near James' rooms—the Middlewich town house being crammed to bursting with all of James' sisters who were going to the ball themselves that night—there had been no time for a nap before having to report to the duke's house for dinner. Once there, Thomas ate and flirted harmlessly with James' sisters and avoided the demon-child Charlotte who threatened him with a lizard and then found himself in one of the many carriages transporting James and his sisters to the ball.

Thomas now bitterly regretted his decision to come to this ball.

He danced one dance with each of the sisters and met Lady Huxley (who was quite mature and *rather* bat-like) and several other widows, including the extremely fetching and dainty Widow Lovelock. She was very attractive to him, a graceful dancer, able to carry a conversation, but he was not at his best, and he allowed another gentleman to claim her for the next dance and lead her away.

He was exhausted. He realized he had slept only four out of the last sixty hours. No wonder his charm was failing.

He stumbled out of the ballroom and went exploring. He had hoped to run into another gentleman or a servant so that he might ask if there was somewhere he could sit in privacy for a minute. He found no one. Well, the good news was that it was unlikely any of the rooms on this floor were private family rooms. It would not be amiss if he tried to find a drawing room, himself.

The first door he tried opened into a dark room. He closed

the door behind him and stumbled forward and felt what he thought might be the back of a sofa. It was. He felt his way around the edge and sat down. Bliss. He would close his eyes for a few moments.

Balls were a highly repetitious sequence of events. Harry smiled and curtsied. She was introduced as Miss Harriet Lovelock to many people. She smiled and curtsied. Lady Huxley sighed when she saw Harry and whispered disapprovingly behind her fan to her own daughter that Miss Lovelock looked destined to follow her mother, the *first* Mrs. Lovelock, as a consumptive. But surely consumptives had better coloring than that? Harry heard it all and followed her stepmother's training and smiled and curtsied.

And now, blessedly, the music had started again. It was a few minutes past eleven. Harry just had to wait until six when the breakfast would be served and then she could be back to *her room* by half past seven in the morning. Her stepmother and Arabella would sleep most of the day, and she wouldn't be bothered.

Harry rarely had partners. She could dance well enough if asked. She had had thorough training in the appropriate things to say to her partners. But most of the time she was let alone. She picked a chair to sit where she wouldn't be noticed. She might think on how to prove that if the product of two relatively prime numbers is a certain power, then each of those relative primes is also that same certain power. The ballroom was so hot, which was so strange since usually she was so cold. She hadn't slept recently. Her eyes were closing a little. She pinched herself and straightened up. Mama Katie would be so disappointed if she fell asleep at a ball. But the music was so soporific. Her eyelids went to half-mast again. The dance ended and the polite clapping from the dancers made her jerk noticeably. The movement of the dancers as they sought out their next partners provided cover for Harry to get up from her chair and flee the ballroom.

Harry had been to Lady Huxley's house many times. She knew where there was a drawing room where she might close her eyes momentarily. She had done so last year, at this very ball, and no one had been a bit the wiser. She found the dark room easily enough. She opened and closed the door softly and crept to her favorite sofa.

It was an unusually long sofa. One that would allow the rather tall Harry to lie at almost full length with only a little curl at her waist. She stretched out and found a curiously firm pillow at one end that was just the right height for her head and went to sleep.

"Ahem."

Harry was sure that this had been one of the best nights of sleep she had ever had. The sofa was so soft and her pillow so warm and firm. And there was the smell of something comforting that she couldn't quite identify. Her nose itched so she scratched it. And it seemed like there was a deliciously warm other part of the pillow that had quite a hard and warm and curious lump in it. Mmmm. She squeezed the lump and it only became harder and larger.

This didn't make sense so she opened her eyes and was confronted by a set of brass waistcoat buttons.

She sat up.

Crack!

"Ahhhh!"

In very short order, there was blood everywhere.

The blood seemed to be coming from the nose of a tall man with dark hair who was sitting on *her* sofa. The top of her own head hurt, but not much.

Harry noted that the drapes of the room were wide open and the gray light of a London dawn was filtering in. The ball was almost over.

"Put your head back," Harry said.

The man obeyed, trying to stanch the blood with his hand.

"You must pinch your nose quite hard."

He was stammering and trying to speak, but clearly the blood was running down his throat, making it difficult.

Harry looked down and saw her white silk dress had several large gouts of blood on it already. Oh, well. In for a penny, in for a pound.

She walked around the back of the sofa and said, "Let me" and seized the man's nose in a pincer grip.

"Arggh."

"I hope your nose stops bleeding soon because I do have to go find Mama Katie. She might be worried about me. And look how light it is outside. It's likely nearly time for the breakfast."

"Glub."

"I used to have nose bleeds every day so I am quite proficient at this."

A pair of confused blue eyes stared up at her as she stood over him. She peered at his face. Really, despite the blood, he had a very good face. Even upside down. Almost as pleasing as his lap.

"I must thank you for the use of your leg as my pillow. I didn't know that was what it was when I used it, but it was quite a good pillow."

Through a mouth full of blood, the man stammered something that might be, "You're welcome."

"I think perhaps it would be best if we didn't mention to anyone that we had slept together."

The man nodded his head in agreement.

"I am not fully conversant with all possible outcomes for this situation, but it is my understanding that it could lead to some quite disagreeable things such as, one," and here she grimaced, "our being forced into wedlock, or two, your death at the hands of my brother-in-law. He is quite a good shot."

The man nodded again.

"Try not to nod so vigorously. I almost lost my hold on your nose, and the secret is constant pressure for at least three minutes."

The man held still and just waggled his very dark eyebrows to show he understood.

"Unless, of course, you're already married and then you would definitely die. It doesn't seem fair for you to die just because the room was dark when I came into it and you have such a comfortable lap. But then, there are many things that I don't understand and that don't seem fair. Such as, why are balls so long and tedious and repetitious when there are so many other useful ways to spend our time? And why are men so opposed to the education of the female?"

Harry leaned down very close to the man's face. Dark stubble on his jaw. That comforting smell again. Almost peppery, somehow.

"I think it's stopped." She released his nose. She wiped her hands on the front of her dress. The man sprang to his feet and spat a great gobbet of blood into his handkerchief, which he had finally fished out of his tailcoat pocket.

Yes, he was quite tall. Taller than Harry was. Big shoulders, too. And, yes, the thighs stretching his tight, blood-stained breeches. One of those thighs being responsible for Harry's good night's sleep.

What strange details to note about another person.

And that troubling lump. She kept her eyes on the lump. "So, mum's the word, yes?"

"Y–y–yes," the man sputtered.

"And I want to make you aware that you seem to have a tumor growing in your lap. I hope you have access to a good surgeon."

And with that sincere wish, Harry opened the door, peeked into the hallway and slipped out. She had no idea why there was a gale of laughter issuing from the room she had just left.

FIVE

Harry, unfortunately, could not leave the house of Lady Huxley on her own. And now her gown was quite bloody indeed. She reappeared in the ballroom where quite a few of the ladies gasped, and yes, one fainted. Harry thought it likely that the lady in question had drunk rather too much punch, so she, Harry, did not bear any responsibility. Fainting was rather silly and certainly an overreaction to a few drops of blood. Of course, if it was one's own blood and one had lost pints of it, that would be a valid reason to fall down.

Her stepmother Catherine quickly appeared at her side. When Catherine looked up at her questioningly, Harry shrugged and said, "Nosebleed."

Harry thought that rather clever. It was not a lie. She was known to be terse at times *and* she was known to have epistaxis herself. And yes, her stepmother drew the wrong conclusion but the conclusion that Harry had hoped she would reach. This was subtle, yes, but not a lie.

On the way home in the carriage, as Catherine fussed over her and Arabella sulked a bit about missing the breakfast,

Harry chortled to herself. When one was as socially inept as she was, no one would suspect her of subtlety.

Harry felt herself punished for her subtlety when her nose began to drip later that day. No, not blood. One of those other humors, she supposed, green and vile. The drip turned to a stream. She had to leave *her room* to ask her maid Smythe for a large stack of handkerchiefs so she could stop dripping on her proof. She thought it odd that she had to sit down several times on her way to her own bedchamber to ring for Smythe.

Smythe took one look at her and made her get in bed. Then there was a great deal of fuss with Smythe waking Catherine up from her post-ball nap and Catherine feeling Harry's forehead and cold cloths being applied and a tray coming upstairs with a steaming cup of beef tea.

It was most unfair that after the first good night's sleep Harry had had in weeks, she should get a cold. It proved that rest was rated far too highly. Work, that's the thing for it.

But her stepmother put her foot down. Literally, Mama Katie stamped and told Harry she was to stay in bed and do what she was told for once in her life. And then Mama Katie had collapsed into the chair next to the bed, her face in her hands.

Harry was astonished and quite meekly drank her beef tea and stayed in her bed the rest of the day. Really, it was quite horrible to waste a whole day.

Thomas escaped from Lady Huxley's fairly easily. He could not go into the breakfast covered in blood, but he found a footman in the front hall and explained that he had suffered an unfortunate and accidental injury and would the footman please convey his regrets to Lady Huxley for his rude exit and also convey a message to James, Marquess of Daventry that he, the Lord Drake, had left and would see him later today at his club? Yes, my lord, the footman would. And Thomas slipped out into the dawn and found his way back to his rooms where his valet Jackson clucked and immediately set to work on his waistcoat, soaking and dabbing, while Thomas ate an enormous breakfast.

Thomas met James at his club later as promised. Tonight was for the fascinating ladies of the evening at Madame Flora's. Tomorrow was for the calls on the ladies of society. But, for now, illegal whisky and masculine conversation.

"Tom, what did you think of the array of females at the ball last night?"

"There was one who caught my eye," Thomas admitted. "Mrs. Catherine Lovelock is everything you said she would be."

James gestured for one of the barmen to bring more whisky. "The Widow Lovelock? Yes, she is . . . a good deal more beautiful than I expected."

"And she is very rich. And for me, that has to be the most fetching quality of all, Jamie." Thomas took out his handkerchief and wiped his nose and looked at it. Blood? No, just some errant moisture. Good.

"Have you ever heard of a 'Mama Katie'?" Thomas asked.

"Mama Katie? Is that the name of that woman who is setting herself up in competition with Madame Flora?"

Thomas shook his head. That peculiar and painfully thin girl who had innocently squeezed his morning priapism was not a strumpet. He didn't know what she was. She had been . . . quite unusual.

"Well, whatever her name is, I hope she gets her establishment up and running quickly. The devil knows you could use some more variety in your whores, Tom. You've gone through them all dozens of times at Madame Flora's. Now that would be quite a good investment, don't you think? Do you think a future duke could get away with funding a brothel? Can you imagine the perquisites?"

And then the conversation devolved into a discussion of buttocks and breasts and birthmarks and who did what with whom.

Thomas thought the rutting that night was nearly as good as the talking about it with James beforehand.

"Good afternoon, Mrs. Lovelock." Thomas and James bowed.

"Lord Daventry, Lord Drake."

Thomas thought Catherine was flattered to have two young lords as callers.

A very pretty fair-haired girl was in the drawing room as well. Thomas remembered seeing her at the ball. A Miss Arabella Lovelock. Mrs. Lovelock's daughter. Her first Season. James quickly monopolized the young Arabella, falling easily into a discussion of dresses at the ball two nights ago. Having sisters was definitely a boon.

Thomas sat and spoke with Catherine. She was as vivacious and as witty as she had been at the ball. She did not flirt, it was true, but Thomas liked that. The Widow Lovelock was quite beautiful with no lines on her face and what appeared to be a firm bosom, but from what James had said, Thomas supposed she might be at least forty-five or so. That momentarily saddened him because he would have liked to have had an heir. But he did have Phillip, his nephew. The bloodline would hold. What mattered now was saving Sommerleigh.

He pulled out his handkerchief to wipe his nose while Catherine was turned away to speak to Arabella and James.

She turned back to him just as he had caught his drip. "Oh, that's too bad, Lord Drake. It must be the London air. I am sure the country air is far more salubrious. My child Harry has been suffering as well and is indisposed. Now, please do tell me more about the geography of Sommerleigh. It sounds quite a picture."

So, she had a son as well. Thomas would like to meet him. He imagined a mischievous rascal of a boy whom he might teach to fly a kite just as he had taught Phillip many years ago. This could work out quite well.

Over the next weeks, Thomas thought he might be making progress with Catherine Lovelock. It was hard to tell. He met her at half a dozen balls, and she agreed to be his partner for at least one dance at each ball. She did not try to divert his attentions to her daughter Arabella. Likely, she knew his reputation. However, she did not spurn his company for herself. He called again several times, sometimes with James and sometimes without, and she was unfailingly cordial, nay, even warm in a cautious way.

Threatening letters from creditors had been forwarded from Sommerleigh to London, and Thomas knew he would have to make a move soon.

Six

arry did not worsen much, but she also did not improve much. The doctors came and went. She moped. So much time wasted on her body. Even if it didn't need to be fed or rested or put on a chamber pot to remove excess water, this cursed vessel could still block her progress with illness. Such a hindrance.

She encouraged Mama Katie and Arabella to continue to go out to balls and dinners and to receive calls. She said to her stepmother that Arabella's first Season should not be ruined by her own poor health. This was a brilliant stroke. She had observed that, unaccountably, Arabella took enjoyment from these activities. Harry now appeared quite unselfish and caring for her sister, which was something her stepmother always encouraged. Meanwhile, Harry could send Smythe to bed early in the evening and get a full night of work in. Of course, she did not have all her books and papers she needed, just the few that she had managed to sneak out of *her room* one night and hide under her bed. She noted there was sometimes a minor deterioration in her condition after a night of work, but perhaps that was the necessary price she must pay.

Then, one afternoon, Harry was where she shouldn't be. She had sent Smythe out for ink so that she could leave her bed and go to *her room* and fetch another book that she needed. However, in the upstairs hallway, Harry had been startled to see Arabella coming out of her own bedchamber, talking to her own lady's maid. Harry had been forced to nip down the main staircase before Arabella could spot her. She was hoping she might use the main floor to run round to the back staircase and get back to her bedchamber with no one the wiser.

There was a knock and a bell at the front door just as Harry reached the bottom of the stairs. She had only seconds before Chelsom, the butler, would appear. She darted out of the main hall and into the nearest drawing room.

She felt quite dizzy. Her breath was short.

Voices. The butler Chelsom spoke. A man's voice. A caller. Her stepmother's contralto.

Blast.

Harry scrabbled for a velvet drape and covered herself with it. It was a good thing she was so thin. She tried to quiet her panting.

The voices were very clear now. She heard a masculine laugh.

"Lord Drake, you are so kind to call. And is James . . . I mean, his lordship, that is to say, I hope Lord Daventry is quite well."

"He is, Mrs. Lovelock. He is just taken up with some family business this afternoon."

Harry shivered. It was cold by the window in just her nightdress and robe, behind the drape. And where was her left slipper? Had she left it on the stairs? What was it about the man's laugh? The closeness of the voices meant they were in this very drawing room now. Her stepmother was asking for some coffee to be brought.

"For coffee is your preference, is it not, Lord Drake?"

Coffee was Harry's preference, too. Harry risked a look around the curtain. The man was tall. Dark hair. His laugh had sounded familiar. His face did not. Well, of course, a face could not *sound* familiar, Harry told herself.

The man moved so that his body was facing Harry's drape but his face was still toward her stepmother.

She saw a well-muscled thigh that stretched the leather of the man's breeches.

It was the man whose leg had served as her pillow at Lady Huxley's ball! It appeared in the intervening weeks that he had seen a surgeon and had his tumor excised, so that was good. He stood and walked with no difficulty so he must have healed quickly.

She was glad. She had mused on him and his thigh, while lying ill in her bed, wishing for a better pillow. She didn't know why, but she was inordinately fond of that thigh. How pleasing to look on it now. She might like to put her head on it again. How that might happen, she had no idea. She would have to think on it.

It was too bad she was too far away from him now to see if he still had that sweet, peppery scent that wasn't pepper. That comforting and cozy smell.

But now she knew that the man with the thigh was named Lord Drake, and he knew her stepmother. How curious, except that her stepmother knew *everyone*. At least, she knew everyone whom Harry knew.

Oh, she was very cold. Was the drape trembling with her shivering now? Would she be revealed? She would be in a great deal of trouble.

The coffee came, and Harry heard polite murmuring over cups and saucers.

And then his voice, quite low.

"May I speak to you alone, Mrs. Lovelock?"

A little laugh from her stepmother. "We *are* alone, Lord Drake."

"It is a matter of utmost delicacy, Mrs. Lovelock. Would you permit me to close the door? I would not want to be indiscreet."

Her stepmother said in a clipped tone, "Yes, Lord Drake."

Harry could hear the man crossing the room and closing the drawing room door and returning.

"What does this concern, Lord Drake?"

"I would be very pleased if you would call me Thomas."

Harry shifted her weight off her cold foot. What was happening?

"In return, I wonder if I might have the pleasure of one day calling you the Countess Drake."

There was a silence and then Harry heard the unmistakable peals of her stepmother's laughter.

Thomas thought he had made a rather nice proposal. Clever and smooth, was he not? He had reminded her that if she were to marry him, she would receive a title and all the respect that came with it. He waited to hear her answer.

He was rather perturbed by Mrs. Lovelock's laughing. Surely, even if she wasn't interested in him and his title, she would demur and say she had to think. Or she would say she was promised to another. Or, she was still mourning her husband. He stood and bowed.

"Oh, Lord Drake, please do sit down and have some coffee. You are quite flattering to me, I am sure." She managed to control her laughter.

He still stood. "Mrs. Lovelock, you must forgive me if I have offended you—"

"No, nonsense, of course not. I am flattered. Forgive me. I just . . . I have made a foolish error, a weak and foolish error, and I regret it." He saw now that Catherine was disconcerted and the laughter may have been a way to cover that.

She bit her lip. "It is just that I did not expect to hear a proposal of marriage. And certainly not from an earl. And from such a good-looking young man. Please sit down and let's talk frankly."

He sat. This was promising. She might still accept.

"I am a most fortunate woman, Lord Drake. I came from nothing. Some might say I came from less than nothing. I found a way to have a profession and my own money in a world run by men. Men who seemed determined to let coarseness rule the day. And then, when I was twenty-eight, and my most valuable asset, my beauty, was fading, I found a very surprising thing." She rearranged her skirts around her on the sofa and stirred her coffee. Thomas saw that she had returned to being as self-possessed as always.

She went on, "I found love. I know that the world thinks I married my husband because he was a wealthy banker and that he married me out of lust. The latter might have been partially true for my husband, at least initially, I cannot say. But for the former—he could have been a tinker for all I cared. He was all that a man should be. True and diligent and careful with me and his children. He was the most solicitous and tender-hearted of men. I came to love him, and he came to love me. I'm just grateful that my beauty brought him to me."

Thomas noted that a softness had come to her eyes and her voice had gentled as she spoke of her husband.

"I am not so vain as to think that you pursue me for the same reason my husband did. I know what I am. A well-preserved and wealthy widow. You're a young man who should be looking at young women. You're not interested in me. You're interested in my money."

Thomas started to protest and Catherine cut him off with a gesture.

"You should know that a peculiarity in my husband's will states that upon my remarriage, my fortune will all revert to Edward's daughters. My husband wanted me to be comfortable and happy, but he felt I could never be so if I married a fortune-hunter. So, he made this arrangement to keep me safe.

"I have been foolish to encourage your attentions. I did so enjoy your and Jamie's, uh . . . Lord Daventry's calls. I was flattered to have such handsome young men spend time with me. Please know I am sorry for wasting your time. I should have made it clear to you immediately that I was not the answer to your difficulties. It was very wrong of me to delay. As I said, a weak and foolish error." She grimaced.

"Your hasty proposal shows that you are likely under some financial pressure. But there are many wealthy young ladies out there, Lord Drake. I encourage you to find one whom you might love. Alternatively, if you feel yourself incapable of love, at least find a girl who might love you. And marry her and do your best not to break her heart."

Thomas stood again, a lead weight of doom in his stomach. He bowed and spoke stiffly. "I am indebted to you for your advice, Mrs. Lovelock."

Catherine suddenly reached out and clasped his hands. "I presume to understand you, Thomas. We are more alike than you know. Since this may be the last time we talk as intimates and friends, let me speak as the farm girl I was and maybe always will be. You are a bull. A restless, angry, hungry bull. You are searching for something. You think it is a cow. No. No." She shook her head impatiently. "You think it is *many* cows. You're wrong. You should be looking for a tree. A lovely graceful immovable tree with strong, deep roots and full, leafy branches so that you can lie in the shade on a hot day and be sheltered from the storms. So you can rest. Then you'll be happy."

SEVEN

Harry had to wait quite a bit of time to make sure she could climb the staircase with no one seeing her. She was tired from standing so long. Her left foot, absent a slipper, ached with cold. She had been very interested to hear her stepmother speak about her father. Harry didn't understand how bulls and cows and trees came into it, but perhaps the Earl Drake had animals on his estate. She was glad her stepmother wasn't going to marry Lord Drake. She agreed with her stepmother that he should have a younger wife. Younger but intelligent. And someone with money obviously. An heiress.

When Harry got back to her bed, she did not feel at all well. Smythe, long since back from the shop with the ink, clucked and fussed and threatened to tell Catherine about Harry's getting out of bed. Harry had no worries. Smythe was a good egg.

Harry's fever was very bad that night and the next. Her stepmother and sister and Smythe and doctors filled the room and then the room was empty again. When finally her bedchamber stopped spinning and she was strong enough to sit up, Catherine came to see her alone.

"Harry, oh my Harry, how you have worried me, worried all of us," her stepmother said, gently touching the top of her head, the one expression of affection that Harry easily allowed.

"Yes, well, I'm better now. I think."

"Yes."

"Will you tell Smythe to let me have my books and papers now, Mama Katie?"

"Will you drink your broth?"

Harry nodded and started sipping from her cup, trying to look helpful and obedient.

"Perhaps one book, a little one that would be easy to hold," Catherine relented.

"Oh, yes, the Euler, it's small," Harry said swiftly. "It's blue, Smythe, you should find it easily, it might be under the bed here."

Smythe did find the book easily in the pile of contraband she had previously collected from under the bed. She handed it to Harry and then left the room after Catherine had nodded to her.

Harry forgot her broth and became quickly absorbed in her book, turning pages, muttering to herself.

Catherine cleared her throat and took a slipper from behind her back and put it down on the bed.

Harry looked at the slipper on the bed. "Oh, good, you found my slipper. Smythe will be glad."

"Arabella found it in the front drawing room, Harry. Four days ago. Do you know how it might have come to be there?"

Harry blinked. "Oh, yes, I was hiding in there. Has it been four days? I thought it might have been yesterday or today."

"Were you in there when I had a caller?"

"Yes, and I was just in my robe and I knew you wouldn't

like that, and I didn't want to be scolded, so I hid behind a drape. I meant to tell you, but I forgot until just now."

"So you heard my conversation with Lord Drake?"

"Yes, I suppose that is eavesdropping but I wasn't feeling well so I couldn't think how to get out of it." Harry went back to her book.

Catherine sat on the bed. "So you heard Lord Drake's proposal of marriage and my refusal?"

"Yes," Harry said, still reading. After all, a polite conversation did not really demand too much of her attention. She might read and talk at the same time.

Catherine took the book from her. "And you know that that was private? And it was exceedingly wrong to listen?"

Harry was perturbed. Didn't she just say she did but it had been unavoidable? She told herself to be still, be still, so she could get the book back.

"I thought you might have some concerns over what you heard."

Harry stared fixedly at the book in Catherine's hands.

"You should know that I have had many proposals since your father died. Your father left me a very wealthy woman, and there are many mercenary men out there. Most of them are not as handsome as Lord Drake, true. Apparently, he is in very grave straits; he is bound to lose his estate soon. He would never have proposed to me, otherwise, I am sure.

"Harry, it's good for a woman to have money. It's security and some power and even the means to have the life you choose. Of course, when a woman marries, her money becomes her husband's. It's one reason that it is so important to choose one's husband carefully, as I did your father. I have never discussed this with you, but you should know that when you marry, you will have a dowry of one hundred and forty-five thousand pounds. This is quite apart from my fortune."

This piqued Harry's interest. Slightly. "I knew I was rich,

but I didn't know how much it would come to. Could I buy an estate—something like the size of Lord Drake's—with that money?"

Catherine laughed. "You could buy several sprawling country estates and town houses for you and your husband."

"And I could also buy a good many books with that?"

"Yes, all the books in the British Museum and—what was that library that burned—the one in Alexandria?"

"That was all papyrus scrolls, Mama Katie, no books."

"No matter. You are a very wealthy woman. And you and I will have to be very careful about whom we let you marry. Someone who will understand you. And who will see you, my darling Harry. Yes?"

Harry really didn't know where all this marriage talk was coming from. She had no intention of marrying. The only man she cared for was Dean George Haddington and he was already married and thought she was a man. And the only thing she was interested in was Fermat's conjecture, that bedeviling problem that had vanquished every male mathematical mind in the last two centuries. What were well-muscled thighs compared to that? She could make do with a regular pillow. But Catherine was still holding *her*, Harry's, book so she didn't argue. And eventually Catherine stopped talking and gave her the book back and went away.

The next day, Smythe brought Harry a letter addressed to Mr. Henry White.

Harry was Mr. White. That was how she had initiated her correspondence with Dean George Haddington of Cambridge. She had written to him seven years ago with a question regarding Gauss' proof of quadratic reciprocity and told the necessary lie that she was a young clerk at the Lovelock Bank who pursued mathematics as an amateur. Dean Haddington had written Gauss himself about Harry's question and then had sent Harry Gauss' reply. Harry kept that letter folded into her copy of Newton's *Principia*. Gauss had praised her question and said it was a sign of "extraordinary insight and talent." From then on, Harry had maintained the correspondence with Dean Haddington, frequently sending lemmas and asking questions. She had Haddington's replies forwarded to the house from her father's bank by a well-bribed courier who had stayed faithful even after her father had died. Smythe, of course, was complicit in this ruse.

And so back and forth the letters flew between Cambridge and London, like fat, white doves bearing symbols that made no sense to anyone except a few dozen mathematicians in the world.

Still bed-bound, Harry tore the letter open eagerly, thinking it must be a response to her last lemma. But the letter was from the dean's wife.

Dear Mr. White, the letter ran, *I received your letter to my dear husband several weeks ago, and it is only now that I have taken up pen to inform you with great sorrow that Mr. Haddington, my George, died a month ago. His illness was brief. He often spoke of your work admiringly and thought that he would soon read your published proof for Fermat's conjecture. It was one of the great regrets of his life, I believe, that he did not live to do so. He said you were the most brilliant mathematician in all of England, a young 'bright shining flame,' and that it was a terrible pity that you were forced to be amateur and so tied to your work at the bank. He often hoped that he would come to London to meet you or you would come to visit him here in Cambridge.*

Before he died, he asked that I send you twenty pounds in the hopes that this might free you to continue your work in an expedited fashion. He had long observed that genius in mathematics is closely tied to youth, and he feared that your youth was slipping away while you labored to support yourself and your family. He also had some concern for your health based on infor-

mation you had included in letters—indeed, he was worried you might be working yourself to such a degree that you might damage yourself. Our time in this realm is fleeting, as dear George's untimely death proves. I have enclosed the twenty pounds herewith. Yours in a grief I feel certain we share, Mrs. George Haddington.

Two folded ten-pound banknotes fluttered to the bed.

Harry cried so long and so hard that Smythe was forced to call for Catherine and brandy had to be administered.

Harry didn't cry the next day. She had what she called "a think," lying flat on her back on her bed. She did not look at her mathematics texts. She did not scribble notes. She turned the problem over in her mind and let her thoughts flow quite freely on the matter. She saw Smythe frowning with worry, so by evening Harry metamorphosed into her difficult, obstinate self again. That made Smythe smile and agree to sleep in her own bedchamber that night as Harry had insisted that she needed "at least one night's sleep without your snoring in that chair."

But the following morning, Harry woke up very early indeed. She dressed herself. She slipped out the front door with no one the wiser. On foot, she made her way south, across Mayfair to Westminster, stopping briefly at Lady Huxley's to leave an anonymous note.

Eight

His valet Jackson had returned to Sommerleigh for two days to gather fresh garments for the earl as Thomas continued, listlessly, to pursue other wealthy widows. Therefore, Thomas assumed his rooms were empty in the morning when he returned from his night at Madame Flora's.

Even though funds were low, Thomas had still managed to bed a whore last night. Madame Flora wisely did not extend credit to her clients, but she had taken pity on Thomas. He was a handsome man, Madame Flora had told him, and her girls said that he was never rough and he was a bit of a favorite. He could be good for her new girl who was shy and from the country. No charge as long as he was patient and taught her some exotic novelties.

Thomas was relieved to find the girl was at least twenty and no virgin. He discovered that the young woman's shyness came from her newness to the city and her fear of being seen as the country maid she was. She grew quite bold in the brothel bedchamber after some wine and fondling. In fact, she had taught *him* a new trick—a quite clever way she had of tickling his perineum just before climax.

In his rooms, he untied his cravat and took off his tailcoat and waistcoat.

"I have a proposal for you, Lord Drake."

The voice was low and throaty. He spun around.

It was the girl who had squeezed his cock and given him that bloody, bloody nose at Lady Huxley's ball. She was seated in a wing chair by the window.

"How did you get in here?"

She stayed in the chair. "I paid an awful lot of money to the porter. He said that my hair wasn't red and I didn't seem like your regular women and I said that he was right and that I was your quote 'irregular woman and here's more money.' Unquote. And he let me in."

"Miss, I don't know who you are but this is very dangerous for you." He fumbled to put his waistcoat and tailcoat back on.

"Dangerous? Will you molest me?" There was no fear in her voice. Equally, there was no coyness. She seemed to be merely gathering information. She went on, "The porter made it clear to me that you were a sexual fiend but surely you would not touch me without my consent."

"You were at Lady Huxley's ball," Thomas said as he buttoned. "So even though I don't know your name, miss, I know that you are either a lady or a rich man's daughter or both. If you are seen leaving my rooms, the rooms of a disreputable rake, you will no longer be welcomed in good society."

"I don't think that will be a problem if we get married," she said flatly.

Of course, Thomas thought. She is an extortionist. "Oh, no, no, no, no, I won't be blackmailed by some hussy—where is your confederate?" He looked around the room to see if others might be lurking.

"Confederate?"

Thomas was slamming open the wardrobe and looking under the bed.

The girl stood up.

"Lord Drake, be at peace. You misunderstand me. It's not your fault. It is quite a common problem for me. With me. To me. I assure you that I have no intention—"

And that was when the wretched girl fainted, crumpling to the floor.

Thomas picked her up and deposited her back in the wing chair, having avoided the bed and all its connotations, and then threw the contents of his wash basin and pitcher on her.

She woke up wet and sputtering.

"Who are you? What do you want?" Thomas paced in front of her as she wiped her eyes.

"I'm Harry Lovelock." Her voice quavered.

Thomas stopped pacing.

"You know my stepmother."

Thomas faced her.

"You . . . you're Harry?"

"Harriet."

"I thought . . . I thought you were a boy."

"No, I'm not."

"I can see that."

She looked dreadful. She had looked quite wan before but now he noted the black circles under her eyes. When he had lifted her back up to the chair, she had weighed no more than a child despite the fact she was rather tall. She had no breasts, certainly no hips, and Thomas would have been surprised if there had been a scrap of excess flesh anywhere on her body.

"Miss Lovelock, let me get you a towel and my dressing gown."

"And could you order some breakfast? I really shouldn't have walked all this way without eating something first."

Harry soon had a dry face and was wearing Thomas' volu-
minous banyan over her own dress. Thomas noted that she
had held his banyan to her face for a moment before putting it
on. And was that a sigh?

He then left the rooms and weathered the wagging
eyebrows of the porter to order breakfast. Thomas carried
the tray of bread and butter and coffee into the room
himself.

Harry ate half a piece of bread smeared with butter, drank
some coffee, and said, "Now, to business."

"Yes." Thomas paced while he waited to see what possible
business he might have with this bizarre scrap of a girl.

Harry said, "Perhaps you could sit. All this walking about
is quite dizzying to me and I want to be as clear as I can in
laying out the terms. I have made quite a bit of effort to work
this out."

Thomas sat.

Harry looked at the ceiling. "You are in want of a wife.
Well, not exactly. You are in want of money, and I assume that
you have exhausted other avenues for acquiring the necessary
funds. *Ergo*, you are in want of a wife because that is the only
way you can get the money you need for your estate. My stepmother has refused you. Honestly, I think she would have
refused you no matter what because you could never be the
man my papa was."

She shifted her gaze to the window. "But certainly, the
peculiar terms of my father's will—*id est*, that his fortune
would revert to his daughters if my stepmother ever remarried
meant that you likely would no longer desire her as well.
Because now there would be no money when you married her.
You would just have a wife, but no money. Do you follow me
so far?" She looked at Thomas now.

He closed his eyes and nodded.

"Keep your eyes open when I talk so I can check to see if

you really understand me. I think I have laid out a very clear scheme of the problem."

Thomas opened his eyes and kept nodding. He briefly wondered why he felt so compelled to do what she asked.

"I am in want of a husband," Harry said. "Well, not really. But I am in want of what a husband can do for me. Namely, put an end to Seasons and balls and calls."

Thomas kept his face very still.

Harry leaned forward, tapping her fingers on the arms of her chair, her eyes burning with a manic fire. "Do you know Fermat's conjecture?"

He noted that her eyes were very large. And hazel. He shook his head no, very slowly. What was this girl on about?

Harry stood and now stalked around the room herself, his banyan flapping around her, her hands clasped behind her back.

"I know you must have heard of Pythagoras. The right triangle, the sum of the squares of the legs equals the square of the hypotenuse? Every schoolboy knows that."

Thomas did have some recollection of Pythagoras and his theorem. But he had no earthly idea what could be the connection between Pythagoras and needing a husband.

Harry went on, "It has been posited that no three positive integers exist, Lord Drake, let us say, x and y and zed, that can make true the equation x to the *nth* plus y to the *nth* equals zed to the *nth* for any whole value of n greater than two."

Thomas had no idea what she was saying. Where was Enth and why were these letters going there?

Harry's words gushed out of her at a rapid rate. "Two obviously works as the exponent—Pythagoras, right? But for exponents greater than two, it is thought—but not proven— that one cannot come up with the integers to fulfill the equation. But one hundred and eighty-one years ago, the French mathematician Fermat wrote in the margin of one of his books, a copy of Diophantus' *Arithmetica*, that he had a proof for this theorem."

A knock at the door came then.

Harry ignored the knock and went on, "But Fermat wrote in his note that the margin of the book was too small for him to provide the proof there."

The knock was now clearly a banging. The door flew open and two hulking roughs stood in the doorway.

Thomas leapt to his feet. "What is this?"

The two large men parted and revealed a bewigged and beribboned elderly gaunt man, putting a small portion of snuff on the back of his hand.

"Lord Drake." The elderly man very slightly inclined his head and stepped into the room. He then saw Harry, dressed in Thomas' banyan. "Oh, I see. Another whore. Your appetite is prodigious, Lord Drake." He then inhaled the snuff.

"Sculthorpe," Thomas said, trying to keep his voice even.

The man wiped his nose. "You know why I am here. You have not been answering your letters. I felt I should make a call. In person."

"I have received your letters," Thomas said, feeling his face go hot. "I did not answer because I do not yet have the funds to satisfy my debts. But this intrusion on my privacy is uncalled for, Sculthorpe."

"But what am I to do, Lord Drake?" Sculthorpe played with his snuff box. "The debt stands. Eight hundred and seventy pounds for the last three years."

Harry stepped forward. "At what interest rate?"

Sculthorpe laughed. "What an ugly looking doxy you are."

Harry cocked her head. "What is the interest rate on Lord Drake's debt?"

Sculthorpe stared. "Seven percent."

"Illegal. The maximum allowable interest is five percent by law. Since 1714 or so. I would have thought you would have known that. Only a hundred and four years old that law. And is that compound or simple interest?"

Sculthorpe looked at the two roughs still standing in the doorway. They stepped into the room now.

Harry threw her arms up and waved them and shouted, "Compound or simple?"

The two men halted in their tracks, unsure what to do next. Thomas stepped up to Harry's side and hissed, "What are you doing?"

"It's a very straightforward question, Mr.—what is it?—Skulltop?" Harry put her fists on her waist, holding her arms akimbo, brow furrowed. "Compound or simple? And if compound, how often is it compounded? Was the eight hundred and seventy pounds borrowed all at once? Or is eight hundred and seventy pounds even the principal? And if it is, has it been exactly three years to the day since the debt was contracted? And are you representing a bank, a private money-lender, a merchant, a house of gaming?"

Sculthorpe was clearly not used to being the one questioned. He put his snuffbox into a waistcoat pocket.

"I will call again, Lord Drake," he sneered, "at a time that is more convenient. And when you have fewer distractions present."

He walked between the two brutes and out the door. After grunting threateningly, the two large men followed him. Thomas went quickly to the door and shut it.

Harry shucked the banyan and went to the table that had the breakfast tray and drained her coffee cup, still standing.

"I apologize," Thomas began, "for the insulting manner—"

Harry waved him off. "So Fermat said he had a proof. He just didn't have room to write it down. But the proof was never found among his papers after he died."

Thomas was lost. This girl was mad. Mad. But she had

scared off Sculthorpe. She had her uses. He crossed to his chair and sat, chuckling to himself softly.

Harry drove her fist into her palm. "But it's there, Lord Drake, I know it is. Some elegant piece of logic just waiting for me to find it."

"So you want to find this—what was it? This proof?"

"Yes, I want to beat them all, and you can help me!" Harry put one hand on the arm of his chair and one hand on his thigh and leaned down, close to his face.

Yes, her eyes were quite large. And rimmed with very dark, luxurious lashes. And she had a strangely generous mouth given the meagerness of her body.

"Well," Thomas laughed nervously, "I've always thought I might be good at treasure-hunting, but I don't think you need to get married to me for that—"

"No!" Harry threw herself back into her wing chair. "You misunderstand me, Lord Drake, I am not looking for a piece of paper. I am looking for the proof here." She pointed to her temple. "If only I could sit and think and think and sit. It's a problem that has baffled every mathematician for almost two hundred years. But I *know* I can solve it."

Thomas wondered what it would be like to be so sure of something. And then he realized he *did* know what it was like. *I feel only that degree of certainty about my love for Sommerleigh. I will not, I cannot let it go.*

Harry went on. "I'll give you my money, you give me peace so that I can do the work I'm meant to do. I just need a few months. It's a fair exchange, but there are conditions. First, I won't have children. I don't have time. The doctors have told me that I would probably die if I did bear children. I'm not so worried about that, because I think I am going to die fairly soon anyway—"

Thomas began to protest.

"Hear me out, Lord Drake. I don't think bodies are of

much importance so it's fine with me if I leave this one behind soon, but I must, must, must leave something of worth behind with it."

"And this proof would be that?"

"Yes! You understand! And you see, ultimately, you would have my money and no wife, and you could do what you want. You could be free, too!" Harry's voice was rising in pitch.

"Does your stepmother know you are here and this is your proposal?"

"Mama Katie?"

Of course. Mama Katie was Catherine.

"Mama Katie thinks I am going to marry some bookish duke and settle down and get fat and have babies." Harry laughed a trifle hysterically. "What do you say, Lord Drake?"

Thomas spoke slowly, "Well, it certainly is very interesting—"

"Oh, no." Suddenly, Harry seemed vanquished. She held her head in her hands. "No, no, it is not interesting. It *is* one hundred and forty-five thousand pounds."

If not for the traffic outside the window, the drop of a pin might have been audible.

"I think we're going to need more coffee," Thomas said.

"So, let's say we marry, Miss Lovelock."

"Yes."

"You would come to the country, to Sommerleigh?"

"Yes. There are too many distractions in London. I mean I'm not distracted, but people like my stepmother and my sister would want to distract me and saying no is very exhausting."

"So, you would come and live with me. On my estate. At Sommerleigh."

"Yes? Is that all right?"

"Well, yes, I mean, we would be husband and wife. That would be quite . . . regular."

"*You* could come to town as much as you wanted. And see the friends you usually see here."

"Ah."

"I would need a room and a place for all my books and papers. And coffee. You have coffee in the country, don't you?"

"Yes, it has managed to filter out from the capital to the provinces." Thomas chuckled a little at his pun.

"You should know I have no humor," Harry said stonily.

"I see."

"But I understand your joke. Filter. Coffee. Yes, it's funny."

Thomas smiled. Harry did not. She hesitated and then—

"The night we met, Lord Drake, or the morning . . ."

"Yes, Miss Lovelock?"

"When I left and closed the door, you started laughing. Why was that? Was it a delayed pain reaction to my contusing your nose with my skull? Or had I said something amusing? People do laugh quite frequently at things I say, and I almost never know why."

Thomas thought for a moment. Why had he laughed? Oh, yes, it was . . . how was he going to explain this?

"I don't know how much you know about men, Miss Lovelock."

Harry raised her eyebrows and shrugged and poured another cup of coffee.

"We have an organ in our laps that we use . . . in the act of pleasure."

Thomas checked Harry's reaction. She seemed interested. She did not seem shocked.

"You may have seen it, perhaps on ancient statues—"

"Yes, yes, I have seen it on statues in the museums," Harry

said. "It's for urination, too, isn't it? It's how the tinkers can urinate standing up against a wall in the alley. Yes. I know what you are speaking of. The phallus, right? From the Greek."

"Yes, well, the phallus can change size. Frequently, it enlarges in preparation for . . . fornication."

Harry had a frown on her face.

"So," Thomas went on, "the enlarging tumor that you wanted me to get examined by a surgeon—"

"—was your phallus?"

"Yes."

"You were planning to fornicate with me?"

Thomas hastened to explain. "No, it's almost always erect in the morning, and in that case it is just a reflex, not arousal. For most men. I think. Well, young men. Any friction or pressure might lead to a response."

"It must be blood flow that makes it swell," Harry said thoughtfully. "Like a goose egg. Does it hurt?"

"Hurt? No, not unless something is done to it . . . to hurt it. The skin is quite elastic and accommodates the swelling."

Silence.

Harry cleared her throat. "I realize now that I have not made my terms perfectly clear. You should know that when I said no children, I meant no fucking."

There was a whistling sound and Thomas realized the sound had come from him. He had gasped. He had never heard that word pass the lips of a lady. He himself did not use the word, thinking it unspeakably crude. And unarousing. It was the word Hugh Drake had used in Manchester for what he had wanted Thomas to do with the whores.

"I mean no fucking for me," Harry explained. "*You* can do anything you want with your friends. Paid or otherwise."

"Miss Lovelock, before we go any further in our discussion, can we agree that we will not use that word, but perhaps instead fornication or coupling or coitus or, even better, intercourse?" Thomas put his coffee cup down.

Harry stared at him. "The rake dictates the vocabulary of the virgin."

Thomas pressed his lips together tightly. "I am, like most people, a hypocrite."

"Fine," Harry shrugged, "it doesn't matter to me. As long as we are clear on the point."

"Yes, we are."

"And no kissing, in particular. Mouths," she made a grimace, "so wet and disgusting. How can you breathe when you are kissing?"

One hundred and forty-five thousand pounds. The solution to all of Sommerleigh's financial woes. And it was most fortuitous that this gawky innocent wanted no part of a marriage bed and had explicitly told him that he could continue whoring. All she wanted from him was a room and peace. He would be a fool not to agree.

He cleared his throat. "Fine, no kissing, no intercourse, nothing between us."

Harry went on, "It's quite easy for you to agree to these terms, of course, because I am singularly unattractive." Here Thomas attempted to object, but Harry spoke over him. "No, this is not a matter of opinion, it is empiric. And I want you to know that I know that I am ugly, I am skinny, I am sallow, I am stooped, I am sickly. There is no need for polite contradiction. I have no false ideas of beauty. I have mirrors, and I have ears."

Thomas felt quite sorry for her at that moment.

Harry continued, "Therefore, it is quite useful that I also have one hundred and forty-five thousand pounds. I have been thinking this would be quite a good agreement between us since we both will get something we want."

"Yes."

"With very little trouble to ourselves."

"Yes."

"Since we will both just continue to do what we have always done."

Thomas was silent, but Harry went on to explain, "I will be a mathematician, and you will be a whoremaster."

With that comparison hanging in the air, Thomas felt a great deal less sympathy for Harry in that moment.

Still, when she stuck out her hand, meaning to make a contract with him, he took her thin hand in his own and shook it.

NINE

Catherine thought it was unfortunate Lady Huxley and her daughter should have been passing in a barouche just when Harry stepped out of Thomas' rooms. It was even more unfortunate that one of Lady Huxley's footmen suddenly became eager to spread the scandalous and rather grotesque story of two people at Lady Huxley's ball last month who had mysteriously disappeared for hours and then reappeared, both covered in blood. Behind closed doors, the gentlemen of the *ton* discussed those they knew who enjoyed making urine with their coupling—could blood be the new flavor of the erotically unspeakable? And, finally, it was *most* unfortunate that Thomas was well-known to be an insatiable cocksman.

However, as Harry said to Catherine, it put paid to any possible hindrance to their wedding. They were now committed, and why not? She and Thomas had made the contract already in Thomas' rooms.

Initially, there was a great deal of shouting by Catherine. Harry sat through it dispassionately and then replied, "You said no. I said yes. It's that simple." Of course, it wasn't that simple, but Harry didn't budge.

Catherine won one and only one argument. No special license. There would be three weeks of banns. Harry fussed. Thomas shrugged when Catherine told him that and said his creditors would be reassured by the impending marriage.

Three weeks. Catherine turned all her energies to persuading Harry. She coaxed and threatened and pleaded. To no avail. Harry would go in *her room*, lock the door, and ignore her knocks.

Catherine then planned two conversations. She thought the one with Thomas would be easy. She knew the one with Harry would be difficult.

Three days before the wedding, Catherine asked Thomas to come and see her the following day. It was a matter of a detail in the transfer of funds, she wrote. It must be cleared up before the wedding. Would he come?

Catherine told her butler Chelsom that she was not at home to anyone else. As she had asked, Lord Drake came at ten o'clock the next morning, a time she knew Harry was unlikely to be out of *her room*. And Harry never looked down out of her window at the street to see arriving carriages and visitors. She only looked out at the sky.

Catherine made sure the door to the drawing room was firmly closed.

"Let me allay your concerns. There is no difficulty with the funds," Catherine spoke coldly. "Your banker will receive the monies the instant the wedding is over. There will be no problem with the transaction. But I must speak to you of Harriet."

Thomas interrupted her. "And I must speak to you as well. I want you to know that I have done nothing improper with your stepdaughter. I understand my reputation. I understand that it must seem unlikely that nothing untoward has occurred. I am going to marry her as I have promised her, but I felt you should know that she is wholly unspoiled."

"I know my stepdaughter. I know Harry. I know she is unspoiled."

"Good, so she has told you." Thomas smiled in relief.

"No, she has told me nothing. Except that you are to marry. When I asked her why, she said that she was tired of balls. And since I know Harry, I know that is the truth. I offered that she might not go to balls any longer and stay unmarried. She then worried for Arabella, which I thought was quite good of her."

"Arabella?"

"Yes, Harry was worried that my daughter Arabella might never receive an offer of marriage herself since Harry had been seen coming from your rooms. I reassured her. I told her that Arabella's dowry would still attract suitors. And then Harry said she had already given you her word."

"And I have given her my word, too."

"But I have not agreed to this marriage, Lord Drake," Catherine said through clenched teeth. "You are not the man I would want for Harry."

"Harriet does not need your consent, Mrs. Lovelock."

"She is a child, Lord Drake. I know you must know this. One can't spend fifteen minutes with her without noticing it."

"She is twenty-three. She is of age. She seems to know a great deal of certain things and nothing of others. But is that not the way with all young ladies? Certainly, she has read more books than you or I or anyone I know. Or maybe more than all of us put together."

"But Harry's mind—"

"She is not mad, is she?"

Catherine considered lying. Finally, she shook her head. "No."

"So, we will be married. It may not be the kind of marriage you had with your husband, but it will be Harry's marriage."

"Lord Drake, I warn you that there has never been such a child as Harry before in the history of the world. At least, none that I have heard of. Yes, there is the mind that captures everything with absolute accuracy and with lightning speed. But then, with it, the rages and the tempers and the frustrations that cannot be managed. The inability to understand the most basic human interchanges at times, the failure to read a face or a mood or an emotion of even a beloved sister or a father. I have had the training of her, you see. Far beyond the training that most young ladies require, Lord Drake. I have trained her to create a facsimile of the behavior of others. I have taught her how to act, in essence, like a normal woman. To sit. To speak. To smile. Her differences go far beyond anything you may have witnessed in your brief time knowing her. She is an aberration."

Thomas bristled as he spoke, "I find her frank, and yes, startling at times. But she is not some inhuman creature, Mrs. Lovelock."

"I love Harry, Lord Drake." Catherine's voice was steely. "And Harry loves me. She has never said so, but she does. I don't know why she is so set on marrying a degenerate like you, but I know that she loves me more than she will ever love you."

Thomas held up his hands. "I have no expectation of love from your stepdaughter, Mrs. Lovelock. Nor she from me, I assure you. She asked me for something. I promised it to her. And she promised to marry me for it. That is all. Good day, Mrs. Lovelock." He moved toward the door.

"And what was that, Lord Drake? What did Harry ask for from you? What could a debauched man—an animal—like you possibly give her?" Catherine spat her words.

"Time." He bowed and left the drawing room.

.   .   .

That afternoon when Harry emerged from *her room* to seek coffee, her stepmother was waiting for her. She asked Harry to come with her, and Harry complied.

Catherine took Harry to her own pretty boudoir and asked her lady's maid Wright to bring coffee. While Harry was pouring out a cup, Catherine opened one of her bureaus and took out a nightdress trimmed with Valenciennes lace.

"Isn't this lovely, Harry?"

Harry shrugged politely. She felt that if she could get through tomorrow and the day after that without too much fuss, she would be in the clear. But it didn't hurt to be courteous, Mama Katie always told her.

"I'd like you to have this, Harry. I had one made with the same lace for your sister Mary for her wedding night."

Harry took the nightdress. She was confused. Surely, the wedding dress was what was important. Arabella certainly thought so.

"As you know, Harry, I grew up on a farm and since there were so many animals around, I quickly learned about bulls and cows and stallions and mares and sires and dams and boars and sows."

Harry grew quite dizzy with the number of animals her stepmother was listing. She had a sudden thought and said, "Does this have anything to do with Lord Drake's bull looking for cows when he should be looking for a tree?"

"In a manner of speaking." Catherine gulped. "And this is quite difficult because I don't remember anyone ever having *this* conversation with me when I was young, and by the time I was your age, I had been on the stage for so long and had already suffered so many indignities . . . ." Catherine trailed off, her voice betraying her emotion.

Harry took a little pride in the fact that she could recognize her stepmother's upset. She patted her on her knee. "Oh, Mama Katie, don't think about those bad times and those bad men. Papa found you and protected you, didn't he?"

"Yes, he did, Harry." Catherine smiled.

"Well, Lord Drake will make sure I don't run across any bad men, I assure you. I don't think he is a very good shot, but I understand he is a skilled boxer."

"Harry," Catherine said slowly, "do you know that some might consider Lord Drake a bad man? Not evil, but not what a husband should be?"

Harry looked at the ceiling and reviewed what she knew of her future husband. "Lord Drake? No, that is surely a mistake."

"Do you understand why everyone thinks you have to marry him?"

"Because I was in his rooms alone with him? Or because we slept together?"

"Harry!"

Harry looked at Catherine's face. "Yes, didn't I tell you? At Lady Huxley's ball? We fell asleep on the same sofa. The room was dark and I thought that his leg was just a superior sort of pillow. He didn't snore at all. And in the morning, I was so startled, I gave him a bloody nose."

"Yes, the nosebleed story that has now run rampant around the *ton*. So, you slept in the same room?"

"Yes."

"Nothing else happened?"

Was her stepmother deaf? "Yes, I told you, I gave him a bloody nose. With the top of my head. Then I held his nose. Then he laughed at me."

"Harry, do you understand how people come to have children?"

"They get married. Oh, no, that's right, you can be

married and have no children, and you can have children and not be married. I think the first one is better, don't you?"

"There is an act, Harry, that women and men perform together so that the woman will bear a child."

"Oh, yes, don't worry, there will be none of that."

Catherine blinked several times.

"I discussed it with Lord Drake, Mama Katie. It's part of our arrangement. No kissing and no children."

Harry put her coffee cup to her lips and drank. There was a long pause and Catherine appeared to be searching for words.

Harry swallowed her coffee and spoke first. "And no fucking either, of course."

"HARRY!"

"Oh, yes, I am not to use that word. It seems a perfectly good, even euphonious, word to me, but Lord Drake has forbidden it. He said that perhaps the word 'coupling' might be better or 'fornicating.'"

"So, you do know about coupling, Harry?"

"I've read some books, Mama Katie, that might not have met with your approval. I didn't understand everything I read but I think I understood enough. I only wish there had been some illustrations. And I listen to people talk. I have very good hearing. It seems like many people like fu—fornicating very much, but I don't think it would be to my taste. You know I often get very irritated about touching." Harry shivered in disgust. "I explained that to Lord Drake after he answered my questions about his phallus. He is amenable to a chaste marriage," Harry looked at her stepmother's face to make sure she understood, "and I know he has other avenues for fornication."

"And does that bother you, Harry?"

"Why should his whoring bother me? I'm sure he has a cook. That doesn't bother me. I'm sure he has a tailor. That doesn't bother me. I'm sure I'm grateful—and he would be too, if only he knew how little I care for food and how useless I am with a needle—that I am not making his soup and sewing his shirts. By extension, I am also grateful that I will not be the one fu—tending his phallus."

"Harry, Harry, Harry." Catherine smiled but the smile looked strained. "I thank you for not using that word."

Harry shrugged. "It's a bodily function, isn't? Like going to the privy. I'm just glad I have no need for that kind of evacuation. It seems to absorb a great deal of time and energy for men." Then she had a hopeful thought. "Perhaps that will give me the advantage in proving the conjecture." Harry touched the top of her stepmother's hand lightly. "Now, my mind is firm, Mama Katie. And you know that I am stubborn."

Harry had become the unstoppable force.

"I hope you know I love you. And I wish you happiness, my darling girl," Catherine said after a long pause.

Harry gulped the last bit of her coffee and stood. "Is this interruption at an end? I have so much to do."

She made for *her room* as quickly as she could and stayed there long into the night.

TEN

Arabella's gift to Harry on the wedding day was several pieces of embroidered linen—tablecloths, pillow slips, handkerchiefs.

"My trousseau chest is overflowing," Arabella said, "and yours is a trifle bare, Harry."

Harry tried very hard to be gracious but when would she ever have much call for linen? She had been planning on using the trousseau chest for books.

Harry did manage to smile during the wedding but it was unfortunately when the bishop said, "nor taken in hand to satisfy men's carnal lusts and appetites" and then she had snorted when he said that marriage was "to avoid fornication." Harry listened quite carefully to Thomas' vows and noted that Thomas had vowed to forsake all others. Forsake is a very vague word, Harry thought. Convenient. Harry was still thinking about that when it came to her vows and didn't pay attention to the obey and serve part.

"I will," she said in much too loud a voice.

It was a relief when it was over and they had all signed the register.

Arabella said it was a lovely wedding and wasn't Harry lucky to have such a handsome husband. Harry chuckled to herself. It had nothing to do with luck. Hadn't she arranged it in just this way, to her own satisfaction? However, why she wanted a handsome husband as opposed to an ordinary one didn't bear thinking about.

The nuptial couple were quite late in leaving London after the wedding breakfast because Harry said she had to pack her books herself. She explained to Thomas that she couldn't have packed them earlier because she might have needed one this morning. So, after much delay, Thomas and Harry finally found themselves headed by carriage to Sommerleigh. Smythe and Jackson had gone ahead with Harry's clothes that morning but Harry had a small bag. And three trunks of books.

The late start meant they would have to break their journey at a coaching inn. Thomas had not anticipated this, and when they stopped at the only decent inn within five miles, there was a servants' bunkroom available for the coachmen and the footmen but only one private bedchamber available for the wedding couple.

Thomas came back to the carriage yard to tell Harry, who was directing the coachmen on the safe unloading of her trunks.

"These will have to be stowed in the room," she said.

"I'll bunk with the coachmen tonight," Thomas said, slinging his leather bag over his shoulder.

"Why?" Harry asked.

"I assumed—"

"We've slept together before. A bunkroom doesn't sound very comfortable. Not up to an earl's standards. There will be enough space in the bedchamber for both of us, and the books, too." Harry strode into the inn.

They ate in the room. Well, Thomas ate and Harry had one bite of her meat and pushed it away. Thomas then ate her portion as well. It was unseasonably cold and there was a fire in the hearth, but it burned weakly and did not warm the chamber. Harry dug a book from the bottom of one of the trunks, and sat near the fire, trying to use the firelight and the light of a candle to read. Thomas was tempted to go down to the innkeeper and buy a bottle of wine, but then felt circumstances were such that he had better keep his wits about him.

"What are you reading?" Thomas asked after he had hung his tailcoat up, looked out window, paced the small room, crowded with the piles of books Harry had pulled out of the trunks to find the one she wanted.

Harry did not answer. Thomas studied her.

Her hair was the nondescript brown of a field mouse. It had been in some elaborate arrangement for the wedding with flowers woven into it but Harry had taken it down in the coach, and Thomas had been surprised by the abundance of her hair. So many curling tendrils flying everywhere. Such a contrast to the spareness of the body. As her eyes were. And her mouth.

In the swaying coach, Harry had then smoothed and fastened her hair back into a plain arrangement. As she had raised her arms up to pin the last curl in place, Thomas had experienced a sickening lurch in his chest. He had seen many women in his lifetime perform just this gesture—strumpets sitting at dressing tables, applying rouge and then arranging their hair. But a vision of Jane, his sister, had suddenly come before him—Jane brushing her hair and pinning it as he had watched, fascinated, a boy of six or seven.

Nonsense, Thomas told himself now. Look at this girl. His Jane had been a beauty. Her hair as dark as his. Her eyes blue.

Her skin fair and rosy. This girl was some peculiar blue-stocking scarecrow with delusions of grandeur. She thought she was going to solve some perplexing problem that the finest minds of Europe could not penetrate? Bah. Perhaps she *was* mad.

No, Tommy. Be fair. His wife was odd, but not mad. And she had saved Sommerleigh. And so, she had saved Thomas. And Phillip. And even Octavius.

Harry placed a finger on a line and looked up.

"Limits."

"Pardon me?"

"You asked. I'm reading about limits. And before you ask, limits are something mathematical that you will have absolutely no interest in or need to know."

She went back to reading.

"Well," said Thomas. He left and went to the privy.

When he returned, he carried a bottle of wine. And four more candles he had bought from the innkeeper. He put the candles down next to Harry.

"Good," she said. "I'll be able to read longer. I don't sleep much."

"I don't sleep at all, a few hours a night at most," Thomas said, pouring himself a glass of wine.

"I sleep far less than you," Harry said.

"I seem to remember that I woke up before you in Lady Huxley's fourth-best drawing room."

"Ah, but you must have fallen asleep before me!" Harry was triumphant.

Thomas swigged his wine.

"Well, you should sleep. And you should eat more," he said.

Harry looked toward him.

"I did not spend one hundred and forty-five thousand

pounds on a husband just to exchange one stepmother for another. That was not the bargain."

Thomas subsided into silence. He drank all of the wine. It had been inexpensive but it was not rough on his tongue. It was probably watered. He felt barely tipsy. He was so long accustomed to spending his nights with female company or, when at home at Sommerleigh, with an excess of drink or abusing himself into exhaustion. None of these options would be possible tonight. How would he pass the hours until dawn?

He decided to put on his nightshirt. He thought of warning Harry. The devil take her, she was the one who had insisted on sharing the bedchamber. He stripped down and put the nightshirt on.

Harry did not even look up from her book as he took off his clothes.

Thomas reminded himself of the women who had looked at him and openly admired the muscles in his arms and legs, the size of his shoulders and chest. He was not mistaken. Many women—of all stripes—looked at him with lust. This girl had not even cast him a glance.

He threw himself into the bed and covered himself with the counterpane. Why should he care that she had not looked at him nor even uttered a maidenly protest and turned away? He thought briefly of using his own hand so that he might sleep. The girl was an innocent; she would never know what he was doing under the covers.

And then he felt the deepest kind of disgust. He *was* well and truly a degenerate.

He gritted his teeth. He would keep his word and more, he swore to himself. He would keep his end of the bargain with this girl as she had kept hers. He would give her time and peace, and he would not expose her to evil. She would have her mathematics, as much as she wanted, until she died. Which she seemed very determined to do given how little she cared for her body.

Thomas tossed and turned in the bed for hours. He occupied himself with thinking of the improvements he might bring to Sommerleigh now that he had funds. And he might buy a new thoroughbred colt. Octavius would always be his favorite steed but although the horse was still vigorous, he was getting older.

The bed moved ever so slightly. A body next to him. A fragile thing. He turned to look and saw a mass of curly hair and a ruff of lace. And nothing else. Harry was buried under the counterpane and appeared to be trying to burrow into the feather tick. She let out a low groan.

"Are you all right?" he asked.

She peered up at him. "Oh, I should have come to bed a long time ago, Lord Drake. This is pure delightfulness. You are better than any bed warmer I have ever used. You might hire yourself out as such."

He had forgotten how husky her voice could be.

"But then I might not have needed to marry for money," he joked.

Harry said seriously, "I don't think the potential remuneration would be adequate." Then, "Oh, I see, that is a joke."

"Yes."

He lay still so as not to touch her, even accidentally. Although she had drawn quite close to him, she too did not touch him.

"Lord Drake," she began.

"Yes," he said and his mind raced. What could he call her? She was no longer Miss Lovelock. Harriet? Harry? "Lady Drake," he finally said.

"You are an earl," she said. "What does that make me now?"

"A countess."

"I thought so. How apt."

Suddenly he got a sharp elbow in his ribs.

"Ow!"

Harry sat up and then quickly lay back down again.

"I'm sorry, I'm sorry," she said.

"No, it's fine. Am I crowding you?" Thomas said, confused about what had just happened.

"I should know better than that," Harry said, her voice muffled into the feather bed. "I can't make jokes."

"Your assault on my rib cage was a joke?"

"No." She stuck her face out. "But I elbowed you to show you that I had made a joke. That is what my sister Arabella does to me when someone makes a joke. And that is a signal for me to laugh. You didn't laugh so I elbowed you."

"But . . . but what was funny?"

"Me, a countess."

He still did not understand and did not laugh. "Please don't elbow me again!" he said, half in fear, half in jest.

"*Count*-ess," she repeated it slowly, emphasizing the first syllable. "Me. See? Because of counting and numbers and me?"

"One might think you had planned to marry an earl just to get the title."

"Oh, really, anyone with some sense about him and a big house in the country would have done."

Thomas felt first unaccountably wounded that anyone might have done, and then unaccountably pleased that she thought he had some sense.

A silence had descended on the bed.

"What time do you think it is?" Harry asked.

"It can't be three yet," Thomas replied. He turned over several times, almost violently. Would this night never end?

· · ·

After Thomas' thrashing in the bed, she definitely sensed some chill now that had not been there before.

"I feel a draft," Harry said.

"You do?"

"There is some cold air leaking in under the counterpane from somewhere."

Thomas swung his legs out of bed and stood. He walked around the bed tucking the counterpane in tightly on all sides.

The dim light of the fire allowed Harry to observe that something was tenting Thomas' nightshirt.

When he got back into bed, Harry said, "You're having a reflex."

Thomas said brusquely, "Yes," and promptly turned over so that he was facing away from her.

Harry considered the situation. It had been so thoughtful of him to get her the candles. And to turn the bed into this heavenly snug nest. Next to her, the Earl Drake radiated heat like a bonfire. And there was that lovely warm smell of him. That spiced smell that was like pepper but was too sweet to be pepper.

Yes, being married might agree with her. Certainly, the first night of sharing a bed was revelatory. And cozy.

And if he would just stop tossing and turning, she *might* be able to sleep a bit.

Besides, she was curious.

"Should I relieve you, my lord, manually? I don't know how, but you can tell me. I know it will not lead to children. And then you might be able to sleep. And stop moving around so much."

"No, Lady Drake."

Harry wondered why his voice sounded so strained.

Thomas went on, "No, Lady Drake, I want you to put your mind to rest on the matter. I promise you that I will never call on you to perform that function."

How curious that he should use that word.

"Do you know that we use the word function in the calculus? Of course, it was Herr Leibniz and not Newton who first used the term. And Euler coined the current system of notation. It is a most useful concept."

Silence from Thomas but she could tell he was listening.

"It is the word used to talk about a process whereupon a group of numbers is transformed into another group of numbers. It is like a machine where you feed threads in and get length of fabric out. I'll give you an example. Say that you bred rabbits on your estate—"

"Rabbits?"

"Yes, and you noticed that your number of rabbits was doubling every day—"

"I don't think it happens that quickly—"

"Hush, Thomas, that is irrelevant."

Thomas hushed.

"And let's say that you wanted to be able to anticipate how many rabbits you might have on succeeding days. You would define the function f of x equals n times two to the xth power with n being the number of rabbits you started with and x being the number of days that had passed. You see? And, of course, you are going to eat some of the rabbits and sell some of the rabbits so you could introduce some additional terms to the function, but at least in this elementary example, it would be best if those numbers were either zero or some other constant or some fraction of x. I think it is far too early to start talking about introducing other variables. We can depict this function using Descartes' system. Now, of course, with rabbits, it is really a discontinuous function because you can't have a fraction of a rabbit, can you? Except when you're eating one, I suppose, as a whole rabbit is a quite large amount of food.

"Let's just put rabbits aside so our function is not just

restricted to non-negative integers. That will then let me explain limits to you because the limit of f of x will approach zero as x goes to negative infinity. I do wish I could draw it but you'll just have to imagine a horizontal line with hatch marks on it labeled with numbers starting at zero and then one, *et cetera*. The negatives will be on the other side of the zero. And then a vertical line intersecting the horizontal line at zero and having its own set of hatch marks going up, sharing the same zero as the horizontal line—we call that the origin—and then one, two, three, you see?"

But Thomas was silent, having fallen asleep long ago.

Harry crept slightly closer to his heat and in time, she, too, slept.

Eleven

To Thomas, Harry seemed a little overwhelmed by the formal staff greeting upon her entrance into the main hall of Sommerleigh.

"So many people. I see why you needed the money," she said under her breath to Thomas.

"You don't have to learn everyone's name at once," Thomas said, taking her arm and leading her toward the imperial staircase at the far end of the hall. Smythe followed them through the main hall, carrying Harry's small bag that she had retrieved from a footman.

And then Harry proceeded to name off everyone in the hall that she had just met. "Of course, as soon as they change their clothes, I'll be lost." She then stopped and turned to Smythe, panicked. "My books! The trunks!"

Smythe said smoothly, "The trunks will be brought to your bedchamber for now, my lady. Your bedchamber is the bedchamber meant for the lady of the house, and as such was predetermined. But I am sure that his lordship and you will want to select *your room* for your books. Then, the trunks can be moved."

"Yes, good," Harry said. Smythe then curtsied and headed off for the servants' staircase.

Thomas noticed Harry was leaning on him and panting a bit as they climbed the first half-flight of stairs, even though the steps were wide and the risers were low. The day was not hot but drops of perspiration were beading her forehead. Halfway up that first set of stairs, she had to stop. He thought for a moment that she might collapse. Then, she took a deep breath and looked up at the stairs still left to mount until they reached the grand landing with an enormous window that faced the grounds that led to the lake.

"I'm looking forward to seeing the view from that window, Lord Drake," she said.

And then she started up again, Harry leaning more and more heavily on Thomas' arm with each passing step. As they reached the landing, Harry crossed to the window on her own power, and collapsed onto the window seat.

"This is nice," she panted.

"I'm hoping that the grounds will meet with your approval, Lady Drake," Thomas said.

Harry looked out. Thomas looked out too and saw the familiar sloping green lawns, the glimmer of light on water, and beyond, forests and farmers' fields. He was glad to be home. He was grateful that his wife had saved this place for him. Unexpectedly, he felt the pricking of tears in his eyes.

"Pretty," she finally said.

Thomas blinked rapidly.

"How tall is this house?"

"I don't know, my lady."

Harry looked down at the garden directly under the window.

"If you ever need to know," she said, "I will find it for you."

Thomas had a picture of Harry standing on the parapet at

the top of the manse and lowering a massive tape measure, plumbing the air.

"It's quite a good trick and I have always thought it would be fun but I could never do it for Papa's house because the buildings behind and across the street were both higher than our house. Of course, I would have to do it earlier in the day when the shadow is slightly more pronounced. Or later, but round the other side."

Harry stood, teetered, and then sat back rather hard onto the cushion of the window seat.

"Oof," she said.

"If my lady will permit." Thomas stooped and put one arm under her knees and wrapped one arm around her back and swiftly picked her up.

Good God, was it possible she was even lighter than when he had picked her up after she had fainted in his London rooms?

Harry held herself rigidly as he easily carried her in his arms up the next flight of stairs.

"After all, this is traditional." Thomas smiled. "It won't hurt us to follow some traditions, would it?"

"Mmmf," Harry said, staring at the ceiling. "Based, of course, on the story of the rape of the Sabine women, the custom of the groom carrying the bride across the threshold of the bedchamber reflects the woman's natural reluctance to submit to intercourse and the man's eagerness to perform it upon her."

Thomas marveled at her ability to speak in such long sentences when moments before she had not had the strength to stand.

"Does not the rape of the Sabine women really refer to the Latin for seize, *rapere*? Weren't they kidnapped?" he asked.

Harry eyes widened, and she looked at his cravat rather

than at the decoration on the hall ceiling. Her eyes were more brown than green today.

"You remember your Latin?" she asked with some evident surprise.

"Very little. I did have some tutoring. Had to read Cicero. Dreadful."

"And so you think your noble Romans kidnapped these women and didn't force them into fornication? They just wanted some nice ladies around, to look pretty and maybe do the cooking?"

"That was my impression when I was nine." Thomas laughed.

Smythe had reached the bedchamber, had opened the door, and was standing in the hall, waiting. It was, of course, Thomas' mother's bedchamber, not used since her death and his birth. He could only remember being in the room a handful of times, sneaking in as a boy, curious. His mother's personal effects had long lingered, likely due to his father's wishes, but then had disappeared around the time Jane was married.

He carried Harry over the threshold of the room now and deposited her in a chair by the fire. The butler Whitson or the housekeeper Mrs. Dewey must have arranged to have the bedchamber freshly painted and the carpets and drapes cleaned after the first announcement of the banns in the church of Sommerleigh three weeks ago. There had been time for some womanly touches, too. Flowers on a table. A cozy chair by the window where the light was best for reading. Likely, his staff had arranged for the flowers and Smythe had moved a chair to the window upon her own arrival yesterday. Smythe knew Harry.

His mother's furniture remained unchanged—the delicate dressing table, the mahogany bed where she had given birth to him and died. He shivered.

"My lady," Thomas inclined his head, "welcome to Sommerleigh."

"Thank you, Lord Drake," Harry said absently. She stared into the fire, not even noticing the lovely room that had been prepared for her, the best room of what many thought was the most beautiful manse in this part of England.

When Thomas reached the door, he turned back and said, "I'll arrange for some luncheon to be sent up."

Harry waved her hand in an abstracted manner as if he were a footman and said, "Coffee."

Smythe curtsied and said, "Thank you, my lord."

Fifteen minutes later, Thomas asked to see one of the upstairs chambermaids. She had been in his service for a year, and he had never had occasion to speak to her, nothing beyond a nod and "Good morning" to her curtsey if they passed in the upstairs hall, her carrying coals or linens or a duster.

She looked rather astonished at his request. But an hour later, there was a knock at the library door.

The butler Whitson opened the door and entered, the chambermaid following behind him, holding a covered tray.

"My lady's luncheon dishes, my Lord," Whitson intoned.

Thomas lifted the lid off the salver. A bite of meat gone, perhaps. A pristine pile of roasted potatoes. The butter and the cake untouched.

"How many bread rolls were sent up with this?" Thomas knitted his brows.

The chambermaid looked at Whitson fearfully.

"Answer Lord Drake, Ellen," Whitson said firmly.

"Pleasing to say, my lord, two rolls." She bobbed her head and curtsied.

Two rolls still lay on their plate, nary a crumb missing.

"Send for the doctor," Thomas growled.

When the young doctor came, Harry refused to see him.

Thomas had met Dr. Alasdair Andrews a few times before. The first time had been over a dislocated kneecap sustained while playing cricket drunk with James and some of the other fellows during hunt season. Thomas felt Dr. Andrews was a sound physician. A transplanted Scot, like many of the best doctors, and quite a sensible sort.

Dr. Andrews seemed embarrassed to come back down the main stairs and apologize to Lord Drake, but the lady widnae permit his examination, her maid had said that the lady had said that she was working on a lemma.

A lemma? What the devil was that?

Thomas went up the stairs, two at a time. He knocked on Harry's door. Smythe answered, saw that it was Thomas and curtsied.

Harry's voice floated out to the hall, "Smythe, do tell that doctor to stop being such a bother."

Thomas moved to come through the door, and Smythe stepped out of his way.

Harry was sitting in the same chair where he had left her, but now her feet were on an ottoman, her knees drawn up and a writing board propped there, covered in papers.

"I'm busy," Harry said, not looking up.

"NO ONE . . . in MY house . . . least of all MY WIFE . . . is going to die of neglect!" he roared.

Harry was not in the least bit cowed. She took her feet off the ottoman and put the writing board down. She looked up and met his eyes and knitted her brows together. She looked as fierce as he felt.

"Fine," she growled.

"Fine!" Thomas thundered. He stalked from the room and walked down the stairs.

"Go," he said to the doctor and jerked his thumb in the direction of the stairs. "Examine everything. I'll be back in an hour to hear your report."

He went out to Octavius, who whinnied at his return after such a long absence. Thomas rode him at a gallop until they were both lathered.

"Have ye always been this thin, my lady?"

Harry looked at Smythe who shook her head no.

"No, Doctor."

"When did ye stop eating?"

"I never stopped, but I have no time for it."

"Ye are starving yerself, my lady."

Harry shrugged.

"'Tis a curious thing," Dr. Andrews said. "The Roman physician Galen was the first to suggest that the brain was the seat of thought almost two thousand years ago. Two thousand years and it is still such a mystery. How does this hacket thing —it has the look of a slimy cauliflower, my lady—how does it produce the pyramids and aqueducts and *Beowulf* and our beloved calculus? And yet it does. I suppose that some see the hand of God in it. Of course, my lady kens the work of Descartes."

"*Cogito ergo sum*," Harry murmured.

"Aye."

"I know his mathematics well, but not much of his philosophy."

"My lady, have ye ever entertained the converse notion? Aye, *cogito ergo sum*. I think, therefore I am. But why not also —I am, therefore I think? I'm just a country doctor. I widnae presume to argue against Descartes in a formal setting. But I have seen many things and I cannae believe in Descartes' notion that the mind and body are separate. When the body eats, it gets nourishment and that nourishment is for the brain and, subsequently, the mind as well. When our vital humors course through the body, they also flow to our brain and to our mind. When the body is strong, the mind is made stronger, more quick, more graceful. If the body is weak, the mind can be weakened and made dull."

Harry was thoughtful.

"What do you suggest, Doctor?"

TWELVE

W hen Thomas returned to the house, the doctor was standing in the library. The butler Whitson had brought him some tea.

"My lady respectfully requests that my lord see her first, before we speak together," Dr. Andrews said.

"I don't doubt it. Although I think the 'respectfully' is a polite fiction on your part." Thomas went to his room and splashed some water on his torso and changed his shirt before rapping on Harry's bedchamber door.

"The doctor was quite meticulous," Harry said. She was lying in bed, in a nightdress unruffled by lace, thin wrists poking out, her hands folded in front of her. Except for the dark circles around her eyes, her skin almost matched the white lawn of her nightdress.

"It should be observed, my lord, that despite our agreement about the nature of this marriage, within a day of our wedding, you have managed to force the examination of my body. I might not have been penetrated, but I was thoroughly prodded and palpated. By a man."

Smythe chose that moment to step out of the bedchamber and into the hall. She closed the door.

"I . . . I, uh . . . I am sorry if the doctor—" Thomas felt he had very definitely been put on the back foot here. Unfairly. Was he not in the right to insist on her good health? In a way, it was very . . . sacrificing of him to try to keep her alive. She had told him that she would die and leave him free. He was working against his own best interests, wasn't he?

"The doctor did nothing wrong. In fact, Dr. Andrews is quite magnificent, and is much more skilled and knowledge-able, I believe, than the fashionable London physicians Mama Katie hires. I am quite happy to have him attend me in the future. He knows the calculus."

"He does?"

"Yes, he studied it during his medical training. He said that the beauty of the calculus helped him survive the dissecting rooms."

"I see. Well, I am glad he meets with your approval." Thomas was, strangely, not glad.

"Yes, we had quite a good talk. And I have agreed to the utility of many of his treatments. He was quite persuasive."

Thomas wondered *how* the doctor might have persuaded her.

Harry went on, "To spare Dr. Andrews discomfort, knowing that you will be paying his bill with my money that is no longer my money, I have told him that he can tell you the results of his examination of me."

Thomas was lost. Why would information about his wife be withheld from him?

"You see, Lord Drake," and Harry looked directly in his eyes, "I now know that I have been quite right, all along. Bodies are of no real importance since this one will never belong to me. It belonged to my parents, I suppose, and it now belongs to you. I have just one thing that is really mine."

She lay down flat and rolled to face away from him.

"She's a canny lass," Dr. Andrews said and then bit his lip as if he regretted saying it. "I meant to say, the Lady Drake is quite extraordinary, my lord."

Thomas was in no mood to discuss Harry's lack of ordinariness with Dr. Andrews. He noted then for the first time that Dr. Andrews was as tall as he was, if slimmer in his build. A full head of wavy, auburn hair. That damn charming burr. Dimples when he smiled, as he was doing now. Women liked dimples.

"She says that her other physicians, the ones in London, told her that she was to die soon," Thomas said.

"She told me that, too. And, aye, she might, if she dinnae have a change in her ways. Her habits will be the cause of her demise."

"What does she need, Doctor?"

"Simple things. She needs to eat good food. She needs sunshine. She needs to walk and strengthen her heart and lungs and legs. She needs rest."

"Rest? Should I take away her books?"

"Good God, man!" The doctor was shocked. "Do ye want to kill her?"

"No, no, I see what you mean," Thomas said hastily. "So she could get better, stronger?"

"Aye," Dr. Andrews said and smiled. Thomas smiled, too, and clapped him on the shoulder and went to pour them two glasses of whisky.

Dr. Andrews took his glass. "Ah, the illicit milk of the motherland." He hesitated with his glass at his lips. "But I must tell ye, my lord," the doctor said and gulped the whisky.

"Yes?"

"'Tis very bad news, my lord."

Thomas refilled his glass. What could be bad news? Hadn't the doctor just said that Harry might get better?

"I was glad to find that ye had been careful with yer wife on the wedding night and that she remains whole. In my opinion, my lord, she should not bear a child at this time. That could be fatal to her, as she is now."

Thomas felt a rise of blood to his head.

"You looked, down there?" Thomas took a step toward the doctor. "At my wife's nether regions?"

The doctor stammered a bit but held his ground. "Ye told me to examine everything. Her maid was present the entire time, my lord."

"And what did Harry—Lady Drake—do, when you . . . ?"

"She said that she dinnae mind and could her maid pass her a book."

In fact, Dr. Alasdair Andrews had been surprised by the nonchalance with which Lady Drake had pulled up her nightdress and spread her legs wide. It had put him in mind of the many whores he had treated during his training in Edinburgh —their complete lack of concern for who might see their pudenda as he lanced their pustules.

Based on Lady Drake's detachment, Dr. Andrews had felt sure that he would find that she had been ravished many times before. However, he had discovered no physical evidence of that. She was merely a malnourished innocent with the mind of a prodigy.

Dr. Andrews had drawn down her nightdress and told Harry that she should try to avoid pregnancy.

"I know," she had said. "No kissing and no children. And no fu—of the other thing." She had looked at her maid, who had raised her eyebrows at Lady Drake.

"Aye," Dr. Andrews had said and then had gone on to feel

Lady Drake's extremely large skull, really the only large thing about her besides her eyes.

However, now in the library, Dr. Andrews was dealing with a husband who was not at all nonchalant about a display of genitalia.

The earl took a deep breath and let it out. "Just so." He seemed to force a smile on his face. "Well, it's her body, isn't it?"

"Ah—aye," Dr. Andrews stammered, afraid of being lunged at again. But Lord Drake just laughed and poured the doctor more whisky. He did not seem at all concerned that his wife should not bear children.

Dr. Andrews wondered that the empire could sustain itself with the aristocracy having so little concern for successful reproduction. No wonder England had lost the colonies of America.

Thirteen

Harry was confined to her bedchamber for several days. Dr. Andrews attended Harry in the morning. He would examine his patient and then come downstairs and give Thomas a brief synopsis of Harry's progress. She had better color and her pulse was not racing as it was before. She was doing as she was told, drinking the broths and the tisanes that Dr. Andrews had told the cook Mrs. Haversham to prepare. With the assistance of Smythe, she was walking in her bedchamber a bit every day, to strengthen her legs. However, she was still weak.

Thomas, for his part, would visit Harry before dinner every evening. She had not been cordial, exactly, but had received him and thanked him for his inquiries regarding her health. On the evening of the fourth day, he found Harry pacing up and down before the fireplace in the room, Smythe standing off to one side.

"Ah, Lord Drake," Harry whirled and her robe flared out for a moment, revealing very slender ankles, "see how fit I am. How I walk? So steady. Such long strides!" Here, she took quite a long step and teetered for a moment, unbalanced, and

Thomas caught her around her waist before she fell into the fire screen. Harry glared at him.

"Yes, I see, you are quite the Pheidippides," Thomas said and made sure she was upright and stable before he released her. But she had been against him for a few moments. Such a small waist under her robe.

"Yes," she was breathing a little hard, "I think it's time I find *my room*."

Thomas looked at Smythe.

"A room for my lady's books, Lord Drake." Smythe curtsied.

"A room for the mind that will prove Fermat's conjecture," Harry corrected.

"Of course, you shall tour the house tomorrow, if Dr. Andrews permits," Thomas said.

Harry turned around and stalked back to the bed. "Dr. Andrews will permit it."

Dr. Andrews *did* permit it. Thomas thought perhaps he had taken one look at Harry's knitted brows and had known what was good for him.

First, Thomas suggested the morning room. Surely, that was traditionally where the lady of the house received visitors, did her correspondence, approved menus proposed by the cook. Harry scoffed. *Her room* could not be a place where she might be bothered with menus. Besides if she had her way, they would all eat porridge every meal of the day, every day of the year. The food must be managed as it had always been before she came here. And, besides, she needed something far more private.

And so, Thomas led her on a slow tour of all the rooms. If Harry was astonished by the size of the manse, she did not say so. Thomas was very careful to insist that she sit in most of the rooms for a few minutes. "To see what it is like," he said diplomatically, rather than saying it was for her to rest.

"*My room* should be big," she said and gestured with her arms. "I have been thinking that perhaps my mind has been cramped by the narrowness of my space in London. This one should also have a good view, perhaps like the view I saw my first day here, from the window on the landing."

After luncheon, up one of the smaller staircases, among a set of small, modestly furnished bedchambers, Harry said she had found the room. It was at the very top of the house. A spacious room with some odd angles. Wide smooth wooden planks on the floor. Well-plastered white walls and ceiling with nary a crack. It was empty except for a wooden chair and dust floating in shafts of sunlight coming from one of the two strangely large windows.

"These attic rooms were for the servants of guests who come to stay. It has been a long time since bedchambers have been needed in such abundance in this house." Thomas looked out one of the windows and swiped at the dust on the sill. "But this room . . . my older sister Jane told me that my mother once used this room for watercolor painting."

"You have a sister."

Thomas did not turn from the window. "I did have one. She was more mother than sister to me. She is gone now. But you will meet her son, Phillip. He is at university. Cambridge."

"Cambridge?"

Harry's voice was pitched higher than usual. Thomas turned and thought her face might be a trifle paler than it had been before.

"I need twenty pounds," she said.

"Of course," Thomas said.

Harry sat down abruptly in the lone chair.

"And I need the money sent to Cambridge," Harry said.

"Cambridge?"

"It's a debt. A return of a gift. I forgot until just now. I was given twenty pounds by someone who thought I needed it.

But I didn't, of course, and I don't know where the banknotes are now. I might have used them to mark my place in a book."

"You must tell me the name of the person, and I'll arrange for the funds to be sent."

Harry looked relieved. "Good. But it must be anonymous. No, it must be from Mr. White. I will write a note."

"Who is Mr. White?"

She hesitated. "I suppose I should have no secrets from my husband. I am Mr. White."

And then the whole story came tumbling out. How Harry had first written to Dean George Haddington seven years ago. How she had used the name Mr. Henry White. How the dean had then begun a correspondence with her about number theory, all the while thinking Mr. White was a clever clerk in Harry's father's bank. And then the dean had died, and his widow had sent twenty pounds to her so that she might prove Fermat's conjecture.

"And I don't think that the Widow Haddington is likely to be very rich, my lord."

"No," Thomas said. "It will be arranged, don't worry."

"Good," Harry said. And then, "Thank you" and her eyes skittered away from him.

The large attic room was cleaned that afternoon, and Smythe supervised the moving of the trunks of books and the installation of a large table by the west-facing window. When Thomas came to see Harry in her bedchamber before dinner, she was sitting by the fire, and, was it possible? She looked happy.

"There must be a lock put into the door on the room, and I must be the only one to have a key," Harry told Thomas peremptorily.

"Do you suspect a rival mathematician will sneak into the house to crib your work?" Thomas asked, amused.

Harry just glared at her lap.

"It will be done, Lady Drake," he assured her.

Harry then looked at the ceiling and smiled. "I have decided to call it my aerie."

"I am glad you have found a nest, my lady." Thomas turned to leave.

"Perhaps . . ." At the sound of her voice, Thomas paused at the door. "Perhaps I shall dedicate my proof to you, Lord Drake, since you have made it possible."

Thomas bowed his head, sensitive that this was a great honor being bestowed upon him. "Thank you." And then, "Oh, and I go to London tomorrow."

"Oh?" Harry said diffidently.

"I tell you so that you will not expect a visit from me tomorrow evening."

"Just so, Lord Drake."

"Goodnight, my lady."

Thomas closed the door behind him. Harry was improving. He could now depart Sommerleigh with a clear conscience. The urge to get back to London had been building since their arrival. This was the longest he had gone without a woman since his father died. He relieved himself, of course, but his need seemed to abate for only seconds.

He would leave in the morning, so as to be in town quite early and have his choice of the doxies.

From then on, at least once a week, Thomas went to London. He would ride up on Octavius, indulge in a night of debauchery, and ride back the next day. It was two days of hard riding with a sleepless night between. It made no sense. He could afford to stay in London for a week or two. He often took the clothes and coin to stay a week. But without fail, the day after his arrival in London, he found himself saddling Octavius back up for the return to Sommerleigh.

Staying in town a week didn't agree with Octavius. Although it was true that Octavius had, for years, spent many weeks at a time stabled in London while his master grazed on female charms.

The estate needed his attention, as he would never let it fall into the financial disarray that his father and his grandfather had.

And Lady Drake. He must see to her health. She was his responsibility.

If Jackson had noted that his master, on his return from London, was quick to ask for a bath to remove the dregs of perfume and rouge left on his body, the valet said nothing. Thomas would stand outside the aerie, shaved and clean, and wait for Harry to come out. He would come down to dinner with Lady Drake. He would eat heartily and then retire, able to sleep through the night. It was often his only full night's sleep until the following week, when he would repeat the cycle again.

Fourteen

arry found her new life to her liking. She still
thought breakfast very difficult, wanting only her
coffee. She tried to persuade Smythe to eat the
breakfast—toast and eggs and ham and kidneys and porridge
—that was brought to her in bed on a large tray. Harry could
not believe the amount of food she was expected to eat. There
was enough for a farmer's family. But Smythe wouldn't touch
it, saying Harry had to eat it all, Smythe had already eaten her
breakfast which had been twice the size of Harry's breakfast,
and his lordship would have her head if he found out she was
eating Lady Drake's portions.

When Thomas was at Sommerleigh and Harry tried to
scrimp on breakfast, without fail, he would then eat luncheon
with her and encourage the footmen to bring her dish after
dish. He didn't insist but he did *promote*. He would smack his
lips over a meat pie or a wedge of cheese or bowl of raspberries,
telling Harry that the food was succulent and that Dr.
Andrews had said meat pie or cheese or whatever it was he was
eating at that moment was vital for health.

She suspected from this that he inspected her tray after it

left her bedchamber, and she did not want to disappoint him with a poor showing at breakfast. He had helped her find her aerie and had sent the money to Dean Haddington's widow; she must show him that she was making an effort.

So Harry ate as much of each breakfast as she could. In time, she found eggs could be agreeable to her if the white and yellow were mixed together before cooking so that both the color and texture were uniform. She told Smythe this and noted that her eggs came to her that way every morning thereafter.

After breakfast, there was walking. On fine days, it must be outside in the gardens, so that she could have the sun on her face. On wet days, she walked in the gallery, up and down, up and down. Many fine mornings, the doctor would happen past Sommerleigh to check on his patient and then he would join her for her walk on the grounds. They talked mathematics frequently, or rather, Harry talked mathematics. Specifically, theories about the natural numbers. The doctor, Harry felt, did his best to ask intelligent questions but quite frequently he was silent until the conversation was steered, by her, to a topic of more general interest. Like celestial mechanics.

Sometimes, during her walks in the gallery, Thomas would join her if he were at home. He might offer his arm and be close to her as they walked. In this way, she could feel a bit of his heat. He would explain the provenance of the pictures if she asked. But mostly they lapsed into silence. If the day was more than wet, if it was storming, he would stand on the landing of the main staircase and watch and wait. When the storm stopped, she noted, even if it was luncheon, he would go out and ride Octavius.

Harry was in her aerie before and after luncheon, before and after dinner. Thomas had had a lock fitted to the door of the room and she wore the key on a chain round her neck, where it joined a sister key, the one to *her room* in London.

The aerie was now filled with her books and stacks of paper and an assortment of inkpots and quills. It smelled of ink and old leather bindings and dust. Harry thought the aerie itself, the smell, the view were all extremely conducive to hard work. And perhaps the morning exercise helped her to sit quietly for longer periods of time in the afternoon. She certainly felt less agitated.

The hours in the aerie flew by in a way that they had not in London. Harry relished her life of no balls, no calls.

Thomas would ride Octavius in the afternoon, if he were home. She would often look out from her aerie as the sun was descending in the western sky and search for a horse and rider coming back to the manse for dinner. And when she would spot him, knowing that soon she would be joining him in the dining room, she had the most peculiar feelings in her stomach.

She didn't tell anyone, and certainly not Thomas, about those peculiar feelings. It turned out, after all, that there were some secrets one should keep from one's husband.

It was not going well. It was very much not going well. It could not be going any worse. Why couldn't she see? Why wasn't the path clear? How could she fail at this?

Thump, thump, thump, thump. Head on wall. Get it clear. *Thump, thump, thump.* Not any clearer but her head hurt and *that* was clear.

Blast Fermat. Damn him to hell. And Diophantus, too.

Thump, thump, thump, thump, thump, thump, thump, thump. Almost uncontainable.

A knocking that sounded different from her head knocking and, "Harry, Harry, Harry." A man's voice.

And, "Let me in, damnit!"

Thump, thump, thump.

And, "I'll break this precious lock if you don't let me in!"
Thump.

Harry walked to the door and unlocked it and opened it. She walked back to the wall where she had been thumping her head. *Thump, thump, thump.*

She could feel herself on the verge.

Thomas was then in her aerie. "See here, Harry, stop that, you're scaring everyone, what is wrong with you?"

Harry stopped thumping her head and held still. But Thomas said, "Be quiet, stop it!"

Only then did Harry realize that she had been keening. With enormous effort, she quieted her voice. She went back to thumping her head.

Thomas grabbed her by her shoulders. "Stop doing that. You're hurting yourself."

Close, so close. Harry slid out of his grasp and collapsed onto her knees and rocked back and forth, bending down so that her head almost touched the floor.

Thomas crouched down next to her. "What's wrong? Are you ill?"

Smythe in the doorway. Smythe's voice. "She's upset, my lord. She's not ill, she's not mad. She's just trying to feel better."

Yes, she agreed with Smythe. Just trying to feel better. No. Just trying to think better. Who cared about feeling better?

"Well, there has to be a way for her to feel better without pounding her head to a pulp and howling like a banshee!"

Smythe again. "Her stepmother had a way. You must ask her if you can help her."

Thomas said, "Can I help you, Harry?" His voice seemed very far away.

Harry bobbed and bowed and rocked and nodded yes. Could she manage to speak? Yes. She squeaked out a single word. "Yes."

Smythe said, "Kneel behind her. Yes. Now, wrap your arms around her waist."

Harry felt the warmth of Thomas behind her and then the tentative touch of his hands. Oh, that heat. His scent.

"No, no, my lord, you must wrap your arms very tightly. You must constrain her so she can't move."

His arms tightened. A cinch around her waist, holding her. She tried to rock and she could not. She was stuck fast. Yes.

"Are you sure?" His voice came from behind her. "Harry, is this right?"

Harry nodded and leaned back into his chest and then pushed her body forward trying to break his grip. But she could not. He was much stronger than Catherine so she could push with all her force. His grip did not break. It would not break.

Her breathing slowed. She felt her muscles start to relax. She was safe with him. Safe with his arms around her, holding her here, keeping her compressed so she did not break off into a million spinning pieces and crumble into dust.

"Don't let go yet, my lord," Smythe said.

The overwhelming need to thump and keen and rock was dissipating. And yes, there it was, how Euler's totient function might be of use. She went to get up but Thomas' arms still held her to him. She thought it might be agreeable to have him do this sometime when she didn't have an important mathematical *coup de maître* in mind. But she had no time right now.

"You can let go," Harry said, voice hoarse. There was a silence and she suspected Thomas was looking to Smythe.

"Yes, my lady," Smythe said. Thomas let go. Harry got up and went right to the desk and dipped her pen in the ink and began writing while standing. She must get this down.

. . .

Thomas didn't know what to make of the episode. Harry's eyes had been so wild, almost mad. But Smythe said it was not madness.

"How often does this happen, Smythe? You seem to know all about it."

They had come down the stairs away from the aerie.

"Not often, my lord. Maybe now once every six months. More often when she was younger and more subject to frustration."

Thomas took out a handkerchief and wiped his forehead. She had been so tense, vibrating in his arms, putting him in mind of a frightened, skittish, unbroken filly.

"I think her stepmother tried to warn me. I've never seen a fit like that."

"My lord, it is not a fit. She is trying to calm a strong emotion. Some people cry, some people drink wine, some people strike others. Harry hits her own head and howls."

"I am surprised she allowed me to hold her. She does not like touch, she says."

"No, my lord, she does not."

"Well, thank you, Smythe." She curtsied, and he turned to go.

Just then he heard her say in a low voice, "I am surprised she let you in the room at all, my lord."

FIFTEEN

"I think we will need to go to London soon, my lady," Smythe said as she helped Harry put her dress on over her head.

As far as Harry was concerned, that was an impossibility.

"Why?" Harry's gruff voice was muffled as she sought her arm holes.

"Your clothes, my lady. You are much more shapely now. You need proper accommodation."

"Bother." Harry's head had finally popped through. She looked at the cheval mirror, something she rarely did. "You can see the top of my bosom!"

"Yes, my lady."

"Well, that's rather horrid. I should cover it up. I might catch cold."

"Not today, my lady. It is so warm."

"That's true," Harry said and strode to the window. She looked down at her own chest. Such a nuisance.

"And you need some new corsets, including one that can take a busk."

"A busk? No, Smythe, no, I will not wear a piece of wood down my front so that I can't lean over."

"Just for formal occasions, my lady. We will have some corsets fitted and at least one made so that it could have a busk. Then you could try it once and see if you could tolerate it."

"All right." Harry conceded and turned away from the window. "But I am sure I'll never wear it."

On one point Harry was firm. She didn't want to go to London. Too long of a journey. Too much wasted time. Smythe, after discussion with some of the other servants, then suggested that they go to a dressmaker in Tavishbourn, a town of some size, only an hour away by carriage. Harry agreed.

At luncheon, Harry told Thomas of the planned trip.

"Why are you going to Tavishbourn?" He was curious. Harry had gone nowhere since she had come to Sommerleigh.

"Smythe says I must have new clothes."

Thomas leaned forward. "But you won't get the latest fashions in Tavishbourn. Much better to take several days and go to London. You can see your stepmother and your sister and your usual dressmaker. Perhaps I'll come with you."

"I don't care for fashion, my lord. And I don't have the time to go to London." Harry threw her napkin down in exasperation.

"Then why the new clothes? We do not entertain here."

Harry looked down.

"Smythe says . . . I must."

Thomas steepled his fingers. "Does Smythe have some magical power to persuade you to do things that I don't?"

"I have . . . That is, my clothes . . . I am getting fat! I knew all this food was a mistake. I waste time in eating it and now I must waste time in getting new clothes." Harry's face became pink. "If you must know, my bosom grows!"

Thomas did not need Harry to inform him of that fact. He had, for some time, been privately tracking the development of Harry's chest. She had gone from being completely flat to having two subtle protuberances. Very subtle indeed, but Thomas felt himself a connoisseur and thus well able to appreciate the change.

He saw now that the shoulders of her current dress were quite strained. There was no rupture of seams but the dress did look uncomfortable.

"I beg your pardon, my lady. I defer entirely to Smythe's judgment." Thomas wanted to find a way to tell Harry that he liked her fledgling breasts and that she was still much too thin, but he could not. Instead, he said, "Do you not find yourself enjoying your meals?"

"Enjoy? Enjoyment is not the ruler by which I measure my life, Lord Drake." Harry's voice was rising. "In a hundred years, no one will care about the number of potatoes I eat. Or, for that matter, the number of whores you've bedded. But they will care that a woman solved Fermat's conjecture!"

"It seems hard to give up so much of one's life in a bid for posterity."

"You think that this is all about self-glorification!" Harry was seething. Thomas had never seen her like this. Even her episode of keening and head thumping seemed calm compared to this. This was red-faced screaming with spittle flying from her mouth. "You know nothing!" she shouted now and stormed from the room.

A half an hour later, Thomas went up to Harry's aerie and stood outside the door. He thought he heard a pen scratching, her muttering. He walked down two flights and went in search of Smythe. He found her coming out of Harry's bedchamber, carrying a pair of boots caked in mud.

"Well, Smythe, I see that at least my lady had a good walk this morning."

Smythe curtsied. "Yes, my lord."

"She lost her temper at luncheon," Thomas said. "Or I should say, she lost her temper at me."

"Yes, my lord."

"I was astonished."

Smythe bit her lip and curtsied.

Thomas crossed his arms in front of his chest and leaned on the doorjamb. "Say what you like, Smythe. You're the one who knows her best. Give me the benefit of your wisdom."

"In truth, my lord, I am surprised it has taken so many weeks for her to have a rage at you. But it will pass quickly. She won't apologize to you, but by dinner, she will be quite calm, almost sweet, and will act as if it never happened."

Thomas thought it might be interesting to see Harry's version of "sweet." He smiled at that idea. "Since my lady seems to resent having to have new clothes made, perhaps you could induce the dressmaker at Tavishbourn to make several dresses in the same style and color but increasing in size? I would not want my wife to stop eating just to avoid a trip to the dressmaker."

"Yes, my lord."

"And perhaps, you could make sure . . ." He turned his head to the side and squinted at her.

Smythe waited.

"No brown, no gray, no green, no yellow. Blue, I think. And none of your faded, insipid blues. A good strong blue. Yes, at least one blue gown. And pink. And red."

"Yes, my lord."

"And two warm cloaks, one with a fur lining, one without. I want her to be able to continue her walks in all weather. I think, perhaps, red wool?"

"Yes, my lord."

"And get her measured for some new boots as well."

"I will do my best, my lord." Smythe curtsied.

Thomas looked at her now. Neat, tidy. A sensible woman of middle age. "You've done very well for Harry, Smythe. I suspect she does not thank you, so let me."

"It is a privilege to wait on Lady Drake."

Thomas turned to leave but was arrested by Smythe's voice.

"And if I may be so bold, my lord, you've done very well for her, too."

Thomas nodded and walked down the hall.

Later, Jackson told Thomas he had to stop grinning because it made his lordship devilishly difficult to shave for dinner.

Sixteen

Harry went out into the garden one late morning with a stake and a ball of string. Thomas spied her from the library and strolled out to join her.

"Good morning, my lady," Thomas said. "You have already walked?"

"Yes," Harry said. She found a soft place in a flower bed near the manse for her stake.

"I did not know you had a fondness for gardening."

Harry looked up then. "I don't."

"Then what are you doing, Harry?"

"I am measuring the height of your house, Thomas."

It was the first time she had called him by his Christian name since their wedding night. He was pleased. Very pleased. Far too pleased. He had no business being that pleased.

Thomas looked up at the towering manse. He shielded his eyes with his hand, squinting as he stood in full light as the sun peeked over the crest of the roof. The sun was fairly high. The shadow of the house right now only extended about eight or so feet from the house itself.

"I had imagined that you would need to go to the roof."

"No." Harry had placed the stake so that the shadow of the house fell across the stake, dividing it. She leaned over and placed the end of the string at the point where the shadow hit the stake and let the ball of string fall to the ground.

"Do you have a knife?" she asked. Thomas fished a small folding knife with a white handle out of his pocket, opened it, and handed it to her, handle first. Harry squatted and cut the string where it brushed the ground and hung the string around her neck. Then she measured a string from the house to the base of the stake and a string from the base of the stake to where the edge of the shadow of the house fell on the ground.

She folded up the knife, looking at it briefly. "Nice." She handed it back to him. "Do you have a Bedwell ruler? Or really anything to measure feet and inches?"

Thomas did. He took her to the library and she measured her strings there.

"Seventy-six," she said.

Thomas looked at her blankly.

"Feet. That's the height of the house."

"What trickery is this?"

"Do you have paper?" Harry drew a picture and explained. It helped that Thomas had studied geometry at some point with one of his tutors, long ago. He grasped the concept but was still confused.

"But the number seventy-six. You did no calculations to arrive at that number."

"Yes, I did."

Thomas smiled. "Are you a mental calculator? How splendid."

Harry shrugged and left the library.

Thomas then began to look in some of the large drawers in the library that contained different documents, ones that did not need to be in a vault. He seemed to remember . . . yes. He laid his hands on drawings of the house, made by an architect long ago, before he was born, when his father had apparently thought of adding another wing. Nothing had come of it as his father had soon realized his finances were contracting, not expanding. The drawings showed the height of the roofline as seventy-six feet.

He was not surprised that the number matched Harry's. He was surprised by the degree of delight he felt that it did so.

An hour later, a message came from the house of the Dunbars, his nearest neighbors. Mr. and Mrs. Dunbar would be pleased to call on Lord and Lady Drake this afternoon, if it might be convenient to them. Thomas waited to send his reply.

He broached the subject to Harry at luncheon.

There was a plump brown partridge with Mrs. Haversham's bread sauce and red currant jelly sitting on Harry's plate. She was cutting into the breast when Thomas said, "We may have some visitors this afternoon for tea. The Dunbars. My neighbors. I suspect they are anxious to meet you. We cannot make an excuse of your illness any longer. You are looking so well."

Thomas was surprised to see Harry's face redden. "I look so well?" she said and quickly put a forkful in her mouth.

"I don't want to be accused of being a Blackbeard and keeping you locked away."

Harry chewed and swallowed. "I see." A pause. "Is Mrs. Dunbar a gossip?"

Thomas was startled. "What?"

"Is she a gossip? And is she popular and gregarious in the neighborhood? Will all the other local gentry hear of this visit? Will she recount what I wear and what I say to the other ladies, the shopkeepers, any tramp who might be passing through?"

"She is popular, yes, I believe. I don't know whether she is a gossip, but she is . . . voluble."

Harry continued to eat, steadily. After she had eaten most of the bird, she said, "I suppose I better be done with it. If she will come and tell the others what I am like, I will not have to entertain the rest of them individually in the future. Their curiosity should be satisfied."

Thomas didn't think that was true but was relieved by her answer. "Yes."

"And will there be coffee in addition to tea?"

Thomas knew that Harry did crave coffee in the afternoon.

"I will make sure of it, Harry."

Thomas told Smythe to inspect for ink on Harry's face and her hands and to dress her hair quickly in a becoming manner when it was time for her to descend from the aerie. When Harry came into the drawing room to meet the Dunbars, a hearty couple in their forties, Thomas thought that Smythe had done a good job picking the dress—a pale-pink one that was soft and hid a great deal of Harry's remaining angularity. He also thought there might even be a bit of a flush on Harry's cheek. She looked much better than she had at their wedding, and he felt a bit of pride over it.

Harry remembered a great deal of her lessons at the hands of Mama Katie. She curtsied and smiled. She answered questions and asked her own. She hoped that Thomas noticed how well she was doing. But he didn't really understand how difficult this was for her, so he couldn't possibly fully appreciate what she was doing for him.

She learned that the Dunbars had seven children. Harry made the appropriate sounds of awe. Their three oldest were daughters that Mrs. Dunbar had named Faith, Hope, and Charity.

"Just a silly fad of mine at the time," Mrs. Dunbar said,

sipping her tea, "but the girls have been so good as to say they like their names. Although, at times, people think that we are Puritans." Mrs. Dunbar laughed at that—a big, jolly laugh—and Harry smiled to be polite.

"To be sure, Charity is only fifteen. Faith has married and lives in Tavishbourn but we see her often. Hope is out in society and a lovely girl, beautiful red hair like my own mother's, so very sweet and so kind. You two might become friends."

Harry murmured politely.

"She is very sociable. She will call on you soon when she returns from London. She enjoyed the last bit of the Season at her aunt's house and then decided to stay on through the early autumn."

"I am sure she will be very busy upon her return. Perhaps with suitors or an engagement."

"We had hoped, that is—" Mrs. Dunbar's glance went to Thomas who was engaged in a conversation with Mr. Dunbar regarding the amount of rain and the effects on the local farmers. Mrs. Dunbar then suddenly seemed to remember something and pulled up sharply. "Yes, yes, very busy. But we will see. She returns next week in time for her birthday. She will be just twenty."

An upcoming birthday. Harry had one, too. She had forgotten. A pit opened up in her stomach.

Mrs. Dunbar went on to discuss the different balls that Hope had been to during the Season. It seemed unlikely that Harry would have met Hope in town since Hope had traveled to London just as Harry and Thomas had made their way to Sommerleigh. Mrs. Dunbar chatted away about minutiae even as Harry directed her mind to that which was most crucial.

She had very few days left on her schedule. She must work harder, longer. She had no time for anything else. Especially not for thoughts about her husband.

SEVENTEEN

After the call from the Dunbars, Thomas noted a rapid decrease in Harry's appetite. Her breakfast came to him with just a few mouthfuls gone. She picked at luncheon and dinner and rushed away to go back to her aerie. She still walked but she made the walks quite short. She would come back into the house, muttering and agitated. Long after midnight one night, Thomas wandered out to the front drive to enjoy the crisp air. When he looked back at the house, he could see a lamp burning in the aerie's windows.

Thomas made his weekly trip to London and upon his return, he was startled. The Harry who came out of her aerie that evening was different. Her shoulders were stooped. The rings under her eyes were, if anything, darker, more deeply carved into her pale skin. And her dress looked slightly loose. He selfishly mourned the dwindling of her breasts.

The next day it rained.

Although Harry did not look well, she no longer took Thomas' arm when they walked in the gallery, as she had in her first weeks at Sommerleigh. He found himself missing that delicate pressure of her presence, how she would curl her arm under his at the elbow and then rest her hand on his forearm. She had been close against him then, and he could feel when her breath was short, when she might stumble. Now, they walked six feet apart.

"He's coming," Thomas said that morning as they walked. "Phillip's coming."

Harry focused her gaze toward the other end of the gallery, their goal.

"Phillip?"

"My nephew. My ward. My heir."

"Heir to your title? But you said he was your sister's son?"

"Yes." Thomas bit his lower lip and said nothing else.

"Then how can your nephew be your heir?"

"His father was a distant cousin. Next in line. He married my sister."

"I see. This is how you can marry me and have no concern for having a son. Unless, of course, I die, then you can have a son by your second wife," Harry said flatly.

Thomas did not know what to say to that.

"But you're not going to die, Lady Drake."

"The average death rate per person is holding steady at one, my lord."

"But in the near future . . . I mean to say, you had seemed improved. For a while, at any rate. Are you not feeling well?"

Harry sat down to rest in one of the chairs that dotted the gallery.

Thomas stood in front of her, waiting.

"I *had* felt better," Harry said. "But I had not seen the miraculous improvement in my powers of cognition that Dr. Andrews promised me. There is so much still that eludes me."

"Perhaps," Thomas said, "when one is a genius as you are, there is so little room for improvement in your mental prowess, that you must be happy with incremental change."

"How do you know I am a genius?"

"Pardon?"

Harry cleared her throat and looked up, straight at him, meeting his eyes, a rare occurrence. Her eyes were decidedly more green today than brown, he noted.

"I don't think you have the competence to judge my mathematical mind, my lord. Do not take offense. Very few would have that capacity. Perhaps, I am only brilliant *for a woman*. And not brilliant full stop."

Thomas was shaken. He had never heard Harry speak this way. Where was her conviction, her absolute surety that if she could just sit and think and think and sit then she could solve any mathematical problem? Where was that damned arrogance?

"It would be ironic, would it not," Harry went on, looking away from him now and at the wall just behind his left leg, "if I were to outlive you and deny you a real wife and children and yet still not prove Fermat's conjecture? All this, for nothing. Better I should die."

Her voice sounded a note of despair.

"Lady Drake. Harry." Thomas knelt in front of her and intentionally blocked her view of the opposite wall with his head so that he could hold her gaze. "It would not be for nothing. You have saved my estate, and for that, I will always be grateful. Sommerleigh, it is all that I care for. You have done me a great service. I know that is small comfort, if any, to you." He impulsively seized her hands, which were lying limp in her lap. "Take heart, Harry."

She removed her hands from his and stood up on her own, shakily. Thomas scrambled to his feet.

"My heart's not the problem," she said and turned.

There was no good explanation for why his own heart skipped a beat as he watched her narrow figure walk away from him, down the long gallery.

· · ·

The next day, Harry willed herself to stay in the aerie and make *some* progress, any progress. She must. At her request, Smythe brought luncheon on a tray. Producing a half-empty plate, Harry thought, was perhaps the only thing she was good for today.

In the late afternoon, feeling both simultaneously that she could do no more and yet she had done nothing, she heard a creak on the stair. As she came out of the aerie, Thomas was standing two steps down from the top of the stairs, waiting. His hair was sticking up a bit on the side and she thought she might put her hand out and comb down that one tuft of dark hair with her fingers.

But she thought better of it. She would not want him to touch her hair.

Or maybe she would. She did not know her own mind right now, she was so tired. She would go straight to her bedchamber and lie down.

"My lord," she said.

"My nephew Phillip is here. I'd like you to meet him. He wants to meet you," he said and he held out his arm.

"Yes." She took his arm. She would go downstairs to meet his nephew because he said he would like it, but she wished he would carry her on the stairs, like he had on the day after their wedding. She had not fully appreciated her husband and that experience at the time. And besides she was about to drop with fatigue and melancholy.

"Perhaps you would prefer to meet Phillip tomorrow, my lady?" he asked her when they had descended one flight.

"No, no," she said and straightened herself up. "I must meet my nephew."

Phillip was an ordinary-looking youth of nineteen. Ordinary height for a man, which meant the same height as Harry. Already a little heavy around the middle. Flat brown eyes. Straight brown stringy hair. An empty smile.

"Mr. Phillip Drake. My wife, Lady Drake."

Phillip bent low over Harry's hand and she pulled it back quickly, afraid he would kiss it. He laughed. It had been a while since someone had laughed *at* her. And it was in her own house. Of course, it was Phillip's house, too. He had grown up here. He would inherit it.

She looked at Thomas. Thomas was smiling, delighted that they were meeting, saying they should have sherry before dinner and wasn't this splendid?

"You are most welcome, Phillip," Harry said.

"I should hope so." Phillip smiled his empty smile.

"Phillip is at Cambridge." Thomas led her to a chair in the library and seated her in it. "You two should have a lot to talk about."

"And why is that, Uncle?" Phillip asked.

"My lady is—"

"—was an acquaintance of Dean George Haddington, the mathematician," Harry interrupted. "He recently died. Did you know him?"

"Dean Haddington? No, not to speak to him. Mathematics? Blech. I hope I have better ways to spend my time than in finding the sine of thirty-nine."

"What is that?" Thomas turned to her.

"Zero point six two nine," she said and tried to sit up straighter.

Her husband was showing her off. And she didn't mind.

Thomas turned to Phillip and raised his eyebrows. "My wife is a bit of a wizard—or should I say witch?—with numbers."

"Did you calculate that in your head, Lady Drake?" Phillip leaned forward with interest for the first time.

"No." Harry supposed she could have, employing a McLaurin series. "I learned it from a table."

"You must have a prodigious memory, Lady Drake. Could you tell me, say, the sine of five hundred and three?"

"It's nearly the same thing. Zero point six zero one eight."

"That's impossible." Phillip got up and strode to a shelf. "Let's see what Pitiscus says."

"Yes," Thomas knit his brows, "five hundred and three is so much larger than thirty-two, Harry."

Harry bit her tongue.

Phillip placed a large volume on a table and began to leaf through it. He stopped and ran his finger down a page. Then he slammed the book shut and put it back on the shelf.

"Well?" Thomas asked.

Phillip shrugged. "It's a good trick, isn't it? And I had forgotten that it all repeats starting at three hundred and sixty, doesn't it? So three hundred and sixty one is the same as one, and so forth. So you really only have to memorize three hundred and sixty values, Uncle Thomas."

"If you stick to degrees and ignore minutes and seconds, fewer than that, since the sine function has a great deal of symmetry. The values between zero and ninety are the same as those between ninety and one hundred and eighty but counting up instead of down. And the values between one hundred and eighty and three hundred sixty are just negatives of the values from the previous one hundred and eighty degrees, but again ordered in an opposite fashion," Harry said. She did not want Thomas to think she had pretended to memorize more than she actually had. He should know how really simple it was.

"Can you do it with cosine, as well?" Phillip asked.

"In truth," Harry cleared her throat, "I think sine is the only trigonometric table I've memorized."

"So you don't know the other functions, then? That's a pity, you could have been of use to a navigator," Phillip said, his lip curling a bit.

"But the cosine of thirty-nine and five hundred and three are zero point seven seven seven and negative zero point seven nine eight six, respectively."

Phillip laughed. There was something wrong with his laugh but Harry didn't know what exactly.

"All the other trigonometric functions are trivial calculations if you know sine," she explained, "and can do square roots in your head."

Phillip looked her over from head to foot carefully. He made a face. It was quite like the face her stepmother would make when the cook presented a menu that contained turnips, a food Catherine despised.

They were eating turnips that night, among other things. Harry didn't mind turnips; one soft white vegetable was near enough to another. She picked at her food.

Philip peppered Harry with questions initially, asking her to perform mental calculations during dinner, but he couldn't check her answers. Eventually he stopped and only spoke to Thomas, asking about the estate, gossiping about the *ton* and Princess Caroline's affair with her Italian servant. Thomas tried to draw Harry into the conversation at times but she answered with only a few words.

Thank goodness for this very rare female privilege. She stood, Whitson pulling out her chair.

"Please excuse me, gentlemen, I will retire and leave you now."

Thomas looked up at her. "Phillip, go ahead and pour yourself some port and take it to the library. I'll escort my lady upstairs."

Harry waved her hand as if to say not to bother but she was really too tired to protest much. And when they reached the stair and Harry looked up and felt her knees buckle, she was very glad of her husband who picked her up in his arms with so little effort and carried her against his warm chest up

the stairs to her bedchamber where Smythe was waiting
for her.

And Thomas was strangely moved that when he picked Harry
up, she put her arms around his neck and nestled ever so
slightly into his chest, rubbing her cheek against the lapel of
his tailcoat. Just before they reached her bedchamber, without
her noticing, he dared to lower his face to the top of her head
and smell her wild brown curls. Coffee and ink. He should
have known.

He would have Dr. Andrews come and look in on her
tomorrow. She had regressed dangerously back to her old
habits. Not eating, likely not sleeping. And now as weak as a
kitten.

Phillip was thumbing through the book he had pulled
down earlier. When Thomas came into the library, he
slammed it shut.

"Rot," he said.

"You won't get very far with Harry by dismissing mathematics, Phillip," Thomas handed him a glass.

"And who is this Harry?"

"Lady Drake," Thomas said. "Harriet, Harry."

"Harry," Phillip said. And then, "I was very surprised to
hear that you had married, Uncle."

"Well, it happened very quickly."

"I assume the Lady Drake then will be blessing us with
another Drake soon, perhaps in fewer than nine months?"
Phillip's voice, usually so jovial when speaking with his uncle,
had an edge to it.

Thomas goggled at him.

"What . . . why would you say that?"

"The apparent illness of the lady this evening. The haste of
the wedding. And my new Aunt Harry? Is decidedly *not* what

I thought might be your usual type. In physiognomy, anatomy, temperament. And she definitely has the wrong color hair."

Thomas felt a need to defend Harry. "Lady Drake is a woman of many positive qualities."

"Oh, so she's rich as well as pregnant."

Thomas felt Phillip, wonderful boy, was being a trifle impertinent.

"It is none of your business, Phillip, but I assure you my wife is not pregnant."

Phillip raised his eyebrows. "All things being equal, I would love to have a cousin. But all things are not equal and not to put too fine a point on it, it *is* my business. My entire future. As of now, I am your heir. If you die right now, I get the title and Sommerleigh. If you have a son, he gets the title and Sommerleigh."

Thomas now understood Phillip's probing. He gave out a laugh.

"Have no worries, Phillip. You will inherit Sommerleigh, just as I promised you."

"I see. Well, no, I don't really see. Is she incapable?"

Thomas paused.

"I have already said more than I meant to, Phillip. Lady Drake has been the means to save Sommerleigh. I pray you be satisfied with my assurance that your inheritance is safe."

Phillip shrugged and held up his glass. "Right-o, Uncle Thomas. Then let me toast your marriage in a belated fashion. To the best uncle in all of England and his bride."

And they drank.

EIGHTEEN

T he next day, Thomas and Phillip went out riding. Thomas insisted. He said he wanted Phillip to see a small stone bridge on one of the estate roads. The bridge went over a stream that had jumped its banks during some hard rains last spring. Some of the stones on the bridge were loose. Thomas feared a heavy wagon with a full load might bring it crashing down. Perhaps Phillip might have an idea about whether it could be shored up or whether it should be rebuilt entirely from scratch. Phillip shrugged.

"I know nothing about bridges or masonry, Uncle, but I am always happy to ride with you."

In truth, it was a chance for Thomas to show off Sommerleigh. It was his heart's blood. He wanted Phillip to love it as much as he did.

"I'm in a bit of a pickle, Uncle Thomas," Phillip said, as they looked at the small bridge.

"Perhaps some new mortar on this side where it's crumbling a bit," Thomas said to himself. "What's that, Phillip?"

"Well, I am in need of money."

"Again?" Thomas laughed. "Didn't you get thirty pounds three months ago?"

"I am in need of another fifty."

"Tell me the truth, is this going to food and robes and books? Or does some of it go for wine and ale?"

"Yes," Phillip admitted. "And some to dice and some to cards."

"Don't worry about the money, Phillip," Thomas said as they got back onto their horses. "You shall have it. But I want you to be careful. Don't be a wastrel. I have not been a good example to you. But I mean to be careful from now on. No more debts."

"And no more whores?"

Phillip said it lightly. But Thomas' face grew serious and he slowed Octavius.

"No, I have not reformed, but I'm glad you do not follow me, Phillip, in that way. It is not what I would want for you. I wish . . . I wish so many things for you."

"I was just teasing you, Uncle Thomas, don't worry." Phillip laughed.

"Your mother, she was your age when she died. I can hear her disappointment in your voice, that's all."

"I'm not disappointed in you. Now shall we have a race, old man? I think my Romeo can beat your Octavius. Shall we wager on it? A pound?"

"Yes, to the race. No, to the wager. I can't afford to pay your gambling debts even if they are owed to myself!" And with that, Octavius was off across the meadow, Romeo following, both men bent over their horses, intent on victory.

That afternoon, Harry came out of her aerie suddenly, wondering if a cup of coffee might sharpen her brain and lift her spirits. Phillip was standing in the hall, about ten feet away, his back to her.

"Phillip," Harry said, surprised.

He moved slightly to one side and she saw that one of the upstairs chambermaids—Ellen, her name was, with the same apron, cap, and shoes as the day Harry arrived—was behind him, holding a pile of linens, her back pressed against a corner.

Phillip turned and smiled at Harry.

Ellen slid along the wall out of her corner, curtsied, and disappeared.

"Lady Drake, I'm surprised to find you up so high. What are you doing up here?"

Harry pulled the chain from her neck and turned and locked the door of her aerie.

"Working."

"Oh, yes, the French mathematics competition. For that conjecture. What is it? Uncle couldn't remember. Oh, you're going down? Let me join you. I think some tea would be delightful."

"Where did Ellen go?"

"Ellen?" Phillip had already moved toward the stairs but then he turned around and looked at the wall where Ellen had been standing. "Oh, is that her name?" Then he kept walking down the stairs. "I have no idea."

Harry meant to follow him. She also meant to ask Smythe about what she had seen, to ask Smythe to find out if Ellen was quite well.

But she was lost in her own despondency. Tomorrow was the day. Her final day. And she had run out of time and out of ideas.

But perhaps she might be able to prove that the Fermat equation had no integer solutions when the exponent was a prime less one and the prime took the form of a multiple of eight plus seven. Of course, this case would not be enough to constitute a complete proof but it might pave the way for the comprehensive solution.

She pulled the chain from her neck and unlocked the door to her aerie and went back to her desk.

She mustn't waste a minute. The coffee could wait.

NINETEEN

Phillip left the next day, having secured both fifty pounds and the assurance that he would someday be the Earl Drake.

That night at dinner, Harry stirred her soup in front of her. She did not lift the spoon to her lips. Thomas, for his part, ate his soup hungrily as he had missed his luncheon, having spent the whole afternoon riding Octavius. He eyed Harry.

Suddenly, Harry put her face in her hands and burst into tears.

Thomas stood, unsure what to do. Damn. He had forgotten to have Dr. Andrews look in on Harry yesterday as he had planned. He had become neglectful, distracted by Phillip's visit. He would never have ignored an illness of, say, Octavius. Couldn't he treat his wife as well as he treated his horse?

Finally, he looked at Whitson and jerked his head toward the butler's pantry. Whitson and the footmen left the dining room.

Harry continued to sob.

Thomas went to the sideboard and poured two glasses of

port. Then he crossed to Harry and put a glass in front of her. He sat next to her and sipped his port.

He waited.

Eventually, the tears slowed. Thomas handed Harry a handkerchief. She dried her eyes and then found a dry corner and blew her nose. She saw the glass of port and took a sip.

"Thank you," she said glumly.

"For what?"

"Partly for the port and the handkerchief, but mostly for just sitting and not making a fuss."

"Here now, Harry, you must tell me what's wrong."

Her bottom lip began to quiver.

"Today is . . . my birthday." A tear rolled down her cheek.

"I'm so sorry, Harry. I didn't know." Thomas felt relieved momentarily and then cursed himself inside his head. These things were important to women. He should know his wife's birthday. "We should have had a party. You should have gotten gifts. But we can do it next week, eh?"

She sobbed again.

"You must tell me what I must do to fix this, Harry. Shall we plan the party together? Tell me what you want."

"No, no, no! I would hate that, Lord Drake." She wiped her face again with the handkerchief. "I expected that you might know that."

"Well, what's the trouble then?"

"I'm so—old!" she howled.

"You're what? You're twenty-four?"

"Yes."

"That's not old, Harry."

"But the *anno mirabilis* for Newton was the year he was twenty-three, Lord Drake. 1665. Calculus, gravity, light as a spectrum. All three of those things he did in one year. Three brilliant strokes. Three miracles, any single one of which would lead you to become the most celebrated mind of your day. I was of a mind to prove Fermat's conjecture when I was twenty-three."

"Yes. But you didn't," Thomas said calmly.

Harry looked at his cravat, tears still welling in her eyes.

"There's no magic in the number twenty-three, Harry. You know that. So perhaps, when you are twenty-four?"

Harry hiccoughed.

"Or twenty-five? Or twenty-six? Harry, you told me that Fermat's conjecture has been around for one hundred and eighty years. Now, I am no mathematician, but I know enough of gambling to know that the odds that someone else —some puling man somewhere—solves the conjecture this year is very low. You are still in with a chance."

She looked in his eyes then.

"You are an eminently reasonable man, Thomas Drake. I did not expect that from you."

With that, Harry began to eat her soup. At Thomas' ring, Whitson and the footmen returned to serve the rest of the courses. Harry ate a very good dinner that night.

Thomas did not understand her about-face but was pleased by it, nonetheless.

A few weeks later, after a long morning walk with Dr. Andrews, Harry came in for luncheon and found Thomas in the dining room. She was surprised. She had eaten well at breakfast so there was no reason for him to join her. Since her birthday, she had needed no cajoling to make a good meal. And didn't he say yesterday that he was going to London today?

Harry caught sight of herself in one of the many mirrors in the room. She had some good color but her hair was a fright. There had been a good deal of wind on the walk and her hat had blown off and she and the doctor had chased it, laughing, across the lawn. Now she took her hair completely down and twisted it and repinned it quickly. She could see in the mirror that Thomas was looking at her.

She looked down at herself to see what he might be looking at.

"It's one of my new dresses."

"Yes, I see that. It's very pretty."

Harry sat and filled her plate full from the offerings presented to her by the footmen. Thomas was still looking at her. She had that feeling in her stomach that had nothing to do with appetite. She turned her attention to her napkin, the floor, the cuticle on the third finger of her right hand.

Thomas broke the silence. "What do you talk about?"

"Pardon?"

"On your walks with Dr. Andrews, what do you discuss?"

Harry looked down at her plate and picked up a knife and fork.

"Oh." She cut a piece of trout and peered at it, looking for bones. "Nothing. Everything."

"Do you discuss the calculus?"

"Sometimes."

"Do you know, you never did finish telling me about the rabbits."

"Rabbits?" Harry felt brave and looked at him and forked a piece of fish into her mouth.

"The rabbits that were multiplying in a place called Enth. Or was it Exth? At the inn. On our wedding night."

"Mmpf." Harry tried to summon the function that she had been trying to create in that warm bed. Had it been f of x equals n times two to the x? Yes, that was it. Not a very good example. She should have chosen a linear function for Thomas. That he might have understood. And what a pity he didn't come to her bedchamber nowadays and toast up the bed before she got into it herself. She had some notion on her wedding night that the future might hold some version of that. But she supposed you couldn't ask an earl to do those things. Not if you weren't going to do all the other things that went along with sharing a bed.

It was a pity.

Thomas stood suddenly. "I'm off to London."

He was going after all. But it had nothing to do with her. That was not her function. She was not a rabbit. She would do some good thinking on consecutive residues.

"Goodbye, my lord."

Despite his late start, Thomas made good time to London and to Madame Flora's. In the parlor where gentlemen selected their whores, he looked around the room and chose the shortest, plumpest, and silliest of the women available.

As the woman led him to the bedchamber and began removing her rather scant clothing, she kept up a constant stream of giggles and chatter about how his lordship had missed several weeks at the brothel and all the girls had been wondering if that meant his new wife had learned to satisfy him. Although *she* had been sure he would come back. Men like him always did—

He crossed the room and took her in his arms and covered her mouth with his. He kissed her long and hard. He thrust his tongue between her lips and tasted sherry and laudanum and tobacco. When their mouths broke apart, they were both panting.

"You remember, my lord, that kissing costs extra?"

He grunted and kissed her again. And then he picked her up by her very round buttocks and fell onto the bed with her. She seized his cock with her hand. He bit her breasts, which were four handfuls apiece, at least. He managed the French Letter just in time.

It was a long night. He thought he might have dozed for an hour or so at one point after he had penetrated her for a third time. But mostly, he lay on the bed and stared at the ceiling while Sally—that was her name—slept next to him. He wondered how soon he could go out and saddle Octavius and make the return trip to Sommerleigh.

In the morning, as he dressed, Sally drank coffee by the window. She wore quite a modest dress with an apron. There wasn't a trace of silliness in her manner now.

"My lord, I want to make sure that you are pleased with me."

Thomas was surprised. Wasn't his nocturnal activity with her evidence enough? Hadn't he paid her handsomely? And paid for the kissing as well?

"I do keep myself very neat as you know, and I pride myself that most gentlemen appreciate my appearance. But several times last night you told me that I was hairy, and I wondered if it was my maidenhair or the hair under my arms or some other hair that had offended you."

Thomas blushed, something he had not done in front of a whore for many years. He mumbled some excuse and fled the room.

He was back to Sommerleigh well in time for his bath and shave and to intercept Harry as she was coming out of the aerie. Was he mistaken or had she smiled just a bit when she had come out and seen him standing there?

He must take his encouragement where he could get it, he thought as she took his arm to go down the stairs. They would have a good dinner tonight and he would see if he could convince her to spend more time with him. Especially since she was no longer working toward that absurd completion date she had set herself. He must get her to experience more of

Sommerleigh. Perhaps he might even teach her to fly a kite as he had imagined he would when he had thought she was a boy named Harry.

It would be good for her health, after all. That was his rather wonderful burden and he must make sure that it remained *his*.

At the end of dinner, Thomas looked up. Harry was scraping her dessert plate with her spoon, trying to get up every piece of custard and apple. It looked like she was moments away from licking the plate.

"Whitson, please tell Mrs. Haversham that Lady Drake enjoyed the Apple Charlotte very much and may we have it again tomorrow, please?"

Whitson removed Harry's plate. She had such a hangdog look that Thomas said, "On the other hand, please ask one of the footmen to ask Mrs. Haversham if it's not too much trouble, but might there be two more portions of the Apple Charlotte available now?"

Harry brightened. Really, she had been so easy to please since her birthday. Get her a fire in the drawing room, a cup of coffee, a piece of cake, a book, and she would stretch out like a cat and say, "Lord Drake, this is heaven." And mean it.

"The apples have been quite good this year, haven't they, Whitson?"

"I haven't spoken to the orchard men myself, Lord Drake, but Mrs. H says that they are starting to come in by the bushel and the kitchen staff have been quite busy with laying them into the root cellar and making applesauce."

The footman came in now with two plates of Apple Charlotte that Thomas later learned had been rescued by Mrs. Haversham from under the protesting noses of Jackson and one of the coachmen. "I had to stop them from eating it, my lord," Mrs. Haversham confessed. "I couldn't believe my lady was going to have a second helping of my Apple Charlotte."

In point of fact, Harry ate a third helping as Thomas merely twirled his fork on his own plate and then he got up and carried the plate down to the end of the table and gave it to Harry. He sat in the chair next to her and drank his port. She was wearing another one of her new dresses. As he had suspected, the rich blue was just right for Harry's coloring. Smythe had told him the color was called Mazarine blue.

"Like the butterfly," Thomas said out loud.

"What's that?" Harry asked around a mouthful. Thomas shrugged.

Finally, she pushed back from the table and groaned.

"Are you regretting the three desserts, Harry?"

"No, my lord, I am regretting the soup and the joint before that."

"Dr. Andrews says you are to eat some of everything. "

"And so I did."

"And so you did."

She held her abdomen and said, "There are apple trees on the estate?"

"Yes, there are. Many dozen, I think."

"I've never seen an apple tree."

"Shall we go and see them tomorrow?"

Thomas picked an apple and tossed it to Harry.

"Catch."

She plucked it out of the air and looked at it. "Lovely."

"Go ahead, eat it," Thomas said.

"A whole apple? After that breakfast?"

Thomas came alongside her and took it out of her hand. He reached into his pocket and pulled out his folding pen knife. "I'll eat half." He handily cut the apple and handed half to Harry.

Harry bit into the cream-colored flesh.

"Can I see that?" she said through her mouthful, nodding at his knife.

"This? Yes." Thomas made sure the knife was folded shut and then handed it to her.

The handle was made of mother-of-pearl. Harry held her apple half in her mouth and opened the knife.

"My father gave it to me," Thomas said, looking at it. "I'm afraid I haven't used it much as a pen knife."

She folded it and handed it to Thomas and took another bite of the apple.

"It's a cunning little knife," Harry said with her mouth full. She swallowed. "Feels good in the hand. Easy to open."

He handed it back to her. "You keep it. You have more quills to sharpen than I do. It's a late birthday gift."

Harry nodded and put the small knife in the pocket of her dress. She took one last enormous bite of her apple and threw her core into a clump of briars. She brushed her sticky hands together.

"I'm glad I had pockets put in all my dresses."

"Yes."

"I might ask you to find some pencils for me the next time you are in London. I could put one in my pocket with some paper and then be able to scribble equations when the fancy takes me. I could use your knife to sharpen the pencils."

"Here." Thomas handed her his half of the apple he hadn't touched.

"It's a delicious apple, my lord. You should eat it."

"I assure you that it will give me more pleasure to watch you eat it than to eat it myself."

Harry crunched down greedily and, ignoring Thomas' proffered hand, climbed over the stile without assistance.

TWENTY

hillip arrived at Sommerleigh with no warning. With him came a couple. The man was in his forties with graying temples and a ready smile. The woman was of an age somewhere between Harry and Thomas, redheaded, handsome.

Through one of the front windows, Thomas saw their arrival by carriage as he passed through the drawing room in search of an old newspaper. He was perplexed. He retreated to the library and asked Whitson to bring Phillip to him.

"What is this, Phillip? You've never brought unannounced visitors here before."

Phillip put his hands behind his back. "You've always told me to treat this house as my own, Uncle."

"So I have. But now with your aunt here . . . you know, she hopes for a bit of a quiet life. Her work . . ."

Phillip laughed. "We won't bother Harry a bit. She'll have no idea we're here. And I thought you could do with a bit of livening up. We might have some whist."

Whist. That did sound like a bit of fun. He enjoyed cards.

He hadn't played—was it six months now? On his trips to London, he wasted no time on cards.

"And your studies? You aren't missing too much by being here?"

"No, Uncle, stop your fuss. You're turning into an old biddy." Phillip smiled. "Come and meet our guests."

The man and woman were Mr. and Mrs. Swinton. They were friends of Phillip. They had met—oh, how had they met? Oh, yes, Mr. Swinton and Phillip had met over cards at a gaming house.

As they four sat in the drawing room, Thomas could sense the distant sounds of bedchambers being hastily prepared, Mrs. Haversham sending a footman by horse into the village for a larger joint, a bit of excitement stirring in the bowels of the house.

When Harry came out of her aerie that evening, Thomas was waiting for her. Since he usually only met her at the aerie after a trip to London, she was a bit perplexed. She had seen him at luncheon as she now did almost every day. Surely he had not gone to London this afternoon and returned? No, that would be impossible.

"Dr. Andrews will be here for dinner, Harry," Thomas said. "Perhaps you might wish to change your dress."

"Dr. Andrews? But I feel quite well. And he made no mention of coming to dinner yesterday when we walked."

"Well," Thomas said as they went down the stairs. "Phillip has come with some guests, and I thought that Phillip and I and Mr. and Mrs. Swinton might play some whist after dinner. I know that Dr. Andrews does not play cards and neither do you; therefore, he might sit with you while we play."

Harry thought this was inordinately complicated. Surely,

she could eat dinner on a tray in her bedchamber and then go back up to her aerie to work. However, she was at a good stopping place, having worked out that she should consider her non-exponent variables all to be coprimes. And she always enjoyed talking to the doctor.

And Thomas must want her presence. That thought gave her the feeling in her stomach.

They now drew even with her bedchamber door, and Harry looked at her husband.

He looked well. By that, she meant, she supposed, that she liked how he looked. His coat, as always, was cut to fit his chest and shoulders perfectly. He was wearing the tight-fitting buff breeches he had worn to woo her stepmother. She reached out and touched his leg, just above the knee. A light brush against the muscle there, impulsive. It was the same thigh she had put her head on all those months ago.

She looked up toward his face. Those blue eyes. The pulse visible in his neck, the shadow of dark stubble on his upper lip, under his chin, and on his jaw. She knew Jackson would be shaving him before dinner and then the stubble would be gone, the skin clean and smooth. Until tomorrow morning. But she would not see him before he got shaved again in the morning.

Oh, to see the morning stubble before it was taken away. To stay the hand of the razor-wielding ever-vigilant Jackson for once.

"Yes, my lord." And then she went into her bedchamber where Smythe was waiting for her with one of her new gowns, a daring red one that Harry had objected to as being far too insubstantial in the sleeves and the bosom. Still, she might wear it if Smythe thought Thomas would like it.

Dinner was tolerable. Mr. Swinton and Mrs. Swinton made themselves ideal guests, full of interesting stories about their travels in the Mediterranean in the last year. Dr. Andrews contributed some tales about his time as a physician in the Royal Navy, including a hilarious encounter with a whale while in the Straits of Moyle. The wine flowed. Laughter rose to the top and bubbled over.

Harry looked down the table at Thomas. He was laughing at a quip of Mrs. Swinton's. Harry caught his eye. She picked up her glass of wine and raised it just a few inches to him.

Thomas grinned at her.

In truth, Harry was not enjoying herself. But she was enjoying that Thomas was enjoying himself. And that, she thought, must be enough, for now.

Harry noted how Thomas leaned into Mrs. Swinton and made sure her glass was filled. How he glanced at her bosom. Thomas must like Mrs. Swinton. Perhaps because of her red hair. Or the size of her breasts. It was unclear which of the two was the more important variable.

After dinner, the Swintons and Phillip and Thomas settled to whist in one of the smaller drawing rooms. The Swintons were paired against Phillip and Thomas. Harry and Dr. Andrews were a little apart from the card players, sitting on two sofas. Harry was explaining how consecutive residues might play a part in her proof. Dr. Andrews, who said he had been up since three in the morning to deliver a set of twins to the baker's wife, seemed happy to let her talk while he sipped on claret and dozed a bit with his eyes open.

Harry let the chatter of the card players flow over her as she thought about modular arithmetic. The first game went to Thomas and Phillip. Mr. Swinton then shuffled the cards and proposed that they have a friendly wager on the next game. A shilling a point.

"A shilling! Nay, at least a half crown a point," Phillip said.

At one point, Harry observed that Mrs. Swinton had her hand on Thomas' leg under the table. The doctor was now fully asleep, sitting up, his eyes closed. Harry decided this was a good time to pull a stool up to the table and sit between Thomas and Mrs. Swinton and observe the game more closely. After all, in many ways, she felt that was *her* leg. And she should defend it in her own house.

Thomas had not been completely surprised to feel a hand on his leg under the table. He had been groped before by women during card games, and in many cases, those women had not been whores but respectable wives of baronets and marquesses. There had even been that time five years ago when Lady Rowe had caused him to spend with her hand under the card table. He had lost that particular hand—a large sum— but felt that the thrill had been worth it. The danger of being apprehended in the act, especially by her husband who was sitting next to him, had intensified his own pleasure.

However, he was relieved Mrs. Swinton's hand was currently just squeezing his thigh.

It was the same thigh Harry had lightly touched in the hallway upstairs. What a contrast between that tantalizingly light brush and this firm kneading of Mrs. Swinton's. And then the grope of Mrs. Swinton's hand disappeared as Harry, looking fetching in her red dress, drew up a stool and said "I think I'll watch."

Mrs. Swinton tittered. "Just as long as you don't peek at my hand."

Harry said evenly, "I will do my best but I recommend you keep your hand close to your own chest, Mrs. Swinton."

Thomas had a moment where he thought Harry might have emphasized the word "hand" ever so slightly. But, no. Impossible. No one could accuse Harry of subtlety.

Thomas and Phillip lost the next game. Phillip proposed the stake be raised to a pound a point and Mr. Swinton agreed. Thomas had more claret brought, as well as whisky for the gentlemen. At the end of the very long evening, Thomas offered to settle the wager. He would fetch some sovereigns from his purse. He and Phillip owed the Swintons thirty-seven pounds.

"Oh, no." Harry jumped up. "Surely, you will stay another evening, won't you?" She looked appealingly at the Swintons. "You wouldn't deprive us of your company so soon? That would be most unfair! I must impose on you to extend your visit with us. And you will play more whist, won't you? It is a most entertaining game."

Thomas now marveled at the mastery of Catherine Lovelock in the training of her stepdaughter. If he didn't know Harry, he would have thought her a gay young bride, entranced by the card play and the high stakes, thrilled with her guests, eager for more time with them.

But he thought he knew something of Harry, if anyone could ever know her, so he knew better. What was she playing at?

Of course, Mr. and Mrs. Swinton could be persuaded to stay.

"How delightful!" Harry clapped her hands together in a fair simulation of glee.

At the sound of Harry's clapping, the doctor woke up. He must be off. He had some important reading and a long day in his surgery tomorrow. Oh, aye, if his horse could be saddled?

Thomas walked Harry to her bedchamber door before going to his own. The Swintons were ensconced in the wing that contained visitors' rooms. Phillip's bedchamber was not far from Harry's, and he had come up the stairs behind them. He was turning the doorknob to his room, already loosening his cravat.

"Goodnight, Uncle Thomas, Lady Drake," he said cheerily.

Harry put her arms around Thomas' neck and pulled his

head down. Her lips tickled his ear. "I'll come to your room at midnight," she whispered. And then she disappeared into her own bedchamber.

Thomas gulped. He turned to Phillip. "Uh, good night, Phillip. I'll see you on the morrow."

"Yes, may we have better luck tomorrow!"

"Yes."

Thomas had a jumble of feelings. He got back to his room, closed the door behind him and sat heavily on the edge of his bed. Harry had never come to his bedchamber.

Those arms around his neck, that whisper in his ear, that tickle, her face for a moment so close to his. He looked at the clock in the room. It was barely eleven. How would he pass the hour until she came? There was some cold water in the pitcher. Thomas poured it in his basin and took off his coat and waistcoat. He loosened his cravat and washed his face, then untucked his shirt and splashed water under his arms. What else?

A book. That's what Harry was always doing. Reading. But he could find not a single book, not even an old newspaper, among the things in his bedchamber or dressing room. He contemplated sneaking down to the library and nabbing a book, but then he worried he might miss Harry if she came early. He just sat in a chair then, cracking his knuckles. A few minutes before midnight, he realized he was half-undressed and quickly put his waistcoat and coat back on. He was just retying his cravat when he heard a knock.

Harry, still in her red dress, glided in as he opened the door. She looked around, a bit curiously. She sat on the bed and thumped the mattress.

"Well," she said.

"Well," Thomas said, sitting back down in his chair.

"The Swintons are cheats."

"What? No, I have played cards for years, Harry. I know

sleight of hand and how a man might arrange a deck, sneak cards. The Swintons do none of that."

"Yet they're still cheating. They're quite good at it, very clever. I'm sure no one has ever caught them at it."

Harry explained. The idle chatter the Swintons engaged in was not idle at all. Mrs. Swinton might address her husband by his Christian name, Rodney. This indicated that she was communicating to him about cards she held that were diamonds. The number of words in that sentence told him what number she had. Thirteen words in the sentence indicated king, twelve queen, and so on. So when Mrs. Swinton gasped "Rodney, no!" that meant she had ace diamonds. A remark addressed to Mr. Swinton, using his surname, was about hearts, one to Thomas was spades and one to Phillip was clubs. Mr. Swinton had a similar code for communicating his cards to his wife.

"How did you come to deduce this, Harry?" Thomas shook his head.

"I listened. I saw the cards that were played. I have a bad habit of counting everything. I can't help it. It's like a tic. And the pattern appeared."

"The damnable scoundrels!" Thomas stood. "I have half a mind to throw them out of the house this minute."

"Hush," Harry said. "Sit down."

He did.

"You owe them thirty-seven pounds. That's no small sum. Let's win it back before you throw them out of the house." Harry was a banker's daughter, all right.

"Phillip needs to hear this." Thomas moved to stand again and Harry pushed on that same spot on his thigh where she had brushed him hours ago.

"Thomas," she said. "I think Phillip knows. I think he lost deliberately. For example, the third trick of the second-to-last hand, he played a knave of spades. Only after Mr. Swinton led a queen of spades. Yet, in the ninth and eleventh trick of the same hand he played a seven and a four of spades. Why didn't he play a seven or a four on the third trick and save his knave?"

"He made an error. He's not clever, like you."

"He made many, many poor plays. He wasn't drunk. He didn't seem nervous. Only when you know all the tricks can you see he threw away a lot of good cards on tricks he already *knew* he couldn't win."

"Why would he do that?"

Harry shrugged.

"Perhaps," Thomas said slowly, "he owes these people money. And bringing them here and having me lose to them is one way he has of paying them back. But why wouldn't he ask me for the money? I would give it to him."

Harry held still.

Thomas was even more furious, now. "I can't believe he would do this to me. I'm his uncle—like his brother."

"I suggest that we find a way to get Phillip out of the house tomorrow. He'll know you're angry about something."

"Yes," Thomas said glumly. "I'm a terrible actor."

"Yes," Harry said and looked into his eyes and smiled. "It's quite your best quality."

Later, staring at the ceiling, unable to sleep, he pondered on that look and that smile. He could not recount a time that Harry had done those two things together. At the same time. Smiled at *him* and not the ceiling or a window or a book. He wondered how he could make her do it again.

Twenty-One

Thomas was absent from breakfast, having been asked to settle an issue regarding a boundary between the fields of two tenant farmers. He would be back for dinner, of course. Then, a rider came to the door with a message for Mr. Phillip Drake. He must return to Cambridge. There had been a fire in the building where he had his rooms. Nothing of his had been damaged, but he needed to come and claim his possessions and find new rooms.

Phillip swore and then apologized to the ladies.

"There's nothing for it, I must away." He bowed and then went to make his preparations for leaving.

Mr. Swinton started to grumble that perhaps the Swintons might need to leave, too.

"Nonsense," Harry said. "It's too bad, but we hope he will be back soon. Meanwhile, we will have a lovely day here at Sommerleigh, won't we?"

"But what of the whist? We need a fourth," Mrs. Swinton said.

"Well, I've never played but I was *fascinated* by it last night. I promise not to slow the play too much. And, of course, I will play with my husband." Harry trilled a laugh. "I wouldn't dare to partner either of you."

That arrangement was satisfactory to both the Swintons.

It was now up to Harry to entertain the Swintons for the rest of the day, which she found very heavy going. She felt Thomas' absence terribly. And not just because he would have relieved her of the burden of the Swintons.

She was used to him.

That did not explain everything she felt, but it would serve as a placeholder for now.

She took the Swintons on a walk in the gardens, and around every privet hedge, she expected to see Thomas coming toward her, his long stride, his dark hair, his grin.

Then luncheon. There was no one to encourage her to eat. But she tried to eat as if he were there, to please him.

In the library, she and the Swintons read the papers brought from London. After eons of vapid chat, Harry was exhausted. She had forgotten how really tiring people could be. How wise she had been to leave London for the country.

She suggested they might all nap before dinner. Ever pleasant and accommodating, the Swintons agreed. Harry went to her bedchamber and surprised herself by falling into a deep sleep.

The dressing gong startled her awake from a dream in which she and Thomas were trapped in a rabbit warren where the soft, furry, and ever-multiplying rabbits pushed her and Thomas closer and closer together until the front of her body was rubbing against his and their faces were inches from each other. Strangely, it was not a frightening dream and she had no sense of being trapped or confined, just the feeling of a plea-surable achiness that made her squirm. She thought she might like to go back to that rabbit warren in future dreams. If Thomas were there.

Smythe helped her dress in one of her Mazarine blue

gowns and arranged her hair. As Harry came out of her bedchamber, Thomas was standing there, offering her his arm.

She took it. "I am extraordinarily happy to see you," she said. Thomas put his other hand on top of her hand that rested on his forearm. He had never done that before. She looked up to find his very blue eyes on her. "My lord."

Harry's plan was simple. Because she knew the Swintons' code and her own hand, she would know the exact location of all the cards. And her memory ensured she could recall every card played. She might have enough of an advantage to make sure she and Thomas won enough tricks to win the hand. Thomas was just to play his best. He was not to worry or strategize. However, he might feel Mrs. Swinton's knee every once in a while, just to distract her.

"Maybe I should feel Mr. Swinton's knee as well," Harry had wondered last night but Thomas had dissuaded her from that plan. *Yes, of course*, she had thought later, *I would be a distraction to nobody. In that way.*

It fell to Harry to make the first deal. She fumbled with the shuffling, explaining that she really only played Patience and even that, rarely.

"It's so tedious to beat yourself, isn't it?" she asked. The Swintons, ever agreeable, said yes.

"I have an exciting idea," Harry said as she finally finished shuffling and cut the deck. "Let's make it ten pounds a point!"

Mr. Swinton visibly salivated, and Mrs. Swinton batted her eyelashes and laughed. If that was Lady Drake's wish. It would certainly make for a very exciting game.

Mrs. Swinton and Mr. Swinton talked and talked as they arranged their cards and the tricks were played. Harry listened and would interject occasionally. Thomas kept his mouth shut.

After Harry and Thomas won the first game eight tricks to five, garnering them two points, Harry started to have fun.

While the Swintons were chattering at the beginning of the hand, she would talk to Thomas of five teaspoons of sugar and seven hens and twelve minutes to four. She didn't know if she successfully distracted the Swintons from their counting, but Mr. Swinton started sputtering and Mrs. Swinton repeated herself several times.

Harry and Thomas won the second hand as well, eight tricks to five tricks. That meant that Thomas and Harry had won a total of forty pounds this evening, more than the thirty-seven pounds Thomas owed the Swintons from last night. However, a game was five points and they had scored only four. There must be a third hand. Thomas dealt but as he did so, Mrs. Swinton let out an enormous yawn.

"Are you tired, Mrs. Swinton?" Thomas asked solicitously, pausing his distribution of the cards.

"Terribly so," she said.

"Yes," said Mr. Swinton, also yawning.

"Well," Harry said. "Perhaps we should all retire. Are there any objections to stopping the game without getting to five points?"

There were no objections.

Harry was very sure that the Swintons would leave the next day, their three-pound debt unpaid.

Despite retiring so early, Thomas dozed off very quickly. He, who usually flipped and turned like a Maypole dancer for hours every night, fell into a deep and comfortable slumber almost immediately after lying down.

He dreamed Harry came to him. She kissed the back of his neck and licked the shell of his ear. She snaked her arm around his waist and grasped his cock, rubbing her hand up and down his shaft. He turned to her and kissed her mouth, fondling a large breast.

A large breast.

He leapt out of bed. A naked Mrs. Swinton lay in his bed, smiling up at him.

"Lord Drake, come back to bed. We were just getting to know each other."

Thomas quickly pulled on his breeches. "Mrs. Swinton, I beg you to return to your bedchamber."

"You touched my leg under the table tonight."

Thomas pulled on his shirt. "A harmless flirtation."

"You left your bedchamber door unlocked."

Thomas had never thought to lock his door. "I left it unlocked for my wife."

Mrs. Swinton laughed and waved her hand dismissively. "Oh, Phillip told me all about that. I know you don't bed her. Some illness she has."

Thomas was suddenly aware that someone else had entered the room. There was the scratch and the blaze of a match in the corner near the door. A candle quickly lit.

"Is it an illness . . ." A low throaty voice. The candle held up. It was Harry in a nightdress. ". . . or is it madness?" Harry rolled her eyes and allowed some drool to escape from her mouth.

Mrs. Swinton clutched at the bedclothes and covered herself.

"Oh, don't cover yourself up, Mrs. Swinton," Harry darted to the bed and pulled the bedclothes down. "What fun is that?"

Mrs. Swinton was now out of the bed, searching for something on the floor.

"Are you looking for this?"

Harry held out a robe. Mrs. Swinton snatched it, huddled into it, and ran out the door.

.   .   .

Thomas was grave, his brows knit together.

Harry was suddenly worried that she had completely misread the situation.

"I hope I didn't ruin some liaison you had planned, Lord Drake. She does have red hair, after all. But I couldn't sleep and heard footsteps in the hall and followed her here," Harry said.

Silence.

"Are you angry?"

Then a plosive sound from Thomas.

"You . . . in the corner . . . with the candle . . . madness . . ." He could barely speak. He fell onto the bed, weak. Tears were rolling down his cheeks. Finally, full-throated laughter and Harry understood.

She sat on the bed and watched as Thomas laughed until he could laugh no more. Finally, he quieted and stared at the ceiling. Harry herself fell back so that she was also lying on the bed, facing the ceiling. She turned her head and buried her nose in a fold of the sheet. The bedclothes were warm and had the unmistakable smell of him. That sharp and comforting and sweet smell. Somewhat woody, like cedar, maybe.

Thomas cleared his throat. "I, uh, said nothing to Phillip about . . . our unusual arrangement. But I felt I must assure him that his inheritance was safe, that we would have no children. He must have assumed we were chaste."

"An odd assumption, considering your reputation, my lord. But plausible I suppose, given that I am your wife."

The voluptuousness of Mrs. Swinton's body as she had scrambled out of Thomas' bed had not been lost on Harry. What was that feeling she was having now? The feeling was familiar. It came up when she heard about some frivolous youth going off to Oxford or Cambridge. Oh, yes, it was envy.

A hand grabbed hers.

"Lady Drake, you judge yourself too harshly."

Harry did not like hand holding. She recalled nursemaids forcing her to take their hands. Moist palms. The feeling of being trapped and held to another person's—a stronger person's—side. One hand unable to perform the finger tapping and counting that sometimes kept her calm.

But she had no inclination to remove her hand from Thomas'. His hand was dry. Like the rest of him, it was warm. In her mind's eye, she could bring up the size of his hand, the very faint dusting of dark hair on his knuckles, his signet ring.

She had been tired earlier, but now she felt very much awake.

She turned her head to look at him and saw that his head was also turned and he was looking at her.

The air in the room became very heavy.

"I must to bed," she said and sat up.

"Yes," he said and sat up, too, releasing her hand. "I will make sure there are no strumpets lingering in the hall to attack my mad wife."

At her door, she looked to the side.

"Goodnight, my lord."

Thomas took a step to the side and moved into her view and crouched a bit so his face was in line with her eyes. Those blue eyes.

"Goodnight and thank you, my lady. I promise that your work will not be interrupted tomorrow."

Her work. Yes. She must get back to her coprime variables.

In the morning, the Swintons made a hasty departure, not waiting to bid goodbye to their hosts. They had been invited to a house party in Kent, they told Whitson who reported it to Thomas and Harry. The house party was to be at the home of a baronet and several distinguished guests would be there, including the Ambassador from France and not one, but two marquesses. It should be most entertaining.

Several small knickknacks were found missing from the

Swintons' bedchambers after they left. Nothing of sentimental value, no long-held family heirlooms. Thomas told Harry that he counted himself lucky.

Later that day, Phillip returned from Cambridge. There had been no fire. The message was a fraud, he said, turning accusing eyes on Harry. Thomas then closeted himself with Phillip in the library. When they came out, Thomas' face was grave. Phillip still smiled but the smile was perhaps less sure. He left shortly afterward to go back to Cambridge.

The next morning, it rained and Thomas walked with Harry in the gallery.

"Yes, he owes the Swintons and a few others money due to gambling losses. He had no idea the Swintons were mountebanks, however. Mr. Swinton proposed that he bring the Swintons to my house in exchange for forgiving some part of his debt. He was quite desperate, you see? Well, he has come clean about the whole thing, we have totted up his debts and made a plan for repayment. His future allowance will be scant indeed, poor boy."

Harry, wisely, said nothing.

Could infinite descent work to make a general case against primes? Harry asked herself. And what would she look like with red hair?

TWENTY-TWO

Christmas came. Phillip stayed in Cambridge.

"Probably making merry around the Wassail bowl with friends from his college," Thomas said.

Thomas had urged Harry to invite her family to celebrate Christmas at Sommerleigh. The invitation had long been overdue, he argued, and her stepmother and her sisters should see where she lived. And so Harry had sighed and said she would put her work aside for a bit as the boughs of evergreen and sprigs of holly were gathered to decorate the house on Christmas Eve.

"I'll write to them," she said but she never did, so Thomas himself wrote. The Drakes would have no grand company, he said in his letters. No need for their maids. Let the maids go home for Christmas. Come straight to Sommerleigh from Derbyshire where Catherine and Arabella had been staying with friends.

Harry's older sister Mary and her husband the Viscount Tregaron were at his family seat in Wales this Christmas, but Mary sent her love along with her regrets.

When Catherine and Arabella arrived, Arabella practically

burst out of the carriage to hug Harry standing on the front steps.

"Oh, Harry, how beautiful you look and the house, it's so grand, I can't believe you are the mistress here. Begging your pardon, good afternoon, Lord Drake." She curtsied even as she put her arm around Harry's waist and snuggled to her sister's side. Harry very lightly laid her arm across Arabella's shoulders and made no protest.

"Good afternoon, Miss Arabella, you are most welcome. And Mrs. Lovelock." Thomas turned and bowed to Catherine who had just been helped from the carriage by one of the footmen.

Catherine curtsied appropriately but she did not look at Thomas. Her gaze was arrested by Harry. She came up the steps slowly and held out both her hands. Harry took her arm from around Arabella and gave both her hands to her stepmother. Harry allowed a kiss on the cheek and then whirled and took Arabella into the house, promising her some chocolate to warm her.

Catherine turned now to Thomas. Unexpectedly, he noticed a clenching of her jaw. He gestured toward the door, for her to enter. She reached out and grabbed his forearm.

"Lord Drake, Harry looks . . . so well."

"The country agrees with her, Mrs. Lovelock." Still she held his arm in her grip.

"I am pleased. I suspect I owe you an apology."

Thomas laughed. "Let's hold that in abeyance." She smiled a little uncertainly at that, released his arm, and swept into the house.

They passed a most pleasant week full of walks around the grounds and tramps in the meadows and forest, games in front of the fire in the drawing room, and enormous meals crowned by a monstrously large flaming plum pudding on Christmas Day. The weather was dry and mild, for the most part, but there was the miracle of a few flakes of snow on Christmas Eve. Arabella and Harry had both gone out into the garden and tried to catch the falling flakes with their tongues, laughing and running about.

Thomas thought that was the best bit of Christmas. Seeing Harry laugh for so long.

Dr. Andrews was meant to spend Christmas Day with them but he sent word that he had a quite sick patient whom he needed to tend to throughout the day and the night. And pneumonia and influenza were rampant throughout the surrounding area so he might need to stay away for all of Christmas in case of contagion.

Harry was openly disappointed. "Mama Katie, I did so want you to meet Dr. Andrews."

Catherine said she was astounded by her stepdaughter's appetite and her ability to walk for miles on their rambles and had wanted to meet the doctor as well. "Perhaps you might invite us again," she said to Thomas.

"As soon as I am done with the proof." Harry knit her brows together. Thomas and Catherine exchanged looks behind Harry's back, and Thomas was glad to have the unspoken sympathy and understanding of his mother-in-law.

And then, on the second day of Christmastide, his best friend James Cavendish, Marquess of Daventry, made a surprise appearance. Thomas had written to him to invite him as well, but James had not answered. Thomas and James had not seen each other since—perhaps October during one of Thomas' trips to London?—and James said, "I thought that I must see Sommerleigh again, and, of course, the Lady Drake in her new abode."

James was, as always, full of quips and lively conversation. Thomas thought even Harry was delighted with him. She was, but not for the reason he thought. Harry whispered in Thomas' ear that she was chiefly glad to see James because he quite entertained her stepmother, her sister, and even her husband, and she might manage to snatch a few hours in her aerie.

Thomas felt an unexpected wash of pleasure then. Harry calling him husband. Again, the closeness of her lips, face, body to his as she came up on her toes to reach his ear. Her sharing a secret, even if that secret was that she longed to get away from him and back to her one true love.

Although he had come with very little luggage, James stayed on through Twelfth Night, the same as Catherine and Arabella. James offered to accompany Mrs. Lovelock and Miss Lovelock back to London on Epiphany, and Thomas was glad that the ladies would have an escort.

As Catherine came out the front door on the morning of January sixth, poised to descend the steps to the waiting carriage, she spoke quietly to Thomas, "No, I was right."

He looked at her questioningly.

"I do owe you an apology," she said and curtsied and climbed into the carriage.

Even before the carriage was down the drive, Harry had disappeared into the house and was making her way to her aerie.

Tempus fugit. Time flies.

Twenty-Three

Harry found she did her best thinking just before and after luncheon. She, therefore, guarded her late mornings and her afternoons fiercely. She had long been in the habit of working late into the night, but she found now that most of her evenings in the aerie did not advance her work. She did not know why that might be. She only took a few sips of wine at dinner.

Strangely, the nights that Thomas spent in London *were* enormously productive for her. Her thoughts would flow in an unconstrained manner, and she made the most astounding connections. She even found a flaw in Euler's proof for Fermat's conjecture for an exponent value of three.

One night, at dinner, Harry asked Thomas, "What do you do of an evening, my lord?"

"I drink. I drink far too much."

"What else?"

"I wait for dawn."

"I think it odd you do not go to London more. Your friends are there. And there are plentiful . . . amusements."

"Yes, well, I want to make sure the estate is on a good footing."

"I do such exceedingly good work when you are away," Harry said thoughtfully.

Thomas laughed. Harry thought he laughed a little too loudly, too heartily. Had she hurt his feelings?

She watched him take a swig of wine and thought it unlikely. And then she thought it strange she would like to know she *could* hurt his feelings.

"Do I disturb you when I am here?" he asked.

"No, of course not. You are quite good about letting me be and not fussing when I am in my aerie."

Although, now that Harry thought about it, he *did* disturb her. When she sat in her aerie at night, she could feel his presence in the house. A solid presence. Warm. And . . . comforting. But if it was comforting, why did it disturb her? Because her thoughts would turn to him. And she would lose the slippery train of thought she had about what might happen if none of the bases were divisible by the exponent in question and she instead thought about his new saddle for Octavius or how he had promised to teach her to fly a kite. Or how he had one time held her hand, lying on his bed, looking at her.

"Why should I fuss?" Thomas said. "You have been quite good about following Dr. Andrews' enjoinders about exercise and food."

Harry looked down at her plate of cake which was almost gone. "Yes."

After dinner, as she and Thomas left the dining room, he to go to the library, she to go to the aerie, she laid her hand on his sleeve. "I find it unfitting that you spend so many hours drinking. Surely, you could find some other way to pass the time."

"Shall I take up Patience? Or embroidery, Lady Drake? You know I have not the mental power for your type of fun."

She could hear something in his voice. She took her hand off his sleeve. "I find it strange you do not read."

"What would you have me read, my lady? Archimedes?"

Harry looked down at the carpet. Then she shrugged and began to walk toward the staircase. She had no weapons in her arsenal for this discussion.

She sensed that he had the power to upset her very quickly, and she did not want him to upset her.

And she did not want to upset him further.

"Why do you retreat?" He followed, covering her five paces with two of his.

She began to climb the stairs. "I think you are vexed, but I don't know why. So, goodnight!"

The next day was gray and cold, but there was no rain falling from the clouds. Harry ventured out for her morning walk, dressed in her warm, red cloak, and as she crossed the gardens, Thomas came around the corner from the stables.

"Good morning, Harry." He fell into step next to her.

"Good morning, Thomas."

They lapsed into silence. For Harry's part, it was a companionable silence. She had no emotion attached to yesterday's exchange. She had said something wrong—she knew she had a tendency to do that—and yet he was here and they were friends again. She concentrated on lengthening her stride and on avoiding muddy spots. She had a thought or two about whether or not the sum of fractions in their lowest terms is not an integer if the denominator of each fraction has a factor not dividing all the remaining denominators. She observed that Jackson had not shaved Thomas this morning as carefully as he usually did and there was a lovely little bristly bit under Thomas' chin. She wondered if there would be beef for luncheon.

Thomas cleared his throat.

"I read something interesting last night."

Harry skirted a puddle.

Thomas continued, "*I do not love a man, except I hate his vices, because those vices are the enemies, and the destruction of that friend whom I love.*"

Harry leaned over to brush a clinging burr from her cloak.

"John Donne," Thomas said.

"I'm surprised you were reading his sermons," Harry said. "He has some rather bawdy verse."

Thomas smiled a little then. "Well, I suppose that might be what I will read tonight."

Quite without meaning to, Harry said, "Perhaps we might read together."

That is how, that very evening, Harry found herself opening her bedchamber door to Thomas, who had Alexander Pope's translation of the *Iliad* under his arm. Harry reflected that Thomas had likely thought better of Donne's rather intimate poems. Not fit for a man and his virgin wife.

"But I remember from my boyhood that the *Iliad* is very good stuff indeed. You might like a bit of an epic, Harry."

And she did.

And so Harry gave up her evenings in the aerie in favor of a snug fire in her bedchamber, a glass of cordial, and listening to her husband read. Some nights the *Iliad*. Some nights it was a collection of verse that included Shakespeare's sonnets. Thomas had asked Harry to read to him as well, and she had demurred. "My eyes are tired after a day in the aerie," she said.

In truth, she liked to sit in her chair and let Thomas' voice wash over her. Of course, she remembered every individual word he said but she found she also experienced pleasure from just the sound of his voice. Velvet, she thought, with a little coarse sandiness on the edges. Just like how he looks.

What she didn't like were the dreams she had at night

afterward. She didn't understand them. She didn't like what she didn't understand.

The last weeks of winter were surprisingly dry. Dr. Andrews no longer came to see Harry regularly; she was so well and he was exceedingly busy as there were still so many cases of pneumonia and influenza in the environs of Sommerleigh.

Harry found Thomas joining her instead on all of her morning walks. Once or twice, she stumbled so that he might catch her and her body would be against his, if only for a moment. His hands on her waist, her chest brushing his. Perhaps it was more than once or twice that she did this. In truth, she limited herself to once every other day. Or only twice out of every three days. Certainly, never twice in the same day. She did not want him to worry that she was developing a disorder that made her clumsy. She also did not want to fall.

But he always caught her.

Harry worried aloud that Octavius was neglected, but Thomas promised that he rode the stallion faithfully every day near dawn and in the afternoons.

"I see. A large part of the life of an earl appears to be making sure the inhabitants of his estate all get adequate exercise."

"Yes." Thomas laughed. "That is my principal function."

Sometimes they talked over what he had read to her the night before. Sometimes they talked of the woods and fields and birds they saw. They did not discuss mathematics, as she had with the doctor. She knew he had no interest. Or no understanding. One or the other.

But one morning, she said, "When next you go to London, will you find me a book on the calculus by LaCroix?

There is a translation by Babbage and Peacock and Herschel. I very much want it."

"Yes," Thomas said. "I have not been to London in many weeks. But the next time I go, I promise I will look for the book."

And then she stumbled and his large hands and strong arms caught her.

TWENTY-FOUR

Harry and Thomas were deep in the forest, tramping along a path, when it started to rain. At first, it was just mizzling through the barely budding trees, but the rain quickly became torrential. She had on the lighter of her two red cloaks, but he had not bothered with a greatcoat, saying he expected exercise to keep him warm.

"Follow me," Thomas said. They ran through the woods until they reached the abandoned gamekeeper's cottage. Harry was surprised to find she could keep up with Thomas and not lose her breath.

The gamekeeper's cottage smelled a bit musty but was clean and snug. Thomas quickly opened the chimney's flue and built a fire with the few pieces of dry wood and kindling that had been left by the hearth. He found a tinderbox on the mantel.

Harry pushed back her hood and sat on a wooden chair near the door. Her cloak and her dress were soaked through and dripping on the floor. She shivered.

Harry watched as Thomas knelt by the hearth, one knee on the floor, leaning forward, concentrating on transferring fire from tinder to match to kindling. As he leaned forward, his tailcoat vent split open and gave her a view of his nether regions, hugged closely by his wet buff breeches. She knew how muscled his thighs were—it was perhaps the very first thing she *had* known about him—but she had never noticed his backside. She saw muscles in those cheeks now, muscles that flexed as he adjusted his position and leaned farther forward. She thought what it would be like to touch those muscles, to cup those cheeks, to face him and to use her hands on that backside to pull him close.

She thought it might be very like stroking the haunch of Octavius, his stallion. But infinitely more pleasurable. Her fingers itched to touch him.

She began to tremble more violently and firmly wedged her hands under her own legs, trapping them between her thighs and the chair.

"There, that's going well." Thomas stood from a merrily crackling fire, and as he did so, the vent in his tailcoat closed, and his rear was lost to Harry's view. He put the tinder box back on the mantel and turned to face her.

Harry sat on the chair in an odd posture, with her hands under her legs. She was obviously very cold. Her cloak was pushed back off her shoulders. The wet fabric of her light-pink dress clung to her figure closely, and Thomas was pleased to see she had acquired even more flesh in the last few months. In her legs and her hips. Because, of course, he was well aware of the breasts that were now well beyond the fledgling stage.

But the wet dress did reveal her breasts to him with much more detail than her clothes usually did. And now he was greedy. Her neckline scooped low but not low enough. He wanted to see the top of her bosom. The ever-present keys dangled into what could be a beautiful valley, but it was hidden from view. He could see that each breast was now almost a handful and in his mind's eye, he could see his own hands curling around them. Her nipples pushed against the wet fabric, each about the size of an early spring pea. He knew that this phenomenon was a product of the cold and the wet, but still he couldn't help wishing that those nipples had hardened under his caress, his tongue. Thomas had been cold himself a moment before, but now the room felt close and hot. He could feel blood flowing, his member engorging.

He turned around again hastily, and knelt down once more to feed wood into the fire.

"I think there is a woodshed around the other side of the cottage," Thomas said a little too loudly. "I'll go get some more wood. You should come closer to the fire."

"Do you know . . ." Her voice trembled and then grew stronger. "Do you know if there are some dry clothes here? I am so very wet. I'm not sure the fire will do much good unless I can be dry, too." She stood beside him now, holding her hands out to the fire.

Thomas stood hastily and turned away from her. He went to the bed in the corner of the room. The bed itself had just a straw ticking on it but the cupboard next to it yielded a stack of wool blankets. He crossed back to her, holding the blankets in front of him, shielding her view of his cock straining the front fall of his breeches.

"Thank you." She took the blankets that he proffered and hugged them to her chest, teeth chattering.

"I'll give you time now." He crossed the room and went out the door.

The bulge in the front of his breeches when he had handed her the blankets had not escaped her notice. Again, that fascinating manifestation of masculinity. But it had nothing to do with her. Thomas just had not gone to London lately, had not visited those women who satisfied him. It was, as he had said before, a reflex.

She removed her cloak, unlaced her boots and kicked them off. She peeled down her stockings and started working her way out of her dripping dress while standing in front of the fire. As she raised the dress over her head, the fabric pulled at her breasts. She hadn't worn a corset out for her walk; she had never felt she really needed one, given the paucity of her figure. But maybe now she should always wear one, not just when her stepmother or Smythe insisted. Off with her shift. She touched her own nipples—they were hard nubbins—and as she pinched them, she felt a curious ache spread from her breasts to her groin. How wonderful and strange her body was.

A crack of nearby lightning and the ensuing thunder broke her reverie.

She discarded her petticoat quickly, knowing that Thomas would be back soon and would expect her to be covered up. She took one of the blankets and rubbed herself roughly all over, trying only to use one half of the blanket to dry herself. Her skin warmed under the friction of the wool blanket and the glow of the fire, and her shivering slowed. She then wrapped one of the dry blankets around her waist in a kind of skirt and draped another dry blanket over her shoulders. She pulled two rockers up to the fire and hung the partially wet blanket over one of the rockers and sat in the other. She put her feet up on the hearth, and pulled the blankets around her, allowing her toes to poke out toward the fire.

She needn't have rushed. It was nearly a quarter of an hour before Thomas came back into the cottage, carrying wood.

· · ·

Thomas passed one of the small glazed windows as he walked around the cottage in search of the wood shed. He stopped and stood under the dripping eave and watched Harry disrobe. He tried to assuage his sense that he was a filthy lecher by telling himself that she was his wife and that, in her own words, she didn't attach much importance to bodies. She wouldn't mind him looking.

She stood in front of the fire so most of what he saw was in silhouette. As she lifted her arms and raised the shift off her body, he gasped a little. She stood at just the correct angle so that he could see her right breast. The breast was just as he had imagined it would be, moments ago, inside the cottage. A graceful gentle slope from her collarbone down to the tip of her breast and a luscious, taut scoop of flesh under, pillowing her areola and her nipple. And then Harry put her hands on her own breasts and—was it possible?—pinched her own nipples. As she arched her back, his tumescence surged and he thought he might spend in his breeches with no touch whatsoever.

A flash of lightning with near instantaneous thunder made him duck his head. He didn't think God took much interest in the affairs of Lord Drake so he wasn't worried that he would be struck down for his lust by a lightning bolt, but he was worried that Harry would look toward the window because of the thunder.

When a few seconds had passed, he raised his head enough to peek into the window again. Her petticoat was off now, and she was completely naked in front of the fire. For a moment, he had a vision that she was some slender elf queen dancing in front of a midsummer bonfire. That whimsy dissolved as she took up a blanket and started rubbing at her hair.

It was Harry, *his* Harry, and she was astonishingly beautiful. There was a glimpse of small but well-shaped buttocks leading to slender legs. She turned slightly and just before she wrapped herself into a kilt of blanket, Thomas thought he saw, in the firelight, dimples just above the buttocks. He sank to his knees and groaned.

She wasn't *his* Harry. Not really. She was by law, but Thomas knew Harry didn't give a fig for the law of man. Harry cared only for natural law and cosmic forces. Harry would always belong more to Newton and Euler and Descartes than she would to Thomas Drake.

Next to Harry, Thomas felt like an animal, spurred on by animal appetites. This had seemed tolerable before, but now, with Harry becoming more and more the focus of those appetites, he felt wretched and ashamed.

He eventually got up off his knees, stumbled to the woodshed and considered spending there, if only to prevent further thoughts of Harry. But no. He was no schoolboy who couldn't control himself. He spent ten minutes thinking earnestly about cricket as his manhood waned, and then he gathered a large armful of dry wood and ran for the cottage.

"I, uh, had, uh, some trouble, uh, finding the woodshed."

"Oh?" Harry looked up at him.

Her cheeks were rosy now, and her loose hair was starting to dry in tendrils around her face. Her eyes were as enormous as ever, vast pools of hazel, edged with ebony lashes. She was snugly cocooned in her blankets, blankets he knew were touching her bare skin, those delicate shoulder blades, that flat piece of flesh between her umbilicus and her maiden hair . . . Now he wished he *had* spent himself when he had had the chance of privacy.

"I only used half that blanket to dry myself so you can use the other half." She pointed at the blanket draped on the other rocker. "And there are two completely dry blankets left so you can cover both halves of yourself, just like I did."

"Very practical, Lady Drake, eminently practical." He

picked up the blankets and said stiffly, "I apologize that there is no other room for me to go to."

"Oh, no, you couldn't be at fault for that. And you can't go to the woodshed, can you? You'll just get wet again. And it does seem like it must be exceedingly far away since it took so long to find. But I'll close my eyes while you get dry and I'll tell you what I was thinking about while you were looking for the woodshed." Harry closed her eyes. "I was thinking about these rocking chairs and the problem of developing a perpetual motion device. A force—like my feet against the hearth—starts this chair rocking and what are the forces that slow it?"

As Harry burbled on about friction, Thomas went to the far corner of the room and took off his tailcoat and waistcoat and bent over and pulled off his boots. He stripped off his shirt and his soaked breeches, knees stained with mud from his long stint of kneeling under the eaves after seeing his elf queen. Finally, he was naked. It was cold away from the fire and he picked up their shared blanket to dry himself quickly. But he was arrested as he held the blanket to his face to start drying his head. He inhaled deeply. The blanket smelled of *her*, of Harry. It was the smell of ink and old books and grass and coffee. And there was a tang of feminine—would you call it musk? No, decided Thomas, call it what it was—her sweat. Sweat she had earned by climbing over stiles with him this morning and racing him through the meadow on the edge of the forest. Harry would call it sweat.

It was the most intoxicating odor he had ever smelled.

Harry had kept her word and her eyes screwed shut until she heard a creak from the floor near her.

She opened her eyes and peeped at him sideways. He had come back to the fire, blanket round his waist, but he had not yet covered his upper half. She saw his broad shoulders, the smattering of dark hair across his chest that led to a trail of hair down the center of the muscles of his flat abdomen. A trail that eventually disappeared under his blanket skirt. And then —*whoosh*—he swept the other blanket around his shoulders and sat in the rocker.

There was silence. The fire crackled.

"I'm afraid I didn't follow what you were saying," Thomas said.

"Oh, never mind. I'm sure it is frightfully dull to you."

"Not at all," Thomas said politely.

"No. I know. Mama Katie told me that I had a genius for tedium. But she did tell me the most interesting topic of conversation there is to be had when one is conversing with a man." Harry leaned forward and felt a bit mischievous.

"And what is that? Could it be cards? Horses? Surely, not the weather?"

"Well, the man himself!" Harry crowed and leaned back.

Thomas laughed. "I assure you that I would find myself a very dull topic indeed."

"Well, I wouldn't."

Again, there was silence.

"I do believe that is the very first compliment you have ever paid me, Harry."

"No," Harry said.

"No?"

"It's not the first." Harry looked down at her hands and started rocking a trifle faster, a trifle harder. "On my birthday, I told you that you were reasonable. And that night when the Swintons came, I told you that you were not a good actor and that I liked that. And do you remember our wedding night?" she asked, still looking down at her hands.

"I wasn't completely drunk, so yes, I do remember it."

"I complimented you on your ability to generate heat."

"Oh, yes."

"When I got into the bed, you had made it very warm. I'm always cold. I said to you, 'You are better than a bed warmer.'"

"I see. Yes. That is definitely a compliment. I stand corrected. Are you cold now?"

Harry wasn't, but she said, "Yes."

Thomas opened the blanket that covered his own chest and said, "You are very welcome."

Harry stopped rocking and turned her face toward him. She had trouble looking at his naked chest. Maybe better to look at his forehead. Or the ceiling.

"You don't mind?"

"No."

"I've gotten so much bigger since coming here. I'm sure I will be much too heavy."

"You can't weigh more than eight stone. You're still a sliver of a thing."

Harry got up and crossed the two steps to his chair and, grasping her blankets as tightly as she could, she sat on his lap. And Thomas folded his blanket and his arms around her.

She suddenly knew that her impulsive lie, saying "yes" to being cold when she wasn't, was her greatest stroke of genius yet. Here she was, on his lap, sitting on his muscled thighs. And although she was tall, he was much taller still, and with a little slouching, her cheek could rest comfortably on his hard chest. And his arms held her firmly in place.

"Is that better?" Thomas asked.

"Much."

She was now very warm. The heat came off his body and surrounded her. And suddenly, she was able to place his scent. Cinnamon. He smelled like cinnamon.

She could feel his heartbeat quicken under her cheek. She noticed a pulse in his neck. She traced his collar bone with one finger. She touched the mat of hair on his chest. Soft over hard.

"Men have hair here, I see."

"Yes."

"I didn't know."

"You didn't know that some men have hair on their chests?"

She sat up out of her slouch, letting her blanket slip off one of her breasts on purpose. "In the museums, the statues, the paintings, none of the Greek gods or the Bible men have hair on their chests. How was I to know?"

He nodded gravely. "Yes, I see, certainly, there was no way to know."

Then she settled back down against his chest. *This is extraordinary. My skin against his skin. Maybe it is causing a reaction in his lap.* She wriggled slightly and thought she could feel something swelling.

He didn't know if he should tell her that when her blanket slipped as she sat up, one of her breasts had escaped and he had glimpsed a small, rosy nipple capping a blushing areola before she had settled back down against his chest.

Her left breast, the one that had slipped out of the blanket, was now plastered against his chest with no blanket between them. She must know now that she had been exposed. But she made no move to adjust her blanket around herself.

He gripped her more tightly by a fraction and thought again about cricket.

She now let go of her own blanket completely so she could wrap both her arms around him. This action completely bared both of her breasts against his chest. "Your upper torso has a very large girth. What does your tailor say is the circumference of your chest?"

She had never embraced him before. Her face, her generous mouth, those lips were mere inches from his. He could kiss her easily in this moment. He turned his head away and stared at the beams above them. He concentrated on how cold the keys on their chain around her neck were against his skin rather than how warm and soft her breasts were. "I can't remember."

"How odd. But you have said before that you have no head for figures. Get your tailor to write your measurements down and I will learn them off."

"Harry—" His voice was strained. He put one arm under her legs and stood, holding her, and deposited her, willy-nilly back in her rocker. The blanket that had been around her shoulders was now on the floor and he whipped it up and over her, covering her breasts.

She looked up at him. "Thomas?"

There was no guile there—not in her voice, her eyes. She was not even hurt by what he had done. She was merely curious why he had unceremoniously shoved her off his lap. *My God, despite the breasts, she is still a child. Maybe her step-mother is right and she always will be.*

"I'm too hot now," he said and walked away from the fire, flapping his blanket over his shoulders as if to cool himself. His blanket kilt stayed on, barely.

"Do you like cricket?" he asked too loudly. Away from the fire, he could peer out the window and see the sky was lightening, the rain was less insistent.

She didn't answer. He turned to look at her and saw her in the same position he had left her, staring at the fire.

"Cricket?" she said absently. "I don't understand the rules."

"It's a great game, Harry, a great distraction. You see the point of cricket is—"

She straightened up suddenly in her chair, holding her blankets.

"I'm not interested in distractions. This rain has delayed my work. Do you think there might be some paper and ink here so I might write?"

"A gamekeeper wouldn't have much use for paper, Harry."

"Not even to count the pheasants? Very well. Then until the rain stops, I'll ask you not to talk so that I can work in my mind. I have a very troubling problem to solve."

Harry put her keys in her mouth and sucked thoughtfully.

Thomas returned to his chair and maintained his silence, only moving to put more wood on the fire, until the rain stopped.

That evening, after Thomas had settled comfortably in what he had come to think of as *his chair* in Harry's bedchamber, Harry stood in front of him.

"Thomas," she said. He was thumbing through Pope's *Iliad*, looking for the passage where he had left off and did not look up. "I wonder if I might sit in your lap again."

He looked up then. She had her eyes on his waistcoat buttons. Serious face. What the devil did she mean by proposing that?

But why should he worry about Harry's motives?

He knew he wanted her on his lap. Their clothing should make it safe.

He was immediately filled with self-loathing for the lies he told himself so that he might feel her against him.

But he could control himself. He knew he could. He would keep his part of the bargain. "No fucking, no kissing," she had said. He could do that.

"You may," he said.

She glided into his lap, found a place for her head on his chest, and became very still.

He had greater difficulty than usual in finding the right page, but eventually he did, and he began to read aloud.

Twenty-Five

After weeks of the sweetest kind of torture, he finished reading the *Iliad* to Harry.

They sat in stillness for a moment, she in her usual position, in his lap, head on his chest.

"Helen must have been quite beautiful," Harry said suddenly.

"'Celestial charms,'" Thomas murmured.

"Was she redheaded, do you think?"

Thomas laughed. "I have always imagined her with dark hair, olive skin. Greek, you know?"

"There are many things I don't know," Harry said slowly. "I suppose that in a lifetime, one can learn a small amount about many things or a great deal about a few things. I have chosen quite deliberately to learn a great deal about a few things."

"Yes." He took the liberty of resting his chin on top of her head.

"This has made me very odd in many ways. I think that there are many things about people that I don't understand. I even think that there are many things about myself that I don't understand."

Silence.

"For instance, here, with our position, I am not surprised to feel an occasional hardness under me, in your lap." Thomas shifted slightly. "You made me aware as per our discussion before our marriage, and I am now familiar with the phenomenon. I don't say this to embarrass you," she looked up at him and he looked away, "but I think I *have* embarrassed you and for that I am sorry. I meant to dis-embarrass you, if there be such a word."

"I am not embarrassed, exactly." He tried to laugh and it came out as a cough. "I have been worried about offending *you*."

"Oh, don't worry about offending me. Alternatively, I suppose one could think I should take your hardness as a compliment since you have, after all, likely bedded the most beautiful whores in England. But you have told me before that the flow of blood to your organ is really almost a reflex in response to pressure and friction and even just a night's sleep. So don't worry. I know it's not really me."

"I-I don't know what to say," Thomas stammered.

Harry sat straight up, her face gleaming in the firelight, the top of her breasts straining against her dress.

"Yes, I see it is a conundrum. You can neither say yes, it is a reflex, because this implies I am hideous, nor can you say I have caused it because one cannot imply that a young lady of society is an object of lust."

He was tired of her thinking meanly of herself. Would she believe him when he told her that he thought her beautiful? She would likely snort and get up off his lap. And he did not want her to do that.

Years ago, when he had been foolishly unaware of his father's financial straits, Thomas had staked a thousand pounds on a single hand of cards. That gamble was a trifle compared to what he did next. He reached out and very lightly cupped one of her breasts with his hand. She was not wearing a corset and of this, he was glad. As he had anticipated weeks ago, the breast filled his hand perfectly.

"You are not hideous," he murmured. He rubbed his thumb over the breast and was delighted to feel the nipple harden under his touch.

"No," she said and shuddered. "I am convenient."

But she did not move away. He took heart from this and chose to ignore her jab. He leaned forward and kissed her very lightly on her collarbone. He continued to kiss her collarbone, working his way slowly to her neck, lightly massaging her breast. "And," kiss, "you are," kiss, "not a young lady," kiss, "you are," kiss, "my wife."

Harry very firmly grabbed Thomas by his hair and pulled his head away from her neck.

"Remember. No kissing."

"I thought you meant your mouth."

"I did. As long as you remember." And then she shivered and leaned into him.

But she didn't leave his lap. She lay against his chest again and he repositioned his arms around her tightly. No, by thunder, she was not going to leave his lap. He had touched her breast through her dress and kissed her collarbone and she had not flown into a fury. She had stayed.

She played with the buttons on his waistcoat idly. "I fear the conversation has gotten off the point. I brought up your member, not because it was poking me, but as a way to talk about *my* member."

Thomas was confused. "About *your* member?"

"I don't know what *it* is. But I have to beg you not to interrupt me or I will never get through it. I could wait until I went to London again to ask Mama Katie about it, but I feel it is rather important. If you don't know the answer, I can ask Dr. Andrews."

"No," Thomas said hastily. "Ask me."

"The last several months, I have been troubled by dreams. As I have eaten more and walked more and gotten stronger, the dreams have come. My monthly courses have come back, too. You know that women bleed, Thomas, even though no one talks about it in public?"

"Yes."

"I hadn't bled since before Papa died. But now, I am sure it is because I have gained weight and now my body has the strength to bleed again. In fact, the first dream I had, I thought it was just that my courses had come earlier than usual. But that wasn't it. I woke up and was wet. But the fluid wasn't red. It was like water. I thought perhaps I had waited too long to use the chamber pot but it didn't smell like urine. And I felt a peculiar satisfaction the rest of the day, quite like I had solved a very tricky proof in my sleep. And it keeps happening."

Thomas thought it likely that Harry, after starving herself for years, was now having a long-delayed puberty. He had not known that women could have dreams that resulted in emissions but it certainly seemed possible. Thomas cleared his throat.

"You may speak," Harry said.

"What do you dream of?" Thomas asked quietly.

"Oh, I couldn't possibly tell you that." And she buried her face in his chest.

Thomas' heart sank. She did not dream of *him,* her husband, or otherwise she would say so, would she not? He took comfort in the fact that she had mentioned possibly asking Dr. Andrews about her dreams, because perhaps that meant she did not dream of *him*, either.

"You spoke of a member?"

Harry whispered into his chest, "Sometimes I have dreams

when I am awake and there is the water between my legs and I want pressure or friction or something. I don't know."

"Harry, look at me."

Harry sat up and gazed at Thomas. She looked so troubled. He tried to relax his brows, to make his face kind, to make his voice gentle.

"Harry, those feelings are normal."

"Even for women?"

"Yes, for women."

"And I *am* a woman, Thomas, not a child."

"Yes, Harry. You are a woman."

"Then why is there no mention of these womanly feelings in books?"

"Perhaps because the books are written by men."

Harry nodded, seriously. "Just so." She was silent for a moment. "Thank you, Lord Drake."

Thomas smiled. "You are most welcome, Lady Drake."

"Thomas."

"Yes, Harry?"

She grabbed his hand that was resting on the arm of the chair and pulled it down roughly, pushing up her skirts as she did so. She put his hand between her legs.

He felt her maidenhair. He felt her crease. And he felt wetness on his fingers. He groaned inwardly.

"This is what I am talking about, Thomas."

He didn't move his hand. She looked at him.

"Just so, Harry."

"I need . . . to know what to do. Can you . . . will you . . ."

He found her hooded button at the top of her crease and ever so lightly touched it with his middle finger.

She moaned. He had never heard a sound like that before. It came deep from within. It had none of the screechiness of the courtesans he had bedded. He increased the pressure ever so slightly and began to move his finger in a circular pattern.

"It . . . is . . . what is it?" she almost growled. She clasped her hands around his neck as if she were drowning.

"Is it good?" he asked and again increased the pressure and quickened his circling.

"It is good," she gasped, now hiking her skirts up still farther and looking down and watching his hand move. Thomas, for his part, was watching her face. She was biting her lower lip and her breath was quickening and a beautiful flush was rising up over her breasts to her face.

And down below, he could feel her button engorging and hardening and leaving its hood and rising up under his finger. She began to move her hips, to push herself against his finger.

"Should I do it harder, Harry?" He increased the pressure once again and changed the circling motion of his finger to a rhythmic pulsing.

"Uh." Her speech was gone. Still, she gazed down at his hand where his middle finger flicked quickly over what she had called her member.

And then she started to shake, her chest heaved, and her thighs began to contract.

"Ahhhhhhhhhh!"

A throaty and feral howl. Thomas stilled his finger and felt her quiver and her wetness cover his hand.

She slumped against him, breathing hard. He could see the sweat glistening on her neck, tendrils of hair now damp. Her intoxicating odor filled the room. He inhaled through his nose and waited, still.

She raised her head finally and looked at the fire.

"I think that was the answer I was looking for."

He smiled. "I'm glad." But when he went to take his hand away, she clamped her thighs together and trapped his hand.

"I think now that you've shown me, I might be able to do that myself. But maybe you better show me again."

"Again? Right now?"

"Yes?"

"You've had your pudding and you want another right away?"

"Is that not normal?" She frowned and relaxed her legs.

Thomas laughed and kept his hand where it was. "Harry, when have you ever worried about normal?"

"I have. Before. Worried. But it takes so much energy to be normal that quite often I have to just let myself be. But I am very interested in this and would like to be normal."

"Well, I think your interest is a sign of a very healthy and very *normal* appetite. And I think you should undress and go to bed, like a good girl."

With that, Thomas scooped Harry up as he got out of the chair. He carried her over to the bed and deposited her there carefully.

"Thomas?"

Thomas went back to the fire, sat down and took his boots off. "Don't worry. I'm not leaving. The lesson isn't over."

Harriet tilted her head.

"Go on. Get undressed. It's what you can do for me."

"I don't understand that remark."

Thomas sighed. "Like most men, I am stimulated by the visual." She waited. He said then, "It would give me pleasure to look at your body."

"Oh." A pause. "Would you rather undress me?"

For a moment, Thomas considered telling the truth—that what he would *rather* do was stride to the bed, take her mouth with his, while shredding her dress with one hand and pulling her closer with the other.

"No," he said and leaned back in the wing chair and put his hands behind his head.

Harry did not seem put out by this in the least. She took off her shoes and dress and chemise and petticoat and hose just as she might if she were alone. She spread the clothing neatly over a hard-backed chair and walked to the fire and faced him.

Here again was the elf queen whom he had spied through the gamekeeper's cottage window.

The firelight danced over her skin. Long feet rose to slender ankles and then elongated knees and thighs that were beginning to show some muscle. Muscle but also womanly roundness as the thighs rose into her hips and maidenhair. Thomas spied a glisten of moisture tracking down Harry's inner thigh, evidence of her previous arousal. And then her narrowing torso with what seemed acres of beautiful unmarked fair skin rising to the widening of her ribcage and her bosom. And the blasted keys that she never took off hanging between those glorious breasts. Those breasts. Those beautiful handfuls with their pink peaks. With great difficulty, Thomas tore his eyes from her breasts and looked at Harry's face, to see how she was taking his quite obvious ogling.

Her expression—was it disgust? No, Thomas decided.

It was scientific interest.

"Turn around," he said.

She did. And he found he had been right. Above each perfect small buttock, there was indeed a dimple. He allowed himself briefly to rest one of his hands on her lower back and to brush downward over one of those dimples and one of those buttocks.

Harry bounced up and down on the balls of her feet.

"I'm cold again. Should I sit on your lap once more?" And indeed, gooseflesh was beginning to cover her. He stood up abruptly and took off his coat and rolled up the sleeves of his shirt.

"No, go to the bed and lie down under the covers, Lady Drake."

She almost scrambled into the bed and got under the

counterpane. She lay, facing up, obedient, shivering. Thomas walked to the bed.

"I need to be on this side," he said. She looked briefly at the bedside table, at her stack of books and the lamp there. Clearly, she had a long-established habit of being on the left side of the bed.

He raised his left hand. He wiggled his fingers.

"I'm left-handed," he said. Her face was blank for a moment and then a smile flitted across her lips. Quite like the smile she had given him when he had finally taught her to fly a kite two weeks ago.

She slid over.

Thomas smoothed the counterpane down and got on the bed, on top of the coverings. He lay on his side, facing her, his head resting on his right hand as he leaned on his elbow.

"I'm still cold, Thomas."

After a moment's pause, he got off the bed and slid under the counterpane with her. She pressed against him and he wrapped his arms around her beautifully naked form and prayed he would continue to be a man of his word and not of his cock.

"Your waistcoat buttons are poking me." He let her unbutton his waistcoat and pull it from his body and throw it off the bed. Then, he was surprised to feel her arm reach over him and her hand grasping his buttock. It was fleeting but it was definitely a grope. Now she pulled at the waistband of his breeches and at his shirt. "Take these off, too."

He moved her hands away. "No. These are insurance. So I don't do something we will both regret."

Harry pulled away from him and lay back. "How unfair."

So, in some way, perhaps his body did arouse her.

"Yes, but given our limitations, one of us should be dressed. I would like to be naked, too, but since the lesson is about your body, it makes sense that I am dressed and you are not."

He put a hand flat on her abdomen. Was that an almost pout he saw on her lips?

"Sometimes I wonder how men get anything done when they have so little control over their desires. I mean, did Newton have to prevent himself from fornicating so he could invent the calculus?"

He moved her keys on their chain away from her breasts and off to the side. "Didn't he invent the calculus during the plague year? I am sure that fear of the plague likely kept him from fornicating and helped him concentrate his mind."

Her voice became throaty as he brushed his hand over her nipples making first one hard and then the other. "Please . . . don't speak . . . of Newton . . . while you are . . . doing that!"

"Why?" he said with a lazy smile, teasing her right breast by spiraling his fingers in and out, around the nipple slowly. "Does it insult Newton?"

He now uncovered the breast closest to him and fell on it with his mouth, first kissing, then sucking, then very lightly biting the nipple.

Her skin tasted of a sweet, heady swirl of the sweat he had smelled on the blanket in the gamekeeper's cottage with just a trace of soap.

"Nooo. It's just—" she was panting now "—Newton was so very ugly, while you," she grabbed his jaw and swung it off her breast and toward her own face, "like his calculus, are very beautiful, my lord."

He chuckled and pulled away from her hand and went back to her breast to hide his reddening face. She thought him beautiful. He hadn't known that.

And as he nibbled and suckled, he was pleased to hear her panting turning into mewls of pleasure. He came up for air and murmured, "I am glad I can beat Sir Isaac at one thing, anyway."

Her voice trembled like her body as she said, "And for the purpose of accurate record keeping, please note that was actually the fifth compliment I have paid you."

He winked. "Duly noted." He bent his head again to her nipple.

She sat up suddenly, tearing his mouth from her breast with her movement. "Is this flirtation?"

He sighed. "Yes, it is. Or it was."

She fell back. "My apologies, my lord. It is just that, having never experienced it, I wasn't sure I recognized it correctly."

Then she grew silent. But her pelvis began to wiggle on the mattress, arching upward in search of something. So as Thomas sucked and licked and stroked her breasts, he also slowly moved his hand down her torso toward her maidenhair.

She threw the covers off both of them. "I'm warm enough now, and I need to see," she said.

Thomas decided to change course and moved her legs apart and knelt on the mattress between them and looked at her. His cock was tenting his breeches and he congratulated himself on the wisdom of keeping on some of his clothes because this was very difficult as it was. Every base instinct in his body was telling him to fall on top of her and thrust himself inside of her. The breeches just barely reminded him that *that* was not in the cards for him with her.

She stared back at him steadily. Was it just his imagination or could she be looking at him with some affection? After all, he had given her pleasure and seen her at her most vulnerable.

And now he was going to pleasure her again.

He leaned over and kissed her navel. Then, very slowly he kissed his way over the warm velvet of the skin of her lower abdomen and down to her maiden hair.

She sat up on her elbows.

"What is this?" she asked.

He looked up and raised his eyebrows and said, "You'll see."

"What does it look like down there?"

"You don't know?"

"How would I know? I can't see down there. Everything's hidden and the angle's wrong."

"Well," he breathed, "it's quite beautiful."

She cocked her head to one side.

"But Thomas, I can't do this to myself. You won't be teaching me anything useful."

"Maybe this could be just for fun." And with that statement, he licked her right on her button.

She fell back with a yelp, startled.

Gentle, Thomas, gentle, he scolded himself. *She is so ready that she will pop like a shaken bottle of Champagne with the lightest nudge of her cork.*

He gently pushed her legs apart wider and hooked his arms under her legs. She obligingly drew her knees up to accommodate his shoulders. He pulled her around so she lay crosswise on the bed. He was now kneeling on the floor by the side of the bed with his upper torso resting on the mattress, her legs resting on his shoulders, his face toward her flower.

He began to kiss her inner thighs and as he did, her labia, already swollen and glistening, spread wider, welcoming him in. He kissed her outer lips, lightly sprinkled with maidenhair. He let his tongue run over her wet inner lips. He tasted her and she tasted salty and clean and . . . of herself. He felt her entrance with his own lips and had to restrain himself from trying to penetrate it with his tongue. That would not give her pleasure and there was a possibility that he might frighten her, this woman who did not seem frightened of anything. He could hear her humming—a low gravelly sound—and sensed her hands snatching at the sheet under her. Her thighs began to shake. Her buttocks clenched.

Thomas grabbed her hands and held them so they no longer scrabbled along the mattress looking for purchase. She laced her fingers with his. Carefully, he began to apply himself to the button at the top of her flower. *Her member*, she had called it.

She squeezed his hands. In response to her squeeze, he began to apply his tongue more forcefully, more quickly.

She was close, he could tell, to her release. She arched and thrust her pelvis in the air and the hum became a long, drawn-out, fully voiced howl. He let go of her hands and used his own to push her hips down into the bed so he could concentrate on licking in exactly the right place with exactly the right force and rhythm. She sat up and grabbed his upper arms and the howl stuttered into a vibrato as her flower pulsed and pulsed and pulsed and her body pushed up against his hands, straining. Sweet fluid on his lips. And then stillness. He stopped the movement of his tongue and looked at her face. There was a quizzical expression there and she fell backward onto the bed with an enormous groan.

The fire crackled.

"I must say I like your idea of fun, Tommy," she said. And yawned.

By the time he stood, noting that she had ripped his sleeves almost completely from their armholes, she was asleep, sprawled across the bed, her nipples red from his attentions, her wetness soaking into the sheet under her buttocks. He rearranged her so her head was on a pillow and that she was positioned on the dry part of the bed. He straightened her chain and placed the keys between her breasts. He pulled the coverings over her and tucked them around her body. Smythe might be a little shocked by the absence of a nightdress in the morning but Harry wouldn't be embarrassed . . . and they were married, damnit! Besides, he didn't know where her nightdresses were kept.

He made sure the fire screen was in place and the candles were out. He took his boots, his tailcoat, his crumpled waistcoat from the floor, and left the room.

He went to his own bedchamber. He undid the front fall of his breeches and took his cock in his hand, ready to give himself some immediate relief. But then he thought better of it. He went in search of the leather bag he used when he traveled. His valet Jackson used to keep it with the trunks until Thomas had insisted it be kept in his dressing room. He liked to know he had a few things in his bag, ready to go if he should decide to gallop into town on short notice. He got undressed and took the nightshirt out of his bag. He didn't wear a nightshirt at home or in brothels, only in inns when he might have occasion to traipse down a public hallway to the privy. And he hadn't been at an inn since his wedding night. This was the nightshirt he had worn in the bed he had shared with Harry. He raised it to his nose. There was no trace of her odor.

He cursed. Of course not. It had been ten months. He had not touched her that night and the nightshirt had now had too long an acquaintance with his leather bag for it to retain any of her scent that might have suffused the fabric because she had been only a foot from him.

And now that he thought of it, of course Jackson must have arranged for this nightshirt to be laundered since its last use and replaced in the bag. Or this was an entirely different, clean nightshirt. Jackson's blasted scrupulousness. He deserved the hours of mending the sleeves of Thomas' shirt tomorrow.

Thomas flung himself on the bed.

He took his cock in his hand and using rough strokes, he tried his best to climax while thinking of his last redheaded whore from months ago. When release did not come, he then tried to think of the Mancunian strumpet who had first taught him to touch and lick a woman to give her pleasure. But his thoughts kept turning to the elf queen who slept naked, mere feet away. The elf queen who was his wife. The elf queen who had bewitched him and called him Tommy for the first time tonight. The elf queen whom he had, stupidly, now made self-sufficient.

He hated himself as he let himself imagine taking Harry just so he could be done with this torture. As he finished, he made a small sound. If he was honest, it was a whimper.

TWENTY-SIX

The next night he returned to her bedchamber, a book of verse in hand. He knocked and came in. The fire was lit and Harry was in her usual chair. As he entered, she jumped to her feet and went to pour their usual glasses of cordial.

He sat in his wing chair and took the glass from her and held his breath, waiting to see what would happen next.

She sat in his lap, as if nothing had changed.

He exhaled in relief.

She turned, startled. "You sighed. Am I too heavy now? I have such an enormous appetite. I could have eaten a whole chicken myself tonight." He held her firmly to keep her from leaping up.

"Harry, I have something for you."

"Is it sweets?"

"No. It's a surprise. I'll have it brought to your bedchamber tomorrow."

It was something he had found today in one of the many rooms of this house after a long search. But he thought that it should belong to Harry and be in her bedchamber. She would appreciate it.

She clapped her hands. "Is it the new translation of the LaCroix? Did you order it from London? Has it arrived?"

He had forgotten that she had wanted some book or another and that he had promised to see if he could find it.

"No, it's something else. Probably something not nearly as exciting as the Lacroix."

"Oh, well." Now she shrugged and sighed, too. "As if anything could be."

Thomas laughed.

"Read me sonnet seventeen," she said and leaned her head on his shoulder. "The one that starts *Who will believe my verse in time to come.*"

"I'm glad you are willing to hear it again. I thought you didn't like it when I repeated myself."

"Yes, it's odd, isn't it? But there's something about that one," she said.

"Maybe it's because Shakespeare goes on to say *If I could write the beauty of your eyes, And in fresh numbers number all your graces.* You like numbers."

"Maybe," she sounded doubtful. "But then he doesn't go on to number them, does he?"

When he had finished the sonnet, he closed the book. "I think I am done reading for the night."

"So soon?" Her tone was one of disappointment.

He ran his hand over her back and down toward her buttocks, imagining the skin and the dimples underneath her dress. Those dimples that he had seen last night and only touched briefly. All day he had looked forward to Harry disrobing again. As he had ridden Octavius this evening, he had thought of laying her facedown on the bed and placing his tongue in each of those dimples as he caressed her buttocks.

But Harry jumped up.

"Oh, you needn't bother with that."

He was shocked. She had never pulled away from his touch. True, she had not always shown the normal reactions he had come to expect from other women, but that was a deep part of her charm.

He looked at her. Was that glee he saw on her face?

"You are an excellent teacher, Lord Drake," she said and made a little curtsey. "And that makes compliment number six, mark it well. I had a wonderful morning in bed. Ellen came in with the breakfast tray and I told her that I had been up far too late and sent her and Smythe away. I then used my own hand," she held up her right hand, "and had success four times in three quarters of an hour. I did rest for a bit between number three and four, but I noted no evidence of the law of diminishing returns."

"Well," he said, "you're young."

"I fell asleep last night before I could thank you for showing me how. I didn't think I should thank you in front of the servants at dinner tonight."

"No," Thomas said shortly.

"So, I thank you now. I made some excellent progress today in my work and I can only think your lessons have allowed me to concentrate my mind wonderfully on the problem. I won't have to bother you again for help."

Thomas did not know what to say. He stood slowly. "Well, perhaps since I am done reading and you are done with your lessons, I should leave you." He tried to speak lightly but he knew that some bitterness had leaked through in his tone. He hoped Harry wouldn't notice.

She didn't seem to.

"You won't stay and sit by the fire?"

"No."

"Goodnight, my lord."

He was Tommy no more. He nodded and left.

. . .

The next morning, one of the footmen handed a flat, cloth-wrapped package to Smythe, who brought it to Harry, who was in bed, drinking coffee and reading Gauss. It must be the surprise from Thomas he had mentioned last night. The one that was *not* the Lacroix translation. The label on the outside said, *Lady Drake. Unwrap carefully when alone.*

She dismissed Smythe from the room and unfolded the cloth, which appeared to be one of Thomas' large handker-chiefs. The handkerchief covered a small mirror, perhaps six inches by six inches in a frame and with a cunning little leg attached to the back so it could stand up by itself on a table. Or on a bed.

There was a piece of paper stuck in the frame. She unfolded it.

In Thomas' flowing hand, it said, *For Harry, so nothing is hidden despite the angle.*

She put her coffee down carefully, and began to arrange the mirror and herself into the most suitable position.

Twenty-Seven

That night, long past midnight, he heard a knock on the library door. "Lord Drake, it's me." Harry opened the door.

Thomas had drunk heavily last night, risen late, and spent the afternoon with a bottle of claret, and now he had already had six glasses of whisky and was seriously contemplating downing the rest of the bottle tonight. His chair was tilted back and he had his boots up on the table in the center of the library.

"I have the fire in my bedchamber and have poured the cordial but you didn't come," she said as she crossed the room. "So, I had to find you in order to thank you."

He said nothing.

"For the mirror."

The mirror. He had forgotten. What a stupid idea. She had really wanted some book. He waved his hand in surly acknowledgement.

"Having used the mirror, I think that your description 'quite beautiful' does not really correlate with my understanding of aesthetics. There is vertical symmetry, I suppose, vertical if I lie flat, that is, which was how I was positioned. If I were standing, it would be sagittal symmetry, wouldn't it? I always find symmetry quite pleasing myself, but is that enough to constitute beauty?"

He snorted. What was she going on about?

She stepped closer. "Oh, you already have a drink. Do you want to bring it up to my bedchamber?"

"No," he said brusquely.

Harry clasped her hands in front of her. "May I have some of that?" She pointed at the whisky.

Thomas let his chair's front legs crash down on the carpet. He leaned forward and discourteously filled his own glass again before sloppily filling a second one for Harry.

Harry took it and licked around the rim of the glass.

"Mmm. It's quite strong, isn't it? And illegal. Are you drunk?"

"Yes."

"Listen, my lord, when you didn't come to my bedchamber tonight, I tried to have a good think about why you didn't. You weren't at dinner either, which was odd. I wondered if perhaps I had done something wrong." Her voice quavered. "I have a habit of doing wrong things and only finding out much later that I've done something wrong. It's a bit like transposing some variables right at the beginning and only finding out three pages later that you have to start again."

Thomas grunted.

"But now, I see, it's just because you're drunk." She smiled nervously. "I am much relieved."

She took a drink of the whisky and sputtered a bit. She sat down across from him.

"Yesh, I'm drunk," he said.

"Yes," she agreed.

He gulped at his whisky and eyed her. She sipped and looked around the room.

"This is a nice library, Thomas, I can see why you didn't come upstairs."

Silence.

"And it's only fair, after all, for me to come to you, to a room of yours, once in a while."

Silence.

Her voice shook a bit more. "I thought it was customary for the husband to come to the wife's room but we needn't follow that custom, need we? After all, we have broken so many other rules."

In his drunken haze, he realized she was perseverating on his not coming to her bedchamber tonight because she was *hurt*. He had hurt her. And, scoundrel that he was, he was *glad* that he had hurt her. Because she had hurt him.

"Whatchoo—" he started and stopped. He forced his tongue, thick with whisky, to form the words clearly, if bitterly. "What do you think you might have done that was wrong, Harry?"

"Well, I thought—" she started and then changed tack suddenly. "What difference does it make? Clearly, I am wrong about being wrong. You didn't come to dinner and you didn't come to my room because you are drunk. That's like being sick. So, you didn't come."

"But, Harry," he said and leaned across the table toward her. "Why am I drunk?"

"Why are you drunk? Besides the immediate cause of merely ingesting too much alcohol?"

Thomas put his head back and laughed. "Oh, yesh, Harry, that's the how, not the why."

She sat in silence. He finished his glass of whisky and put it down and reached for the bottle to pour another.

Her hand grabbed his wrist.

"The why is that I *have* done something wrong. And I know what it is."

He pulled away from her grip on his wrist. "Good," he spat. He poured another whisky. He was near to passing out, thank God. He would be able to forget his cruelty toward her tonight. He drained his glass.

For Thomas, what happened next was confusing. And horrible.

Harry came around the table quickly and used all her strength to pull his chair out.

"Ooof," she said.

Then she knelt in front of him and started unbuttoning the front fall of his breeches.

"I see now that it is quite unfair that I have been the only one experiencing pleasure recently. And you have not gone to London, as of late."

"Harry—" he tried to say.

She spoke over him as she struggled with the fastenings. "I was like that as a child, you know, not seeing that my little sister wanted my doll or that my older sister was angry that I had spilled something on her dress. But Mama Katie worked hard with me to get me to notice those things. She said that being me was a lot like being an actress. I had to learn my cues and my lines and I would be just fine."

Thomas was frozen and did not know how to stop her.

She went on, "And I do apologize because I *will* need some training. But as you have seen, I learn quickly, and I will not be offended by any direction you give me since this is for *your* pleasure, and I am well aware I am a novice and you are expert." She paused in her fumblings and looked up at him. "Please do know, Thomas, that I didn't think of it not just because I am deficient in sense but because you *did* tell me before, on our wedding night, that I could not be of service to you in this way. But clearly you have changed your mind, perhaps out of necessity or convenience, and I am glad to help."

.   .   .

And now the buttons were undone and she had uncovered his manhood.

It bore no resemblance to what she had imagined when she had first felt him in her grasp those many months ago in Lady Huxley's fourth-best drawing room. Or when he had gotten out of bed on their wedding night to tuck in the counterpane. Or when he had handed her the blankets in the gamekeeper's cottage, revealing his bulge. Or when she had sat on his lap so many times over these recent weeks and felt that delicious hardening poking at her bottom through her dress.

Instead, it was like the organs she had seen on statues in the museum. It was . . . not of the size she had pictured. She did not like to say it was small but it had certainly seemed of a larger magnitude when it had been hidden from view. It lay against him, in a nest of dark hair, despite being free from clothing. She took her hand and grasped it like a staff. Her grasp was firm but the organ was not. It almost seemed floppy.

She licked her lips nervously. Thomas didn't move. He seemed barely able to keep his eyes open.

"I suspect a circumferential type of friction such as that which you might encounter with entering a woman's pelvic orifice would give the best result?" She looked up at him questioningly.

"So shtupid."

"Thomas, shall I . . .?" She began to move her hand along his member. "Will you tell me what to do?"

"Stop." He seemed to have trouble getting the word out. "Stop."

She rocked back on her heels. He roughly pulled her hand off his member and struggled to cover himself.

"Jussh ssstop." In trying to do his breeches back up, he dropped his glass and despite the carpet, the glass shattered.

Harry bowed her head and started to pick up the glass shards. He was angry. She realized it now. Too late. But surely some pleasure could have calmed that fury? Why had he not let her continue? Why had she failed when it seemed like it would be so easy? Weren't men beasts with insatiable appetites for release? Especially Thomas.

Her face was wet. Was it from a few drops of whisky that had been left in his glass when it fell? She tasted a drop on her lips. Salty. She was crying.

He stood now, wavering. "Jussh leave it, Harry."

He stepped forward.

His riding boot came down and crushed her right hand with the full weight of his body. And then he fell forward, unconscious.

Her right hand had been the one holding the pieces of glass.

Harry felt that she had done very well under the circumstances. Thomas didn't respond to his name or her shaking his shoulder with her good hand. She had rung for Thomas' valet and when he had come, Jackson had quickly checked Thomas' breathing and his head. There was an awful lot of blood from her hand but the valet thought the blood had come from Thomas, and he kept trying to find a cut or a bump on Thomas' scalp.

"It's me, I think," she said and showed him her hand. Jackson had blanched and immediately called for two footmen to come to the library. He sent one footman to get a coach ready to fetch Dr. Andrews. The valet, with the help of the other footman, managed to heave Thomas, who was now snoring, up on the sofa.

"I think he's just drunk," Harry said. "I don't think he needs a doctor."

"My lady," Jackson inclined his head. "The doctor is for you."

"Oh."

Then Smythe showed up in a robe and made Harry sit down at the library table.

"There's still glass on the carpet," Harry said. "Will we be able to get the blood out, do you think?"

Smythe went to fetch towels and a basin and to rouse the kitchen maid to make some coffee for the doctor. Whitson had heard a groom getting the carriage ready and now showed up, red-faced and pulling on his tailcoat, quite the most flustered person so far. Harry could tell that the butler felt strongly that members of the household should retire when he did and then nothing unforeseeable could happen. Harry sympathized.

"It's not too bad, Whitson," she said, holding up her hand, hoping to cheer him up. As she did so, new rivulets of blood ran down her arm and onto the carpet.

"Yes, Lady Drake," he said and slid a silver tray under her arm to catch the blood.

By the time Dr. Andrews had arrived, the valet and a total of three footmen had succeeded in carrying Thomas upstairs to his room, one man for each limb, and an extra maid guarding his head.

"You'll stay with him, won't you, Jackson?" Harry had called after the valet.

"He will, my lady," Whitson had said.

At Harry's insistence, Dr. Andrews first went upstairs to check on Lord Drake. He returned with the report to Harry that Thomas would have a headache in the morning but would otherwise be tip-top. Harry felt just a little tightness go out of her chest. She hadn't even realized that the tightness had been there until it dissipated. Her husband would be fine. But would he really be fine? What about . . . ? She would have to find a way to ask Alasdair privately.

Dr. Andrews then made Harry go into the dining room after the staff had lit all the candles in the chandelier and rolled up the rugs. It was the best lighting available, he explained. Harry then tried to get Whitson and the others to go to bed.

"Smythe can get everything Dr. Andrews needs, right?" She smiled because she knew that reassured others.

"'Twill be the work of several hours," Dr Andrews said as he examined Harry's hand. "There are nae injuries to major vessels and see, the bleeding has slowed. Miraculously, I think perhaps only two metacarpal bones and two phalanges have been broken but the hand will need extensive cleaning, I will need to examine and attempt to repair any tendons that may have been lacerated, and of course, all glass must be removed and the skin lacerations repaired. Only then, can I set the bones and splint the hand."

"And then I'll be good as new." Again, Harry smiled at the staff.

"Some of these tendons can be very tricky, my lady." Dr. Andrews looked worried. Harry clapped him on the shoulder with her good left hand.

"I believe in you, Alasdair."

Whitson dispatched the kitchen maid to make more coffee. Harry's maid Smythe would stay and fetch what Dr. Andrews needed, including more towels and candles. He, himself, Whitson would stay in the kitchen so as to be available at a moment's notice. The horses could be stabled and the rest of the staff would go to bed until it was time for Dr. Andrews to leave.

"But Jackson will stay with Lord Drake, correct?" Harry asked again.

Whitson exhaled heavily and said, "He will, my lady."

The next hours were some of the most agonizing Harry had ever spent. It wasn't the pain, not really, of having her hand probed and washed and finally sewn. It was the tedium.

She had so much energy right now. She drank cup after cup of coffee with her left hand, trying to keep her right hand as still as possible for Dr. Andrews. Finally, Smythe fell asleep sitting up in a chair against the wall.

As Dr. Andrews peered at her hand in the flickering candlelight, Harry looked at the gilt-framed mirrors that lined the walls of the dining room, reflecting the light, over and over again.

"You know, Alasdair," she said. "If you had a curved mirror, you could reflect an intensified light on to something you needed to look at."

"Mmmph," Dr. Andrews said and pulled a sliver of glass from Harry's hand.

"You could have an assistant who would hold the mirror and an assistant who would hold a lamp."

"'Tis a lot of assistants for a country doctor, Harry."

"If you held the mirror, and the patient held the lamp, you wouldn't need the assistants."

"Harry, I need both of my hands for this type of work."

"Or the lamp could be on a table."

"Aye."

Smythe snored a bit in her sleep.

"May I ask you a question, Alasdair?" Harry said in a lower voice.

"Aye."

"It won't distract you?"

"Nae, Harry."

"Oh, good! You see, I have a question about men."

"Men?" He peered at her and then ducked his head to go back to her hand.

"Yes." Harry sighed. "I suspect it is a rather shocking question but you are a physician, and I have no one else to ask. I can't ask Smythe over there, she would have an apoplectic fit and faint. I can't ask his lordship since he is unconscious. I just wondered if there might be some reason a man, some man, far away from here, er, might not be able to . . . function as he should."

"Function? In what way?"

"Perhaps it is just a part of him that will not function."

There was a pause and the doctor nodded. He took a deep breath, "Harry, there are many reasons."

"Does it signal a deficiency in him?"

"It could . . . ." The doctor seemed unsure of what to say next.

"Does it signal a deficiency in the woman?"

"Nae," the doctor said quickly. At that moment, Whitson came into the dining room.

"How does it progress, Doctor?" Whitson boomed. Smythe started awake at the sound of Whitson's voice.

"It goes well. Lady Drake is very brave and has borne the pain with not a bit of complaint."

Whitson said nothing more but continued to stand just over Harry's shoulder, watching the doctor work.

Harry was silent.

"Erm, Lady Drake, have ye read William Shakespeare?" the doctor asked.

Harry thought this was a curious turn in the conversation but she answered, "I haven't, but Lord Drake has read me the sonnets. And my stepmother often took us to see the plays in London. I usually used that time for working through a corollary or a lemma in my head, though."

"Are ye familiar with *Macbeth*?"

"*Macbeth*?" Harry examined her memory. "I have seen a play with that character in it and also a Lady Macbeth. The Scottish play."

"Aye, 'tis set in Scotland, my Lady. I think ye should read that play."

"Oh?"

"Yes, I recommend ye read it and pay particular attention to the comic characters."

Whitson snorted a bit at this. "I didn't know doctors were also Shakespeare scholars."

Dr. Andrews smiled and threaded another piece of catgut onto his needle.

"Everyone should ken the Scottish play. Especially Act two, scene three."

TWENTY-EIGHT

Thomas did wake up around noon with a terrible headache, just as Dr. Andrews had predicted, and a terrible thirst. He sat in bed in just his shirt as Jackson brought him cup after cup of coffee. Jackson also sent one of the stableboys to chip some ice from one of the big blocks in the underground ice house. Jackson used the ice to make a type of cold poultice Thomas favored for his head when he was hungover.

Thomas had a dim memory of something happening with Harry in the library. He feared he had not behaved well.

He finally got up his courage to ask Jackson. "And Lady Drake. Is she well today?"

Jackson was doing something in the corner with Thomas' shaving equipment.

"Yes, my lord, I believe she is as well as can be expected. When I went to make your poultice, Whitson told me that Dr. Andrews is very hopeful that she will have full recovery of—"

Thomas cut him short with a bellow and flung himself off the bed and out of his room and down the hall on bare legs to

Harry's bedchamber. He tore the door open. The bed was made and empty.

"Where is she?" he shouted.

Smythe appeared in the door from the dressing room. She stared at his bare legs. He seized her by the shoulders and repeated as if she were deaf, "Where is she?"

"My lord," she tried to curtsey, "she has gone to find a book—"

Thomas let go of her and whirled and ran down the hallway to the winding stairs that would take him to her aerie. He thundered up the stairs and banged on the door. He rattled the knob. The door was locked, and she did not come and open it for him.

Thomas then remembered with a sickening lurch that Harry had wanted some book and she had thought she might go to London to procure it.

Jackson was coming up the stairs, with a pair of breeches over his arm, at an extremely rapid pace for a sixty-year-old man who had spent the night in a chair in his master's room.

"Where is my wife?" Thomas roared.

"My lord, I believe she is in the library—"

Thomas elbowed Jackson aside.

"My lord, your breeches—"

But Thomas couldn't hear him.

Down these stairs, two flights, down the corridor, down another set of stairs. Damn, why was this house so big?

Thomas burst into the library, sweating, breathless.

A woman in a rose-pink dress stood high on the library ladder on the far side of the room.

"Harry," he croaked.

She twisted halfway around to look at him. She appraised him from across the room.

"You look terrible, Tommy."

He stood there panting, and put his hand to his face. Whiskers. He looked down. No breeches.

"I'm . . . I'm . . . I'm not dressed," he panted.

She was holding a fat book with her left hand so she held out her right hand and said, "I see that. Stay there."

He could see her right hand was bandaged heavily. She turned her back on him to face the shelves and started going down the ladder. Despite her admonition, he started toward her.

She continued speaking, "I'm not sure they've really gotten all the glass up. You might cut your feet."

She was using just two fingertips of her right bandaged hand to hold on to the ladder. She was sure Dr. Andrews would be quite upset if he knew she was using the hand at all. Uncharacteristically, she really had not thought this through. It must be lack of sleep. She had gone up the ladder using her left hand and once the book she needed was retrieved, she had to hold it with her left hand. She thought about throwing the book down to the library floor, but she had far too much respect for books to do that. She had thought about leaving the book and retreating down the ladder using her left hand and calling for a footman to get the book for her, but she was in too much of a hurry.

And then, when she was still eight feet off the ground, it happened. One of her new pink slippers slipped—was that why they were called slippers? she wondered irrelevantly as she fell backward, still clutching the book in her left hand.

And suddenly she was in her husband's arms. She was surprised, and not in a good way. Under other circumstances, she might have enjoyed being held against his chest. His jaw had such a good bristle right now. And she had seen his legs from across the room. She had never seen his naked legs. Her breath caught for a second.

But he had endangered himself. And not heeded her command.

"I told you to stay, Tommy."

He was still panting. "But— You fell."

"Yes, I did. But you couldn't have known I would fall when you disobeyed me." That smell. She wrinkled her nose. "I like the stubble, Tommy, but you stink. Put me down."

He did as she said. She put the book down on a large nearby table. "Now lean over this table and show me the soles of your feet."

Thomas put both his hands on the end of a table, leaned over it, and picked up one foot and then another, like a horse being shod. Harry looked at the back of those thighs and considered running her left hand up under the shirt and feeling a buttock. No, she needed to make sure he was all right first. And he might not like her touching him. He hadn't liked it last night.

She peered down and brushed the bottoms of his feet with her left hand. She was relieved. "No glass in your feet," she told him and picked up the book and walked around the table and sat down.

Jackson cleared his throat just then. He was standing in the doorway to the library.

"Oh, Jackson," Harry called out. "Good, you have his lordship's breeches. And you're wearing shoes? Then bring the breeches here and then would you go back up and get Lord Drake some type of footwear? Because of the broken glass. Excellent. And Tommy, put your breeches on and stay here where I know it's safe."

Jackson having departed, Harry allowed herself one more look before the thighs disappeared under the leather of Thomas' breeches. She opened the book.

"Your hand—" Thomas started to say.

"Tommy, I need to read something." She put the book on the table and started using her left hand to leaf through it. "Act two, scene three, the Scottish play."

He looked over her shoulder at the book. *The Complete Works of William Shakespeare*? What in God's name did she need to read that for? And why was she almost . . . mothering him? He felt he was missing something here. He felt many things, all simultaneously. Confused, frightened, relieved, angry, glad. And very, very hungover.

She smiled and slammed the book shut. "Well, if Dr. Andrews thinks this is medically accurate, it's good news for you. But I'm not sure why it's comic. And it certainly doesn't seem particularly Scottish. Although you *were* drinking whisky last night, Tommy."

"You called me Tommy."

"Yes," Harry said. "I've called you Tommy six times this morning. It's a nickname, right? Like Harry?"

"Y-y-yes," he stuttered.

"Wait here until Jackson brings your shoes."

She stood and turned to go, but he grabbed her left hand.

"Tell me about your other hand," he growled, "in God's name, or I swear I will walk across this library in my bare feet a thousand times over."

"Very," she paused and raised her eyebrows, "dramatic. *You* should be the one reading *Macbeth*."

He got to his feet, still holding her hand, and began stalking around the library, dragging her behind him.

"Where is the glass, where is this glass you're so worried about, hmm?"

And then he saw it. He didn't know why he hadn't seen it before. Gouts of dark dried blood over the carpet, extending on to the floor at the perimeter of the room. Nearby, on another patch of carpet, close to the central table and to a pulled-out chair, small shards of crystal sparkled in the afternoon sun. On the table, an empty bottle and another glass still holding a finger of whisky.

She avoided his eyes. "I-I, uh, cut my hand on a broken glass, my lord. And broke the hand, too. But it's all right, Dr. Andrews reset the bones and sewed me up and he thinks I will be able to use the hand once it's healed. He said, 'Even play the pianoforte again' and I said 'But I didn't play the pianoforte before.' That's funny, don't you think?" She looked at his face now.

He said nothing, at first.

"Harry." He could feel a rage building up. She averted her eyes again. "Harry. I don't want your condescension. I know you think you are the brilliant one in this household, but you have no sense. I am your husband, and you *will* tell me what happened."

He realized then that he was squeezing her good hand, crushing it. He let go of it. She stood there.

Jackson appeared at the door to the library again, holding a pair of boots, and Thomas gestured him over. Jackson very carefully assisted Thomas into the boots.

"Please close the door to the library when you leave, Jackson."

"Yes, my lord."

"And please tell Whitson or Mrs. Dewey that the library needs cleaning. It should not be done now since Lady Drake and I are using this room at present, but it should have been done earlier."

"Yes, my lord."

The door closed behind him.

"Well?" Thomas waited.

"What part don't you remember, my lord?" Her voice was flat.

"Why don't you tell me all of it?"

So, she did. She stood there and told him how she had waited for him in her bedchamber and then, when he had not come after many hours, she had sought him out in the library. He had been drunk on whisky, she said. She felt perhaps he had not come to her room because she had not reciprocated.

"Reciprocated?" he said in a strained voice. "Reciprocated what?"

"I had not given you the pleasure that you had given me, my lord."

He gritted his teeth. It was true.

"I tried to, but I could not arouse you. I mean not you, but your member."

He shook his head slowly from side to side, cursing himself.

"You told me to stop, and you dropped your glass, and it broke. I started to pick up the pieces even though you told me to leave it and you stepped on my hand while I was still holding pieces of the glass. You were drunk, as I said. It was an accident."

He felt like death. But he had to hear it all. He prompted her. "And then?"

"And then you fell and were unconscious. I could not arouse you. You, as in you, not your member."

"I understand."

"And that is when I called Jackson and he called some footmen who sent for Smythe and the doctor."

"I see."

"Whitson showed up, too, and managed everything splendidly."

"Except the cleaning of the library."

"Yes, that got rather forgotten. But the doctor came and I

got fixed, and that's more important than the carpet, isn't it, Lord Drake?"

He lunged out and crushed her to him.

"Be careful of my hand."

He let her go and backed away.

She gazed past him, out the window, mind on something else entirely, he thought.

He cleared his throat. "I must ask . . ."

She turned her eyes on him.

"Why were you reading Shakespeare this morning?"

She hesitated before saying, "You'll be angry. I think."

He turned and walked over to the window and stared out at the grounds. His head pounded. He folded his arms.

"I'm already angry." *At myself, because I injured you.*

"I asked Dr. Andrews if there were reasons why a man's member might not engorge. I didn't use those words but he understood me. I didn't mention you and thought I had been quite cleverly opaque about it all, but I can see now that it would be impossible for him not to realize I was talking about you."

"And the Shakespeare?" He tried to keep his voice even.

"He answered me by telling me to read *Macbeth*. Macduff says, *What three things does drink especially provoke?* And the Porter says, *Marry, sir, nose-painting, sleep, and urine. Lechery, sir, it provokes and unprovokes: it provokes the desire but it takes away the performance.* And then the Porter goes on a bit more about it."

Even as shame fought rage in his heart, Thomas found himself able to marvel at her memory for things she had read once.

She went on, "So, now Alasdair has made me quite happy because I had been quite worried—"

"Alasdair!" Rage won.

She called the doctor Alasdair now.

He moved away from her and toward the door of the library. Alasdair Andrews had made her happy. Had he, Lord Drake, ever made her, his wife, happy? He had given her pleasure, yes, and then, like an angry child who wanted a toy back, he had broken her hand. No wonder she had sought solace from the doctor, a gentle man who fixed things.

His worst fear had come to fruition. He had become something loathsome. Someone who destroyed and ruined things, people.

And she had done it to him. Better he had never married her. Better she had never come to Sommerleigh. She had sparked the monster in him.

He opened the library door.

"Where are you going, Lord Drake?" Her voice was tinged with panic. He took a perverse pleasure in that.

He didn't look back. "To hell," he snarled.

Twenty-Nine

He went out to the stable and told one of the grooms to go into the house and fetch his bag and a waistcoat and a tailcoat. And some money.

Jackson came to the stable himself, carrying the clothes and his bag.

"You should get some sleep, Jackson."

"And you should eat, my lord." He helped Thomas into the waistcoat and tailcoat and insisted that Thomas sit down and let Jackson put some hose on him because his boots were not meant to be worn without some protection for the feet.

"My feet!" Thomas exploded. "Why does everyone care so much about my blasted feet? What about Harry's hand?" And then he collapsed onto the bench next to Octavius' stall. Octavius, already saddled at his direction, came over and gave his hair a friendly nibble.

As Jackson knelt down to remove his boots and roll the hose onto Thomas' legs, he spoke.

"Begging your pardon, my lord, but Lady Drake came to your room as I was fetching your bag and asked me to tell you something."

Thomas held his breath.

"She said—and I hope I am remembering this right—that she is very sure you actually meant London when you said hell, and she said . . ."

Jackson hesitated and then plunged ahead.

"She said that after you are finished at the brothel, please to remember that she particularly wants the Babbage, Peacock, and Herschel translation of the LaCroix and not any other."

Thomas swore, pulled on his boots himself, swung himself up onto Octavius and thundered out of the stable at a full gallop, scattering straw, stableboys, and a few loose chickens in his path.

He rode straight to Madame Flora's and elicited a promise from the most reliable groom at the stable that Octavius was to be brushed and watered and fed. And then he climbed, two steps at a time, to the parlor where gentlemen selected their whores. It was very late evening now.

He considered the women on display. This one was too plump. This one was too short. This one's hair was too dark. This one was also wrong. And this one.

Where was a tall, slender elf queen with curly brown hair? Surely there must be one here. He must find her and teach her to call him Tommy.

And then his voice was hoarse and the room started spinning, and he thought he had really better sit down. Someone led him to a chair. He closed his eyes.

"Lord Drake."

He looked up. It was Madame Flora herself. Over sixty years of age by now and famous for having spent twenty years as the serial mistress to only the most powerful men in the House of Lords. The heavily rouged but conservatively dressed doyenne rarely came out to the parlor. She usually stayed in her office where she kept the books. Thomas tried to stand but she put a hand on his shoulder and kept him in the chair.

"Lord Drake, you are upsetting the other gentlemen." A glass of water was pressed into his hands, and he drank it thirstily. And then another.

"You look quite rough. I am going to arrange for you to have a bath and a bed." Madame Flora turned and spoke in the ear of Nancy, easily the most maternal of the whores. Thomas had rejected her just moments ago as having breasts that were too large.

Nancy led Thomas to a room with a bathtub and ordered the hot water to be brought. She gave him a jar of soap and a banyan and told him to put the banyan on after he had had a long soak. And he really should use the soap. She left the room and, trembling, he took off his clothes and did what she said.

When she came back to take him to a chamber with a bed, he caught her arm.

"Nancy, I will pay, of course, but tonight, I think I just want the bed."

She did not look surprised although he had never asked for such a thing before. She curtsied. "Aye, my lord, I will make sure ye are not disturbed."

He wept a little, alone in the bed that night. For himself. For the ten-year-old boy who had lost the woman who was both his mother and sister. For the thirteen-year-old boy who had thought he had found a cure for his pain and loneliness. And for the man who had then pursued that cure over and over again even when he knew it gave no relief to the gash in his heart left by the ruination and death of Jane at the hands of a fiend.

And then he slept and dreamed he was sitting by the fire in Harry's bedchamber. She was not there. He thought he should go look for her. But something kept him from doing so. *It's all right. She'll come.* In the dream, he was very disappointed that she did not ever appear.

When he woke in the morning, he decided he was done feeling sorry for himself. Now he must find a way clear to repairing the damage he had done. To righting things. He knew where to start.

As he crossed the parlor to leave Madame Flora's, he heard his name.

"Lord Drake!"

He turned. His friend James was coming forward to shake his hand.

"I am very glad to see you, Tom."

"Jamie!" Thomas looked around the otherwise empty parlor. "It's a little early to be starting at Madame Flora's, isn't it?"

"Oh, I'm waiting for you. I heard that you were here. I thought I might catch you this morning so I trotted down here quite early. Shall we find a coffeehouse?"

They walked together out of the brothel and down the street.

"I'm the Duke of Middlewich now."

Thomas stopped and bowed. "Your Grace. I hadn't heard of your father's death. I am sorry."

James clapped him on the back and they resumed walking. "Thank you, but of course, you must keep calling me Jamie. You know one of my sisters is named Grace and it's become very confusing at the castle. No one knows who is talking to whom. And I'm rather angry at the old fellow, actually. He left me with all my sisters still to marry off. Good thing they seem not to be too fussy. Too bad you're not available now."

Thomas was able to laugh at that and then go on to tease his old friend about all the women who must be coming out of the woodwork now that he was a duke.

"It's no joke." James wiped his neck with a handkerchief. "No joke."

At the coffeehouse, Thomas asked James if he knew if there was a bookseller nearby.

James tilted his head quizzically. "Don't you have a library full of books you have never read?"

"I've read two of them now."

James laughed at that.

Thomas finished his coffee. "The book is for Harry."

"Ah." James nodded and paid their bill.

They made their way to a bookseller and Thomas was grateful to find the LaCroix. He was assured by the owner of the shop that it was the only published English translation. The name Babbage on the cover looked familiar. But then he was astonished at the cost of this book Harry wanted. He looked at the few coins he had left after paying for Nancy's time, but not her services, as well as his bath and his bed at the brothel.

"I am the Earl Drake," he said to the wizened bookseller. "Will you do me the courtesy of extending me some credit?"

Before the bookseller could answer, James cut in, saying, "But wait, I never got you a wedding gift," and James bought the book for Harry.

"She'll love you for this, Jamie," Thomas said, picking up the sizable parcel, wishing he would be able to tell Harry truthfully that it was from him, her husband.

James looked down rather sheepishly and said, "Good, good."

As old friends could, they walked together down the street in silence. When they arrived back at Madame Flora's, there was a carriage with the Middlewich ducal arms on the door waiting for James.

"It's going to be tough to be anonymous from now on, Tom."

"I'm sure you'll find a way, Your Grace."

This led to a little scuffle between the two of them with James mock-shouting that Tom was not to call him Grace and Thomas laughing and trying to make sure Harry's book didn't get damaged.

Then they embraced and James climbed into his carriage, promising not to stand on ceremony and that he would come to Sommerleigh soon.

Thomas walked into the stables adjoining Madame Flora's and came upon the reliable groom sitting on an overturned bucket and eating a bowl of a steaming mutton stew. He gave the rest of his coins both as a tip to the groom and to buy a bowl of stew, which he ate like a starved man, standing up, Harry's book squeezed between his legs. He found Octavius well-fed and shiny and he saddled him and headed home, holding Harry's book before him like a tablet from Mount Sinai.

THIRTY

Harry, meanwhile, was not having a very easy time of it. Yesterday, she had managed some sleep and had thought to read the rest of *Macbeth*. Of course, the only interesting character kills herself offstage. Pity how many seemed to commit suicide in plays. So foolish. Perhaps it was just a useful mechanism for the playwright to get rid of untidy people.

And so many of the untidy people seemed to be women.

Then, she had been able to do some very productive thinking about coprimes.

In bed that night, she pulled up her nightdress and made do with her left hand. In every way, her left hand was inferior to her right hand. She tried to imagine it as Thomas' left hand and she was surprised that she did climax more quickly with that thought in her head.

But today, she thought it very unfortunate that just as she had learned to use her right hand in the most marvelous way, it had been broken. And then the man who had taught her to use that hand had run off, taking his left hand and his tongue with him. It was really very unfair.

And it was clear to her that something had been ruined. She didn't understand what had been ruined. She didn't understand how, exactly. But there had been something very fine and very good and now it was broken. Like a whisky glass. Or her hand.

She was working very hard at writing some notes with her left hand on what would happen if one and only one of the bases was divisible by the exponent in question but it was slow going. How did Thomas write so beautifully with his left? Of course, she need not write. She could still think and read without writing, but she was unaccountably distracted. She threw her pen down in frustration and wandered out of her aerie. She would get some coffee.

As she came down the main staircase, she heard Whitson speaking to someone in the hall. It must be the doctor, come to check her hand. They might take a walk on the grounds.

"Alasdair!" she called out as she rounded the landing and hurtled down the last half-flight of stairs.

She was mistaken. Whitson was talking to a woman. At first, she thought it was Mama Katie because the woman had the same short stature. However, she had received no letter from her stepmother, arranging a visit. And this woman had a larger bosom. And she had auburn hair.

Whitson said, "Lady Drake, Miss Hope Dunbar, daughter of his lordship's neighbor, Mr. Frederick Dunbar."

The woman, more a girl really, curtsied as Harry came forward.

"Your father and mother came and called on us many months ago," Harry said. "You were not in the country, then, but in town." She studied the young woman.

"Yes, my lady. I should have called on you before this but—"

Harry cut her off by waving her bandaged hand. "Would

you like coffee or tea? I was going to have coffee but the water might as well be heated for tea, too. Whitson?"

Miss Hope Dunbar looked at Whitson. Whitson nodded and said in a low voice that Harry could hear, "Please follow my ladyship and stay for some refreshment. Do not be startled."

Harry strolled into the largest of the drawing rooms, the one with the best view of the drive. She might be able to see Octavius coming. Harry first positioned herself in a chair with a view of the windows. She then remembered her early lessons from Mama Katie and stood and then said, "Please do sit down." That was nearly automatic by now.

They discussed the weather. The safest of all topics, Mama Katie had said. Miss Dunbar asked about Harry's hand. "Just a whisky accident," Harry cheerfully explained. Speaking of Scotland, had Miss Dunbar read *Macbeth*? Quite a dark story, didn't she think? The lord and lady, both with overweening ambition? And to have the best character, the lady, kill herself? Did Miss Dunbar find that tragic or realistic?

They discussed Miss Dunbar's age. She was four years younger than Lady Drake. Really. Harry felt that she, Harry, must be heaps older than Miss Dunbar. Perhaps because she was a married woman.

The conversation was limping at best. Miss Dunbar was far too polite. Harry was not in a good enough mood to make an effort. Harry could not remember what had possessed her to ask Miss Dunbar to stay for tea. And where was her own coffee?

Just then Whitson had come in with quite a large trolley with coffee and tea and chocolate. Harry was surprised that Miss Dunbar took chocolate instead.

"Why did you ask for tea, then?" Harry wondered aloud.

"I didn't ask for anyth—" Miss Dunbar started and then

Harry saw a look pass between her and Whitson, and Miss Dunbar cut herself off.

Miss Dunbar coughed a little. "I am sorry to have missed Lord Drake."

"Yes, it's too bad he isn't here. He could stay and talk to you and I could go back to work. He is really much more entertaining than I am."

"I . . . I did not know I was interrupting your work." Miss Dunbar put her cup back in her saucer and started to rise. "I do apologize, Lady Drake—"

"No, no, finish your chocolate, I beg you." Harry thought the "I beg you" a rather fine embellishment.

As Miss Dunbar sipped her chocolate with lowered eyes, Harry eyed her carefully. Then, she leaned forward.

"Now that I see you, I'm quite surprised Lord Drake didn't marry *you*. He has quite an *idée fixe* about redheaded women, you know. And you have very good breasts. And you seem like you would have sense."

Miss Dunbar choked suddenly and her cup clattered into her saucer. Whitson sprang to assist her and provide a napkin for the errant drops of chocolate that had erupted from the cup.

"Except you don't know your own mind about tea versus chocolate," Harry added.

"I didn't ask for tea—" Miss Dunbar stood and Harry thought she might be upset. She was flushed. "Excuse me, Lady Drake, I have another engagement. One that is quite pressing."

Whitson ushered Miss Dunbar out into the hall.

Whitson returned to retrieve the trolley. His brows were knitted fiercely together.

Harry realized she had been quite bad. She caught his arm.

"Whitson, please don't tell Tommy—I mean, Lord Drake, what I said. I forgot that he needed such a lot of money, and perhaps Miss Dunbar's father doesn't really have that much. Of course, he would have rather married her. I didn't mean to hurt her feelings by lording it over her that I was married and she was not—well, that's not true, maybe I did. But I tried to make up for it by complimenting her breasts, you see? But of course, I am much more worried about his hearing that I hurt her feelings than I am about hurting her feelings."

Whitson said stiffly, "I am not in the habit of repeating any private family conversations I hear, to anyone."

Harry released his arm.

"Of course."

It was several hours later that Octavius and his rider could be seen coming up the drive. By then, Harry had long since fled to her aerie and was doggedly trying to make her left hand do what she wanted with a pen.

THIRTY-ONE

T hat evening, Thomas was impatient as he waited for Harry outside her aerie. He had been impatient all afternoon. He felt enormous relief when she emerged, even though he had been reassured by Smythe that Harry was well and working in the aerie.

Wordless, he held the book out to her. She seized it eagerly with her left hand and put it down on the table in the hallway and opened it and began to pore over it.

He finally spoke, "It's a very late wedding gift from Lord Daventry—no, excuse me, he's now the Duke of Middlewich. James. My friend. Who came for Christmas, you remember."

"Wedding gift?" She stopped turning pages. "Do you want to look at it first then, my lord?"

She called him my lord. Not Tommy.

"No, he means it for you alone. I'm sure he thinks you're owed some compensation for putting up with me."

Harry shook her head and continued reading.

Thomas knew it was an inadequate apology. He stood as close to her as he felt he could. He longed to put one hand on the back of her neck and bring her bent head around to him and turn her face up and kiss her. No, Harry didn't allow mouth kissing. Well then, he longed to put one hand on the back of her neck and lightly stroke the skin with the tips of his fingers, play with the tendrils of her softest and finest hair that had escaped her hair pins and coiled there. Then he might run his hand down her spine toward her dimples above her—

She held her right hand behind her back, bandaged in stark white except for some spatters of ink. She held it there as if to remind herself not to use it.

He took a step back.

Harry read on, muttering, flipping back to the table of contents and then forward to other chapters in the text.

"Perhaps you could continue reading the book with dinner."

"With dinner?"

"Yes, it's time, we must eat. But we dine alone. I see no reason why you shouldn't read while you eat."

Harry closed the book and Thomas picked the volume up. He went to offer her his arm, but she was already four steps down, holding the banister with her left hand.

Whitson was scandalized, Thomas could tell, by Lady Drake reading at the dinner table. His posture, his sniffs conveyed his disapproval.

Thomas didn't care. *His* wife could read her book anywhere and anytime she wanted. And maybe she might look up at some point and acknowledge him. He would settle for that, at this point.

After the soup course had been cleared, one of the footmen brought the meat course and took it first to Whitson, who stood at Harry's elbow. Whitson placed several pieces on a plate and then the footman brought the serving platter to

Thomas, who helped himself. Whitson then began to cut the meat on the plate.

Of course, Harry could not cut her food herself.

"Here. Stop." Thomas stood. "I'll do that."

"My lord." Whitson bowed. Thomas walked down to Harry's end of the table and began to cut her meat.

"Move my place setting down here, too," Thomas said. "I'll sit here on Lady Drake's right."

After he had finished cutting her meat and sauced it and put the potatoes on the plate as well, he got up, went around Harry's chair, and put her plate at her left elbow.

"Thank you," she said, not looking up.

Thomas went back around and sat and ate and watched his wife mutter and chortle to herself as she read. He cut the fish for her as well as the spring lettuces. The dessert was an ice, which Harry ate with a spoon.

Thomas asked for coffee.

"Whitson, Lady Drake and I will stay in the dining room for a time. I will ring when we are done with the room."

This cleared the room of footmen and the disdainful Whitson.

Harry nodded to herself and turned pages. She let her coffee grow cold.

After half an hour, he allowed himself to speak. "Will this book help with your proof?"

Harry looked up, as if she had woken from a dream.

"This is a book about the calculus."

"Yes?"

"Fermat's conjecture involves the natural numbers, not the calculus."

"But it is the right book, is it not? The book you asked for?"

"Yes."

She went back to reading. The candles in the chandelier

burned lower. Finally, Thomas suggested they leave the dining room. She agreed and he trailed her up the stairs, carrying the book with his two good hands.

At her door, she opened the door first and then took the book from him with her left hand and put it under her right arm.

He held a slender hope that she might issue an invitation to come and sit by the fire with her and read. He had a small book of verse in his trousers pocket, ready for just such an eventuality. What an optimist he had been to put it there this afternoon upon his return to Sommerleigh.

We can sit in two separate chairs, Thomas promised in his head.

Or you can sit in my lap and I won't touch you.

Or I can touch you, if you want, however you want. You can be as my queen, and I will be your faithful slave, worshipping at the altar of your body.

Or we can sit in two separate chairs, and I won't touch you.

She looked just over his left shoulder at the wall behind him. "Miss Dunbar came to call today."

"Oh?" He tried to express a polite interest.

"I think she really came to see you, not me."

"We'll have to return the call—"

But Harry held her good hand up to him as if to say "stop" and then turned toward her open door, saying, "I think I'll be far too busy . . . ." As her words trailed off, she disappeared into the room. Smythe appeared, curtsied, and waited. Finally, Smythe smiled apologetically and said, "Good night, my lord" and closed the door as Thomas stood in the hall.

Thirty-Two

T he next day was bright. Thomas, on the other hand, was in rather a dark mood. He ate his breakfast alone, as usual, in the breakfast room. And Ellen, as usual, came in with Harry's breakfast tray, to show him Harry's dishes. The plates were clean this morning. She had eaten everything.

"Yesterday morning, when I was absent, was her plate clean?"

"Yes, my lord."

Ellen waited for dismissal.

Thomas said slowly, "I don't think you need bother to bring me her breakfast tray anymore. Thank you."

Ellen curtsied and disappeared.

An hour later, he was in the library, trying to understand last year's rents and finding his steward's hand very hard to read indeed, when he heard Harry in the front hall, back from her walk. It must have been a shorter walk than usual. He swiftly crossed the room, noting no trace of blood or glass on the carpet, and opened the library door and walked out into the front hall. It was empty. He turned his head and caught a glimpse of the back of Harry running up the main staircase.

He had missed her. She would go to her aerie now. He might eat luncheon with her perhaps in a few hours. He would need to think of what he could say to her as they ate. Thomas walked back to his desk slowly, considering possible topics of conversation. He sat.

Within a minute, there was a knock. The door opened. Harry, gorgeously flushed from her walk, her chest heaving slightly from exertion, came in with the new book tucked under her right arm.

"Are you busy, my lord?"

Still my lord, not Tommy.

He stood. "No, Harry, I'm not. I'm glad you've come to see me."

She walked farther into the room and pulled the volume out from under her right arm and put it on the central table, the same table where he had been so drunk—was it only three nights ago? She pulled out a chair and sat.

"Come. Bring paper and one of those pencils."

He found a stack of foolscap and a pencil and hastened to her.

"Sit." She gestured to the chair next to her.

He sat. This early in the day, and so close to her walk, she smelled most of grass and her sweat and coffee. The ink would come later, Thomas thought, after she had been in her aerie the rest of the day.

Harry put her hand now to her chest, down the front of her dress. Thomas caught his breath, imagining for a moment his hand there, between her breasts. She drew out the chain, heavy with two keys and now a third object. It was the knife he had given her. She had strung it by a little metal ring that was at one end.

"Handy," Harry said. She opened the blade of the little knife and sharpened the pencil.

She closed the knife and turned to him.

"So," she said.

He waited.

"You wanted to know about limits."

Did he? He didn't remember that. But she was talking to him. And she was sitting close to him.

"Uh . . . yes."

"Our wedding night."

A vague memory tickled Thomas then.

"Let us start from the beginning again," Harry said.

Thomas forced a smile. "With the rabbits?"

"No, not with the rabbits. That was a poor choice on my part. A distraction. Although calculus has a multitude of practical applications, let us stay in the abstract, for now. Let us start with functions."

Harry opened the book to its first chapter and began to define *variable* and *constant*. She did not look at him. Thomas let her speak for several minutes. She was about to flip to the second page when Thomas interrupted her.

"Harry," he said.

She looked at him. "Thomas."

She called him Thomas. Progress.

"Why did you want this book?" he asked.

"It's the first English translation of this text. You know, the French, the Continent, they have far outstripped Britain in mathematics in the years since Newton. And I remembered that when my father finally got me a copy of the first edition of the Lacroix in the original French—it was very difficult to get then because of that greedy French man—"

"Napoleon? You're referring to Napoleon?"

"Yes, he and the war made it devilishly difficult to get

ahold of a copy, but I remembered that when I had read it that I felt it laid out several concepts in quite a useful way. I believe this is now becoming a standard text at Cambridge."

"So, you've read this book before?"

"Yes. It's upstairs in the aerie. In French. I keep it mostly for sentimental reasons. But I thought that the use of English would help you to follow the explanations more closely".

"Help *me*?" Thomas sat back.

"Yes." Her voice was a trifle impatient.

Seconds ticked on the library case clock.

"You wanted the book for *me*?"

"Yes. Well, for me, too, so that I might become a better teacher. Of you."

"You think I should learn the calculus?"

Harry stared at him. "I think *everyone* should learn the calculus." She turned back to the book. "Although there are no pictorial representations of the function described here, I know that you are, like most men, quite visual," and here the corners of her mouth turned up ever so slightly, "so I do think that at this point I should digress and make sure you fully understand Cartesian coordinates."

Thomas did not need Harry's litany of x's and y's to make his head spin, her left hand racing across the foolscap, drawing crooked lines with cross hatching. His head was spinning already.

She had wanted the book for *him*. It wasn't for her proof. Was it possible, could it be possible, that she might care for him a sliver of the amount that she cared for Fermat's conjecture?

He thought of the moment in the library two days ago, when she had confessed that she had discussed his alcohol-induced impotence with the doctor. What cared he for that now? She wasn't going to teach the doctor the calculus. She was going to teach *him*. If only he could go back in time to that moment and turn to her and say, "I am a fool, forgive me." No, that wasn't far enough. Could he go back to the night before where he had crushed her hand under his boot? No, further back, one more night. The night when he had left her bedchamber because she had crowed about her independence from him for her pleasure. Let him stay then, sitting by the fire, sipping cordial, applauding her as a student of her own body. Let him read another sonnet. She likely would have found a way back to his lap if he had just stayed still. Her hand might be whole. He might be Tommy. If he had just stayed still.

"Harry," he interrupted, "you are doing a marvelous job, but could you repeat that last bit again?"

She repeated her last sentence.

"Perhaps we could go back to the beginning of the Cartesian coordinates again," Thomas said.

Thomas decided she should know from the start what a dullard he was. Better she be frustrated by his stupidity than to think he did not care for the calculus. So, Harry started again. Thomas slowed her by asking questions. He listened. He used every ounce of concentration he had to focus on the words she used and the pictures she drew rather than on her scent, her breasts, the curve of her jaw, the tip of her nose. At one point, he suggested that he take over from her the use of the pencil.

"Yes, that's quite a good idea," she brightened, "my left hand is so useless. You draw and write. You'll learn much faster that way."

Thomas felt a sharp pang in his chest from being reminded that she had to use her left hand. Then, he took the pencil and began to create his axes on a piece of foolscap. This allowed him to move away from her slightly since he did not need to peer at the piece of paper in front of her. But she pulled her chair closer to him, and he found that her leaning into him was even more intoxicating than the reverse.

Concentrate, lecher, he told himself.

At one point, he asked Harry how old she was when she had read the Lacroix for the first time. "Eight," she said. "It's too bad you are so dreadfully old, Thomas, it makes it so much more difficult."

THIRTY-THREE

There was no resumption of the evenings of reading in front of the fire in Harry's room. For one thing, Harry said, the evenings were getting warmer, no need for fires. Harry went back to her aerie now in the evenings. She kept their walks short. It was, she explained, how she might fit his calculus lessons in and still devote sufficient time to her proof. She said she was sure that the minds of the Continent were burning the midnight oil in the race to prove the conjecture and she must do no less.

Thomas found it very difficult that those pleasant evenings of poetry had been replaced by mornings of symbols and numbers and feeling quite stupid while his brain ached from exertion.

And Harry did not ask to sit in his lap any longer.

Thomas found that quite difficult, too.

For his part, Thomas did not touch her. His desire to do so was ever-present. The memory of her body that night in her bedchamber would dance in his mind, taunting him. The softness of her skin. The feel of her breasts in his hands and in his mouth. Her smell. Her most private taste. Her exquisite responsiveness to his touch that night. Surely, that was the memory he dwelled on the most—how she had wanted something from him. Something he was uniquely positioned to give her.

The bandaged right hand was more than an admonition. It was a symbol of his brutishness. A show of how a selfish oaf might, without thinking, crush something rare and delicate. It was what had haunted his entire adult life—that he, like his cousin Mr. Hugh Drake, would take something beautiful and destroy it. With his appetites. Like his sister Jane had been destroyed.

And yet, Harry had such resiliency. He wondered at how, the morning after he had injured her, she had treated him with the most affection she had ever shown him. She had been such a *woman* with him. She had been almost wifely.

She had called him Tommy.

She had worried about his feet.

She had tried to shield him from knowing what he had done.

But now, no longer. His anger at her, his abandoning her for London and for his whores, had been a tipping point in some way that his drunken behavior had not been. A point of inflection, Harry might call it. And he had fumbled it, disastrously.

It did not matter that he had not bedded another woman that night. He had planned to, and she knew it. And he could not find a way to tell her that he had not. Harry did not want to hear about what he did or did not do with his cock.

And it would rip his heart in two right now to see that she did not care one way or another what he felt for her.

He did not know how to return them to their former intimacy. And he did not feel he could be the one to do so. At every step of their friendship, from her proposal of an unconventional marriage to her putting his hand between her legs, it had been Harry and Harry's desires that had led the way. He intuited—no, he knew—that it must be Harry who took the next step.

She must choose him. So, he did nothing. He did not reach for her. He did not ask her for anything.

He suppressed his impatience. He studied the calculus. And he waited for her.

"Harry, do you ever wish that you could change something in the past?"

"No."

They were walking on a path through a meadow.

"You have lived a life without regret, then?"

"No. I regret that I have eaten so much that I now, like most other women, have to wear a corset to support my breasts." Harry laughed and looked down.

Thomas felt then that he could also allow himself a glance. He immediately wished he hadn't. His look at the beautiful rounding of her bosom, the creamy skin at the tops of her breasts prompted longing and memories of holding those breasts, caressing the nipples he could no longer see. He felt an ache deep in his groin. And one in his chest. He almost groaned.

Harry went on, "But I think other people attach more importance to the past than I do. Regret is foolish. And it is easy. Because you *know* you cannot change the past. How much more difficult it is to wish to change the present and hence the future. Because the wish demands action."

"Yes."

"I rather like the present. Or at least I am fond of this one."

"I'm glad."

They walked on, Thomas hoping he played some small part in her fondness for the present.

Finally, he said, "For my part, there are many things I wish I could change."

"About the past?"

"Yes."

"There are things I wish to change . . . ." Harry seemed far away.

"Yes?" Thomas said hopefully.

She squinted. "But none of them are in the past. If the present is built on the past and you extract and alter one brick in the foundation, what's to say that the whole thing won't collapse?"

"What do you wish to change, Harry?"

"Why, the future, of course."

"The future of mathematics?"

"Yes. Why not?"

A dozen strides later, she spoke, "Aristotle said that time was the numeration of change and argued that time cannot exist, or has no meaning, without change. And of course, the calculus is the study of change."

"It is?"

"You still thought it was the study of rabbits?" Thomas looked over and saw Harry was looking at him, with a quirked eyebrow.

He laughed and then she did, too.

"You mock me, Harry, but I am in earnest."

"Yes. Well, take comfort, because Aristotle said that in addition to change, for time to exist, there must be a soul to mark the change."

"And?"

"And I will be the soul to mark your change."

Thomas had been walking a few steps ahead of her. He

stopped now and turned to her and thought of reaching for her, taking her hand.

But Harry had vaulted the stile with one hand and was racing across the meadow, back to Sommerleigh and luncheon. Thomas never caught up with her.

While Harry was up in her aerie in the evenings, Thomas spent his time swotting over the calculus, praying he might master enough of it to impress his wife. He had even swallowed his jealousy and imposed on Dr. Andrews several times, asking him for dinner on the nights Harry ate off a tray in her aerie, and then trading smuggled Scottish whisky in the library for tutoring. He found the doctor much easier to understand than Harry, but he would never tell her so. He told the doctor, however.

"Aye," Dr. Andrews had said with a grin, "that is because her thinking mechanism is not in the same class as yers and mine. We are as peasants while she is a fearsome goddess with a mind apart. It must be painful for her to translate the genius of Newton and Leibniz so that ye can understand it."

Thomas held his head. "I think it is a great deal more painful for me."

"Aye." The doctor clapped him on his shoulder and got up to pour more whisky. "But it would be foolish to refuse a gift from a goddess nae matter how many burdens it places on ye."

Thomas groaned. "It's like having Cleopatra as your laundress, scrubbing the shit stains out of your breeches."

The doctor's voice had an edge. "Marcus Antonius, is it then? Marcus, have ye ever wondered why Cleopatra might be willing to do so?"

Thomas opened his mouth and then closed it.

"Recognize yer luck, Thomas Drake." The doctor looked down at his glass.

· · ·

An invitation came. Dinner at the Dunbars.

"No," Harry said.

They were at dinner themselves, in the dining room, eating the first of the spring asparagus.

Thomas protested. It would be rude to say no. They were so clearly free for the evening in question.

"You are free, I am not," Harry said. She picked up her last stalk with her fingers.

Thomas was about to put his argument more strongly. She was his wife. She must accompany him.

Harry leaned forward, her stalk of asparagus dangling from her fingers, and looked at him neutrally, like a teacher not wanting to give away the right answer, waiting to see what he would say next.

He opened his mouth and then he closed it again.

"You are absolutely correct," he said.

Harry sat back and put her tip of her stalk of asparagus in her mouth and bit down. Thomas suddenly felt like he had passed a very important test.

On the night of the Dunbar dinner, Thomas took great care with his attire. Jackson was surprised to have his lordship ask him about which waistcoats were cleaned and which breeches had been pressed.

Dressed, Thomas walked up the stairs to Harry's aerie and tapped on the door.

He heard a grunt.

"I'm off to the Dunbars, Harry," he said.

She said something through the door then. He wasn't sure but it might have been "Have fun."

He stomped down the stairs, feeling that his care with his clothing had been a waste if she would not even open the door to see him.

He did have fun that night. He didn't mean to, but he did. The Dunbars were a convivial family, obviously loving, full of high jinks and laughter. All the daughters —Faith, Hope, and Charity—played the pianoforte and there were enough guests to make up the numbers for dancing after the dinner. How wonderful to be surrounded by simple people, like himself, who did not expect him to integrate and derivate. Who knew how to laugh and sing and dance. Who drank until their cheeks flushed. Who flirted and scolded and clucked and giggled.

Mrs. Dunbar expressed her regret early in the evening that Lady Drake had not been able to attend.

"I hope she is well," she said.

"She is, thank you for asking," Thomas said. "She asked me to express her regrets many times over." Harry hadn't, of course, but Thomas knew the value of a social nicety.

"We are all so happy that you have married, my lord," Mrs. Dunbar said and her gaze rested momentarily on her daughter Hope as she said that.

Later, Thomas waltzed with Hope Dunbar and he was reminded of her beauty. Her red hair glinted most bewitchingly in the candlelight. She must be what? Twenty or so? He had a thought.

"You have met my nephew and my heir Phillip Drake, have you not?"

She looked away. Was it his imagination or did she stiffen in his arms when he said that?

"Yes, my lord."

"When he is home from university again, Lady Drake will invite you for tea. Or rather, I will. We two are so dull for poor Phillip, I am sure he would like to be around lively young people."

"Yes, my lord," she said and met his eyes.

When the dance was over, he wondered why her eyes had been so fearful.

.   .   .

Thomas carried his boots in his hand down the corridor. As he passed Harry's bedchamber, she opened the door and peered out.

"Thomas," she said.

"Hello, Harry."

"Was there fun to be had at the Dunbars tonight, my lord?"

"Yes, my lady."

Harry stood in the doorway to her bedchamber. Her hair was loose and wild, tendrils flying out in all directions. She was wearing a nightdress with a very intricate lace trim. He thought he could see the shadows of her areolas under the delicate fabric. It came to him that this was the nightdress she had worn on their wedding night.

She seemed to be waiting for something.

"Tonight, I decided that I have to prove that there are an infinite number of auxiliary primes for each possible exponent."

"Good." He did not know what to say to his own wife. "Well, good night."

She held out her arm and stopped him.

"You look handsome, Tommy."

His heart was in his mouth. He waited for some other sign. None came.

"Good night," she said and closed the door.

She thought him handsome.

She called him Tommy.

He felt a faint itch of something. It felt like hope.

THIRTY-FOUR

For her part, Harry had no awareness that Thomas desired anything different than the current arrangement. Something had changed, true, but there was no sense in going backward. Something bad might happen again. Better to continue on and see what happened in the future. That is how she approached a proof, after all. In time, she might circle back around and try to correct any inherent incorrect assumptions that she had started with. But for now— onward and try something new. Like standing in a nightdress in the doorway to her bedchamber.

She enjoyed her self-sufficiency with her increasingly skilled left hand in her own bedchamber at night and in the morning. She allowed her husband to creep into her thoughts during those moments, but as soon as she was done gasping with the thrill of her climax, she did try to push away the images of his chest, his breeches clinging to his thighs and backside, his blue eyes and dark stubble.

He had women aplenty. Who was Harry Lovelock Drake to Hope Dunbar or Mrs. Swinton or the dozens of unnamed but beautiful and experienced whores in London? Nothing. She was a null set. Even in her wedding nightdress.

But it had been very good of him to show her how to pleasure herself.

Now, she might pay him back the only way she knew how.

She felt she did quite a good job of leaving carnal thoughts of him aside during daylight hours. There *were* many moments when they sat shoulder to shoulder in the library and she felt his heat and smelled cinnamon. At those times, she thought of straddling his leg or ripping his waistcoat off or sinking her hands into his hair and pulling his face to her breasts. But then the magic of the calculus would catch her and she would be as she was at age eight. How elegant, how beautiful, how useful . . . how uncomplicated by physical sensation. How good of her to show Thomas this.

Two days after the Dunbar dinner, late at night, Thomas went up to the aerie. He did not know why he thought he could, on this particular night, knock on her door and interrupt her. But he steeled himself, and he did.

Harry came to the door swiftly in answer to his light rap.

"What is wrong, Lord Drake?" she said. There was a note of concern in her voice.

"Nothing." Thomas felt like a nervous schoolboy. "I remembered that at some point, Newton wrote about the orbits of the planets around the sun. I think it is a good night for looking for planets. Will you join me?"

They went out to the lawn, Thomas carrying a horse blanket he had stolen from the stables.

"Well, it's my blanket, so I shouldn't really say I stole it. But I have to be sure to put it back so no stableboy is short on the count," Thomas said as he spread it out.

"I'll remind you." Harry laughed as she accepted his hand to lower herself to the blanket.

It was good to hear her laugh.

They lay on their backs, heads close together. The air was warm.

It was quite late, the sun had been down for many hours, so Venus and Mercury were not visible. Harry quickly found Mars and Jupiter and Saturn and pointed them out to Thomas. He thought she might begin to explain the mechanics of their orbits but she didn't. In silence, they looked up into the deep black velvet night and admired those distant twinkling jewels.

A shooting star. Thomas thought hard and kept his wish modest and within the realm of the attainable. He wished that Harry might fall asleep out here on the grass, under the stars, so he might wrap her in the blanket and carry her softly to her bed. On their way up the stairs, she might put her arms around his neck and nestle into his chest.

"I wish . . ." Harry said drowsily on the blanket next to him.

"Yes?" said Thomas and turned his head to look at her profile, her face pointing up to the stars.

"I wish for a telescope."

Her wish was attainable, too. He would make sure it came true.

A letter arrived. Phillip was coming. Worried, Thomas scanned the letter. There were no words that conveyed an imminent crisis. Neither were there words that indicated any contrition. Well, that was a young man for you. Neither looking ahead nor back.

Thomas felt easy when Phillip arrived, though. He was the same as always—smiling, ready with a quip. Phillip greeted

Harry pleasantly, and although Harry did not give him her hand, she curtsied and used the right words.

"Good day, Phillip."

"Good day, my lady."

"It's good to see you, Phillip," Thomas said, clapping him on the back.

"And it's good to see you, Uncle."

It came out eventually that Phillip had decided to leave Cambridge, for good.

"Everyone there is a second or a third son, all preparing to enter the church. I had to think it was a waste of my time."

Harry stomped out of the room.

Phillip raised his eyebrows. "She's a bit petulant, isn't she?"

Thomas glared at him. He could guess why Harry was angry. She would have given her life's blood to have gone to university, to Cambridge, the place where Isaac Newton had been the second Lucasian Professor of Mathematics. But Phillip was not to know that.

"She is working hard, Phillip, that is all."

"Is sitting and playing with paper and numbers work now?"

"What do you know of work, Phillip?"

Phillip laughed. "Fair enough."

"What are your plans?'

"Well," Phillip stretched out, "with all this peace on the Continent, I thought perhaps a year abroad. Venice."

If Thomas were being honest with himself, he felt a bit relieved. He had a hard time imagining Phillip and Harry in the same house together for a long period of time. His and Harry's equilibrium might be disturbed. He held out hope that she might turn to him again one day. Maybe.

That night at dinner, Thomas brought up having Hope Dunbar for tea the next day or the day after.

"Miss Hope Dunbar?" Phillip said. "She, of the red hair and generous figure? One of the chief attractions of the neighborhood, I should think. So many plain bluestocking types of women about."

Thomas thought this might be a sly insult directed at Harry, but Harry had paid it no notice so he didn't want to draw attention to Phillip's words. Later, in private, he would question Phillip about what he had meant and remind him to be courteous to his aunt.

Thomas turned to Harry. "Would you be able to spare the time for some tea, do you think?"

Harry started to answer, and Phillip spoke over her.

"There's no need for the countess to come down from her roost. Two strapping youngish men like us, Uncle, surely we can handle the beautiful Hope Dunbar on our own?"

Thomas thought that an odd response.

"In fact," Phillip said, "perhaps I should entertain Miss Dunbar entirely on my own."

"Miss Dunbar likes chocolate, not tea," Harry said. "Don't give her tea, even if she asks for it."

"Do you know, Lady Drake, at one time, I thought it highly likely that Miss Dunbar might become my aunt. What a cozy family we would be."

"I think," Thomas said loudly, "we have forgotten the bounds of propriety. Miss Dunbar cannot come and have tea here—or chocolate," he added before Harry could interrupt him, "without Harry being present. Or we could invite her mother, as well, I suppose. Or her married older sister."

"Now, it's becoming rather complicated, Uncle," Phillip said and took a swig from his wine glass.

"I suppose . . ." Thomas said, feeling doubtful.

"I will come down," Harry said absently. "*I* will have coffee. I owe Miss Dunbar an apology but I'm not sure what for."

The next morning, Thomas sent round a carefully worded invitation that included all possible beverages as well as the fact that Philip was in residence at Sommerleigh currently. Very quickly the response came back that Miss Dunbar was otherwise engaged for the next several weeks and would be unable to come for tea or chocolate or coffee.

Thirty-Five

Harry was in her aerie when she heard a sound. A mewing. What was it? Had a bird built a nest high up in one of the cornices of the manse? She opened a window with her one good hand and stuck her head out into the early afternoon sun. No, the sound was not coming from outside the house. Then, she heard something that might be . . . a scuffle?

Holding her pencil between her teeth, she opened her door very quietly. The hall was empty. But the sounds were louder. She walked down the hall. This door. What was it to? Oh yes, one of the additional rooms for the servants of guests, should a guest bring a valet or a lady's maid.

She opened the door.

Phillip had Ellen pushed against a wall, his mouth on hers. He was holding both her arms over her head with one hand while his other hand roamed over her body, pulling on her dress.

"Stop," Harry said. She held out the pencil like a sword in her left hand as she walked into the room.

Phillip stopped moving. He let go of Ellen, who collapsed,

sliding down the wall. Phillip adjusted his trousers and inclined his head.

"Lady Drake—" he said.

"Ellen is crying. I think that means she doesn't like this." Harry gestured to Ellen. "Come."

Ellen was trying to pull her skirts down, curtsey and stand up all at the same time. Harry transferred the pencil back to a position between her teeth and then grabbed Ellen and led her by the hand to the door.

"Aunt—" Phillip started to say. But Harry had taken Ellen out of the room.

Harry took Ellen to her own bedchamber. She did not know where else to take her. She rang for Smythe. Smythe arrived very quickly, concerned that something was amiss because Harry almost never needed her services in the early afternoon.

"Phillip was kissing Ellen," Harry explained. Ellen was sitting in the chair by the window where Harry had put her and had her face in her hands. "You must ask her, of course, but I don't think she was wanting that."

Smythe knelt now in front of Ellen and handed her a handkerchief.

"Did Mr. Drake force you to do something against your wish, Ellen?" Smythe asked gently. Ellen wiped her nose and eyes and looked fearfully at Harry.

Harry looked away.

"Do not be afraid of telling the truth, Ellen," Smythe said. "Lady Drake wants you to tell the truth. You will not be in any trouble, no matter what you say. As long as it is the truth."

Ellen's chin wobbled. "He said . . . oh, he said I should come to this room with him to check for mice and then he said if I did not kiss him, I would lose my position . . . and then—" She dissolved into tears.

"And then," Smythe prompted.

"He pushed me against the wall and started touching me."

Smythe said quietly, "Ellen, did Mr. Drake do this?" Smythe touched the front of Ellen's dress lightly.

Ellen looked down and saw that her neat apron had been torn from its strap and was hanging down and the dress underneath had a large tear over her bosom.

"Oh, no, my uniform!" Ellen said and tried to pull the ripped cloth together to cover herself up.

"Hang the dress!" Harry growled.

Smythe quickly said, "Lady Drake is not angry at you, Ellen, do not be afraid." Smythe then turned to Harry, "I am going to clean Ellen up and fix her dress."

"Yes," Harry said. She turned on her heel and left the room.

She found Thomas in the library.

"You are leaving, Phillip."

"Uncle—" Phillip began.

"I should call the magistrate." Thomas gritted his teeth. "I won't, because you are my blood and because I doubt the charge would hold. It would only cause scandal and could harm the girl. But I cannot tolerate cruelty in this house. I will not. You are leaving. I will continue your allowance. Otherwise, there will be no communication."

"So. I am *persona non grata* now. Your heir."

"Yes."

"Really, Uncle, isn't this a bit like the pot calling the kettle black? I would have thought, you, of all men, would understand."

"I am not proud of my appetites. I regret my weakness. Perhaps it is a meaningless distinction that I have always asked and that I have always paid for my pleasures." Thomas hung his head for a moment but then raised it again and stared at

Phillip levelly. "But what I have done in the past does not play a part in this matter. The women in this house and on my land are under my protection. Including protection from you."

Phillip laughed. "For how long, Uncle? You are hale and well, but one day, someday, you will die. If I outlive you, I am the Earl Drake and there will be nothing you can do then."

Thomas clenched his fists by his sides. "Is that a threat, Phillip?"

Phillip faced him. "No, it's fact."

Thomas turned away. "Yes, you are my presumptive heir. For now."

"What does that mean?"

"It means that I have something I hold close to my heart. Hope. Contracts can be broken. New agreements can be reached."

"Hope? A broken contract and . . . a new agreement?"

"You are right that nothing on this earth, including my time as the Earl Drake, is forever. But there is still time for a change, for a cleaning of any and all slates. I must believe that."

Philip said nothing for a long time.

"I think I understand, Uncle. I wish you much happiness."

Thirty-Six

The next morning, it happened. It was clear. Not the proof. But the master plan of *how* to execute the proof. And not a proof for just one integer or one type of integer. But for all integers greater than two.

She trembled. There was a moment when she thought she might cry. Which was odd because she was happy, not sad.

Her first thought after the wash of emotion passed over her was that she must tell Tommy. He wouldn't understand her strategy or her master plan, but he would understand her excitement.

Suddenly, telling him was the most pressing thing she could think of. She would not be able to bear waiting. Even the anticipated applause she would receive when giving the prize lecture at the *Académie des Sciences* could not compare to the grin he was sure to give her. He might embrace her, which she was sure she would be able to tolerate for, say, fifteen or ten seconds.

She might even let him kiss her mouth.

The house was strangely empty as she came down the stairs. Yes, there was a fête today. She had forgotten. Most of the staff had been given permission to go into the village. Now where was Tommy? She went out to the stable.

Octavius was in his stall. And there was a man sitting in the stall, as well, drinking from a bottle. Phillip.

"Where's Lord Drake?" Harry asked.

"He's gone," Phillip said. "He's gone to London. He's gone awhoring."

Harry thought it odd that Tommy had not told her he was going to London. Odder still he had not taken Octavius. And she thought that Phillip had left yesterday.

Oh, well. It had been a long time since Tommy had gone to London. He likely needed the relief. It had nothing to do with her. Nothing whatsoever.

She turned and walked out of the stall.

But Phillip followed her.

"And after he's done at the brothel, I think he's going to see the bishop of London."

Harry turned and cocked her head quizzically.

"Because that's where you got married. In London, right?"

"Yes," Harry said.

Something was wrong with Phillip, but she wasn't sure what it was. It wasn't just what he was drinking from the bottle. It was like he was being eaten alive from the inside. She knew that feeling. But she hadn't had it in a long time. Maybe not since she had had to get new clothes. No, that was a lie. She had had it much more recently. When Hope Dunbar had come to drink tea and had drunk chocolate instead and Harry had hurt her feelings.

She hated that she and Phillip might be alike.

"So, he has to see the bishop in London," Phillip said.

"The bishop?"

"Yes, the bishop. To get an annulment."

Harry suddenly felt very frightened. Like when her mother died. When she was four.

"Why would he be doing that?"

"Why? So he can get rid of you. Marry that redheaded Hope Dunbar, that fecund wench, the neighbor's daughter, have children. Do what all lords do . . . make more lords."

Harry turned from Phillip and began walking away.

He grabbed her left arm and turned her around back to face him.

"You bitch."

Harry jerked her arm away from Phillip, but his grip stayed fast.

"You turned him against me. You told him lies. You made him hate me."

Harry jerked again. Phillip caught her right hand and pulled her toward him. He started mashing her bandaged hand with his own hand. His face was inches from her. His breath smelled of whisky and rotten meat.

"Everything was fine before you," Phillip sneered.

Harry tried not to show the pain that he was causing in her hand. She kept her voice calm.

"Then you should be happy that he is seeking an annulment."

"No! No! Because then he can marry again." Phillip squeezed her right hand. Bright-white pain radiated up from her hand to her shoulder, her neck, her head. "And have a son. And I'll have nothing. You and your virginity! If you had let him bed you, then he couldn't get the annulment. But he probably couldn't even get it up with you. You ugly chit. You whore."

Phillip had now said two contradictory things. Her need to point that out overrode her pain.

"Which is it? Am I a virgin or a whore?"

Phillip pushed Harry to the ground, still holding her. He fell on top of her, crushing her.

"I'll . . . make . . . you . . . a whore."

He was breathing heavily. Harry struggled under him.

He was not an overly large man, but he weighed at least six stone more than she did. He pinned her left arm under her own body. He let go of her right hand and tore the front of her dress open. She tried to hit him with her right hand but she couldn't move the bandaged hand at all and found herself slapping at the side of his head uselessly.

He pulled at her corset, but the material was too thick and unyielding. He swore and began fumbling with his own trousers, pulling them down.

Harry tried to find purchase on the ground with her feet, so she could push up and out from under him or so she could bring her leg up between his and knee him in the groin, but her feet slid on the straw. She then started using her heels on the back of his calves, kicking down as hard as she could. This opened her legs and she felt something push against her inner thighs. Then higher up. She jerked her head up and aimed for his nose with the top of her skull but he dodged her.

He raised his left hand that had been in his trousers and struck her in the jaw. "You," strike to the temple, "vicious," strike to the jaw, "little," strike to the nose, "bitch."

Left-handed like Tommy.

Harry felt warm stickiness from her nose.

He didn't give her much choice.

She used all her strength to try to squirm away and got her left arm free and reached for her bosom.

Phillip fumbled into the straw off to the side, feeling for something.

Harry put her bandaged right hand to her bosom.

Phillip found what he had been looking for in the straw. He raised it up. It gleamed. It was a horse shoe.

Despite her bandaged hand, she got her birthday present open.

And then things were dark and quiet.

Thirty-Seven

A rough, wet cloth on her face. Warm air blowing on her. More of the roughness and wetness.

She opened her left eye. Her right eye wouldn't open. Dust motes floating in the air above her.

And then a long, angular brown thing with big intelligent eyes moved into her field of view and licked her.

A horse's head.

Something very heavy was lying on her. She moved her left arm slightly. She was so sticky. She turned her head to the side to see where she was. She was pierced with pain. She closed her eyes.

When she opened them again, it seemed much, much later. There was a horrible sound. A screeching or screaming or howling. She couldn't tell. She was lying in a man's lap and he was holding her. He was where the sound was coming from. She wanted to tell him to be quiet.

And then it was night. A room. A bed. There were many candles. Low voices. A woman's voice. A man's voice. A low rumble.

That rumble. She raised her head slightly.

The woman's voice. "She's opened her eyes again."

A man's face next to her. Dark-red hair. Concerned green eyes. Wrong man.

"Lady Drake, can ye speak?"

Not the right man. Where was he?

"Harry." Yes. Yes. That velvet, sandy voice was right.

Then a large shadow, getting closer. She lifted her left hand and scrabbled at the shadow. Finally, she grasped a small fold in the fabric of his waistcoat and she tugged. He bent over. Jaw, neck, a pulse. She turned her head slightly. Warm. She inhaled. Cinnamon.

Him.

He waited, hovering. His ear was by her mouth.

She took a deep breath. Pain. She tried to lick her lips. Cracked.

"Tommy," she croaked.

Before she went unconscious again, she felt several small hot splashes of water fall on her face from above.

Thomas and Dr. Andrews were closeted in the library.

"'Tis too soon to know. But she was conscious. She said yer name. These are good signs, Lord Drake," Dr. Andrews said.

"Thank you, Doctor." Thomas felt hollow.

"And I will examine yer nephew's body more closely. But it looks like he died from a sub-xiphoid stab wound to the heart. I believe almost all the blood we found is his."

Dr. Andrews took a bundle from his pocket. It was a handkerchief wrapped around something small. He unwrapped it. A narrow brown object lay there.

"One of the groomsmen found this on the stable floor, crusted into the blood there. 'Twas open, he said."

Thomas took the object from the handkerchief in the

doctor's hand. He scraped it with a thumbnail. The dried blood flaked off and showed a luminescent white. Mother of pearl.

The doctor cleared his throat. "'Twas on a chain with two keys. I took the liberty of removing the knife from the chain and entrusting the chain and the keys to Smythe. I suggest ye keep that until . . . we can talk to Harry. I mean, Lady Drake."

"Yes."

"Ye ken, Lord Drake, that it would take someone with a thorough understanding of anatomy to kill someone with a knife so small."

Thomas said bitterly, "Or someone smart who understood angles and forces."

"Nae, nae, ye misunderstand me," said the doctor hastily. "I meant someone like me, a physician, or perhaps a trained killer, a mercenary, an assassin. I have heard rumors of gambling debts? Perhaps even some cheating. Some ruthless enemies made. Perhaps?"

Thomas thought. "Perhaps."

"A despicable man is hired to find yer nephew, intending to get payment of a debt. He comes to the country and finds Mr. Drake. He threatens him. Mr. Drake says he willnae pay. Lady Drake comes upon the two in the stable and fearlessly tries to intervene. She is knocked unconscious by a blow to the head. The assassin stabs Mr. Drake and runs off."

"But Harry's dress . . . my nephew's trousers . . ."

"I think that if anyone asks, but not a one will, ye will find that the groomsmen and the stableboys will swear they came upon my lady fully dressed. Mr. Drake, as well. And nae weapon was found."

"I think," said Thomas, slowly. "I think it is likely as you said."

"I will alert the magistrate that there is a mercenary

assassin abroad in the countryside, and he has killed yer nephew for his gambling debts."

Thomas hung his head. "Thank you, Alasdair."

"Ye have . . . ye have not asked if Lady Drake sustained any injuries besides those to her head and face and the rebreaking of the bones in her right hand."

Thomas shook his head.

"As her husband, I think ye should ken—"

"No."

"'Tis incumbent upon me to inform ye—"

"No!" Thomas roared.

Silence. The clock counted off the strokes of eleven.

"At this moment, Dr. Andrews, Harry is alive," Thomas said in a strained voice. "That is all that I care for. If Harry wakes up and is of a mind to . . . to . . . tell me what my nephew did, then that is different—"

"*When* Harry wakes up, my lord."

"Yes, when. Right now, the only thing keeping me sane is that her heart beats, her lungs fill. Harry may care about other things. But, at this moment, I cannot bring myself to care."

An urgent rap at the library door.

Whitson. "Begging your pardon, my lord, Doctor. Smythe says to come at once—"

Thomas tore out of the library with the doctor close behind him.

"—my lady is awake," Whitson finished.

Harry was awake. Very awake. Sitting up in bed and thirstily drinking water.

"But that's not what happened." Harry finished her cup of water and looked at Thomas and Alasdair. She wanted another cup of water but Thomas had sent Smythe out of the room. "Phillip pushed me down and I stabbed him and he hit me with a horseshoe. Or he hit me with a horseshoe and I stabbed him. I'm not sure which."

"I think, my lady," Dr. Andrews smoothly, "that yer mind has been confused greatly by yer injury."

Harry did feel sluggish. And she hurt in many places. However, the doctor and Thomas were wrong.

"Alasdair, I'm not that confused."

Thomas sat down on the edge of her bed and took her left hand.

"Harry, you were in the right. No matter what you or he . . . did, I know that you were in the right. What we—what Alasdair and I—want you to do now is to lie."

"Oh," Harry said. "Why didn't you say that?"

The doctor went home then, promising to look in first thing tomorrow. Smythe brought Harry some more water and then went down to have a very late dinner at Harry's insistence. And Harry said that the nurse who had just arrived from Tavishbourn should stay out for now.

She wanted to be with her husband. Just him.

Thomas sat on the edge of the bed, holding Harry's left hand. Even though it was her only good hand, she would let him hold it all night.

"I'm sorry, Lord Drake."

"What are *you* sorry for, Harry?" His voice was even but she thought she could hear some bitterness there.

"Phillip is dead. And you and I and Alasdair, we three will always know I killed him."

"You were protecting yourself, Harry."

"I could have stabbed him somewhere else. The blade is short. Almost anywhere else on his body, save his neck, would not have killed him. Dr. Andrews could have saved him."

"But if you hadn't killed him, he could have gone on hurting you."

Harry stared up at the canopy of the bed. "All right, well then, I'm not sorry."

"Good," said Thomas.

"Good," said Harry and looked him in the eyes. "And he didn't rape me. He was going to but he didn't . . . quite . . . get to it, I think."

"I'm glad for you, Harry."

"I wasn't frightened of it. But I thought it likely that if he had raped me, you would have killed him for it, and that is what frightened me. That you would hang for killing your nephew."

"Yes," Thomas said and looked away from her. "Yes, I would have killed him."

"My killing him before he raped me seemed like a much better plan than your hanging. You see, I really can't do without you."

Thomas then began to sob.

She let go of his hand and used her good left arm to pull him down and put his head in her lap. She touched his hair lightly and clucked her tongue in imitation of her stepmother.

She concluded that he wept for Phillip.

How he must hate me.

Thirty-Eight

Smythe came to Thomas the next day. Very sorry, did not mean to bother his lordship, but my lady has not asked for her books.

Thomas turned from the window in the library to look at Smythe. The magistrate had been there that morning and had agreed that any questioning of Harry could wait until she was stronger.

Smythe continued, "She's sitting in the chair that is at one of the windows in her bedchamber. She walked to the chair herself and said she was only a trifle dizzy. She's looking out the window, my lord."

Thomas still did not understand.

"I showed her the keys the doctor gave me and said I would go upstairs and get her any books she liked. She just took the chain from me and put it around her neck. Thank you, she said. Thank you, but not now."

Smythe's voice was rising in pitch and volume.

"In London, even when my lady had fever and delirium, she called out for her Gauss and Euler, my lord!"

"Calm yourself, Smythe. It is early days. She'll ask for her books soon enough."

But the days passed and she did not. Then she came downstairs for dinner for the first time since Phillip's death.

"How was your trip to London, my lord?"

"London?"

"Yes. The day . . . the day your nephew died. Were you not in London?"

"No, I had walked over to the Dunbars. I had some business to discuss with them."

In truth, Thomas wanted to know if Mr. Dunbar, with his previous experience in shipping, would know of some clever device maker who might make a telescope for Harry. Mr. Dunbar, of course, knew the very man. And Mr. Dunbar would be pleased to assist Lord Drake in making the commission of a telescope.

"Business?" Harry asked.

"Yes," Thomas said.

"Was Miss Hope Dunbar there?"

"Miss Dunbar? Yes, she was."

Thomas was then lost in remembering how Hope had looked at him with fear when he had mentioned Phillip's name at the Dunbar dinner. When they had been dancing. Should he have realized something then?

Perhaps he had missed clues all along about Phillip's true nature. Had he been so desperate for a piece of his beloved lost sister that he ignored how much Hugh Drake there was in Phillip? He began to search his memory for other times when Phillip had lied or cheated or treated someone with contempt. There were so many instances.

So when Harry said, "Hope Dunbar's quite beautiful, isn't she? And she has lovely manners?" he replied in an abstracted, almost wistful, manner, "Certainly, certainly."

"She would make a good wife, wouldn't she?"

Another *certainly* from Thomas, who knew the safest course of action was always to agree with Harry.

But he wasn't listening. He was grappling with his own blindness when it came to his nephew. For so long, Thomas had been worried that *he* himself might become a Hugh Drake. He had never bothered to worry that Phillip might have his father's cruel nature, either due to blood or the eight years he was in his father's care. How foolish he had been.

"And a good mother?"

"Yes, I should think so. What was that, Harry?"

Although she had just come downstairs, Harry thought perhaps she might retire to her bedchamber now. Could Lord Drake ring for Smythe?

Thomas was walking back from the stables toward the manse when he saw Hope Dunbar walking down the drive, carrying a basket.

"Good afternoon, Miss Dunbar," he said, taking off his hat and bowing.

"Good afternoon, Lord Drake," she said and curtsied. "I've brought some elderberry cordial I made last summer. It's for Lady Drake."

"That is most kind of you," Thomas said.

"My father asked me to tell you that your commission— the gift for Lady Drake—will be ready soon. And, also to give his condolences on the death of your nephew."

As she handed him the bottle of elderberry cordial, Thomas decided he must know.

"Miss Dunbar," he said. "I am most apologetic. I know no proper way to ask this, but I feel it is imperative I understand. Did my nephew . . . ever importune you?"

Her face turned the same color as her hair. Her eyes began to fill with tears. Thomas took her hand.

"You need say nothing more, Miss Dunbar. I am most ashamed, and I beg your forgiveness."

"You have done nothing that needs forgiveness, Lord Drake," she said. Her lip trembled.

"May I have my carriage take you back to your house?"

"No, my lord. I prefer to take the air."

Thomas bowed low over her hand.

She walked back down the drive with her shoulders back and her head held high.

Harry stood in her aerie. She paced. She sat. She looked at her notes. She looked at the spines of her books. She went so far as to sharpen a quill and open an inkpot and pull a blank piece of foolscap in front of her.

She knew she had to prove the conjecture for odd prime exponents since the case for four was proven by Fermat himself and all integers greater than two either had four or a prime odd integer as a factor. She knew it had something to do with modular arithmetic. Her notes made that clear.

She understood everything. But she couldn't *see* anything. She put her head on her desk and willed herself to remember her grand plan.

Then she raised her head to look out the aerie window.

Harry watched Miss Dunbar—how pretty she was—and Thomas speak. The window was closed and she was quite high up, so, of course, she couldn't hear anything.

But it was clear the exchange was charged with emotion for both Thomas and Miss Dunbar. Was she crying? She was. But there—Thomas took her hand most tenderly. He bowed. She walked away. How sad that they must be separated.

Hope Dunbar. What a good wife and mother she would make. Such a better Lady Drake than the current one.

THIRTY-NINE

Harry came to Thomas in the library. In her left hand, she held a counterpane.

"I took this from my bed. Let's look at the stars," she said.

Thomas laughed and took the counterpane from her.

"Let's leave that here, and I'll get a horse blanket again. I think that we would both face crucifixion from Mrs. Dewey over the grass stains."

They went out to the stables and he found a horse blanket, but then he couldn't find Harry. The stable was dark.

"Harry," he hissed. Octavius whinnied. He went into Octavius' stall and found Harry there, stroking his mane.

"Such a good boy," she said.

"Yes," Thomas said.

"Yes, he is, isn't he?" Harry laid her head against Octavius' neck and threw one arm over his withers. Thomas had never told Harry that Dr. Andrews had found a post-mortem hoof mark on Phillip's back. He wondered if she knew.

They went out to the lawn and lay next to each other on the horse blanket.

It was not a good night for looking at the stars. The moon was bright. There were some scudding clouds.

"Let's go back in," Thomas said, sitting up.

"No." Harry gripped his arm.

Thomas lay back down. He allowed himself some dangerous thoughts. He had not done so for a long time. He thought about the body of the woman next to him. His wife. He thought of her firm breasts with their small, sweet nipples, of the pink, tender silk folds under her maiden hair, of her dimples that crowned her buttocks. Strangely, as he conjured each body part, he also heard her lecture him and question him and mutter elvish mathematical spells under her breath. Even more strangely, it did not dampen his arousal at all.

Harry rolled onto her side and propped herself up on her left elbow and placed her bandaged right hand flat on his solar plexus.

Thomas held his breath. She had touched him.

"You are a good husband, Thomas Drake," she said.

"Thank you, Lady Drake. I strive to be."

"You have kept your end of the bargain."

"And you, yours."

Harry scoffed. "It was just money. What was I going to do with it?"

"I imagine you could have done a whole host of things with it—books, houses, paper, ink, coffee, a society dedicated to the mathematical education of young ladies of good breeding—"

Harry interrupted him. "But what is all that to Sommerleigh?"

"I'm glad you love Sommerleigh."

Harry took her hand off his abdomen and lay back on the blanket.

"Yes, I should hate to leave Sommerleigh."

Now Thomas got up on his elbow. He was not so bold to

think that he could lay his hand on her abdomen. He was not the gambler he once was. Near-loss had made him cautious.

"But I was thinking, perhaps, you might enjoy a trip sometime, surely? Dr. Andrews says the air on a southern coast, perhaps the south of France, is most salutary. And of course, you will have to go to Paris anyway once you prove the conjecture so you can get the prize and give the lecture at the *Académie des Sciences*."

Harry's face had no expression and her voice was even. "Yes."

Thomas lay back and let his mind roam over the host of future pleasures that lay before him that had nothing to do with copulation and yet still revolved around the woman lying next to him.

FORTY

Harry woke to a note under her door from Thomas saying he had been called away early to the next county. Some business or other. He would endeavor to be back late tonight or tomorrow.

This fit in perfectly with her plans. She ate a very good breakfast quickly and had Smythe dress her in traveling clothes and walking boots.

Smythe looked worried. "Where are you going, my lady?"

"Oh," Harry said airily, "just for a walk."

Harry walked as quickly as she could to the Dunbars. It was not many miles. However, she was not as accustomed to walking as she once was. And she was in a hurry. Consequently, when she arrived, she was sweating and out of breath, her hair hanging around her face, a dirty smudge on her cheek, and mud on the hem of her dress and boots. Her bruises on her face from the horseshoe had not faded completely either.

She presented herself to the butler and asked for Miss Hope Dunbar.

The butler sneered, "And whom should I say is calling?"

Harry drew herself up as best she could. "The Right Honorable Countess Drake."

The butler bowed very low indeed and ushered her immediately into the best drawing room.

Hope Dunbar appeared and Harry darted forward and closed the door behind her. If the pretty redheaded Miss Dunbar was startled, she showed no sign of it.

"My lady," Miss Dunbar said.

"Miss Dunbar, you have a great deal of equanimity, I admire it," Harry said. "I beg you forgive this very early call with no warning. At this time, I must, as I am wont to do, abandon propriety."

"Please sit, Lady Drake."

Harry went to sit and then thought better of it and jumped up. "No, no, you sit, Miss Dunbar. I am covered in mud and don't want to injure the sofa. It's better if I walk around the room. You don't mind if I do that, do you?"

Miss Dunbar demurred. Of course, she did not, my lady.

"I planned out what to say but it is exceedingly more difficult to say than I thought it would be. That shows increasing maturity, on my part, I think. I used to take great delight in saying enormously startling things in the most impulsive manner. I am wiser now and more solicitous of the comfort of others."

Miss Dunbar murmured politely.

"However, I would like to do this quickly, so I don't lose heart," Harry said. "My question to you is," she took a deep breath, "if my husband, er, if Lord Drake were free, would you marry him?"

Miss Dunbar's mouth fell open.

"I assure you that he is a very high-quality husband. And I feel sure, that with your great beauty and attractions, you would be able to induce him not to roam. Or, you could do as I did, and just let him. He doesn't mean anything by it. Quite literally. Think of it as like going to the privy. That's what I do."

Miss Dunbar seemed to teeter on the edge of the sofa.

"Please, Miss Dunbar, forget that *I* am the one asking the question. Just embrace the hypothesis. If he came to you, unencumbered, and asked you to marry, would your answer be yes?"

Miss Dunbar found her voice.

"If he came . . ." she repeated.

"Yes, if he came to you and asked you to marry, what would your answer be?"

"I would . . ." she said.

"Yes?" Harry prompted.

". . . say yes." Miss Dunbar finally gasped.

It was the answer she had come for. "Thank you, thank you, Miss Dunbar. I assure you that you will not regret it. Just don't let him drink too much at the wedding breakfast. Whisky, that is. Chocolate or tea or coffee are all fine though. Now, do you think that I might impose on your hospitality further and ask that your carriage take me to Dr. Andrews?"

Miss Dunbar seemed relieved that Lady Drake wanted to visit the doctor. But she had a question for Harry. "Why might Lord Drake be unencumbered, my lady?"

Harry did not want to answer that.

Then Miss Dunbar asked if Lady Drake wouldn't prefer to wait here and they would send for the doctor? She seemed to be in a great deal of distress.

"No, no, I must go at once."

Miss Dunbar must, of course, speak to her mother, Mrs. Dunbar. Mrs. Dunbar must speak to Mr. Dunbar. All the Dunbars were in agreement. Yes, Lady Drake should see the doctor.

And so the Dunbar carriage was made ready and Harry was put in it. Harry could hear Miss Dunbar instructing the coachman that the Lady Drake should be delivered directly into the doctor's safe hands, and if that was not possible, she must be brought back to the Dunbar house as there was some concern she might do herself an injury.

Harry remembered then her discussion with Miss Dunbar regarding the Scottish play. Surely Miss Dunbar didn't think Harry was that stupid?

And then, she wasn't quite sure why, she cried all the way to the village.

Thankfully, Harry found the doctor was in. It was not yet eight.

"Harry!" he said as she stumbled into his surgery, the Dunbar coachman on her heels.

She knew she was a sight. Tear-streaked face, mud, hair surely a mess. But she had recovered her breath, and she had managed to slow the crying.

"Alasdair," she said, as calmly as possible.

The Dunbar coachman approached the doctor and bent his head to whisper something to him.

"That's pure rubbish," Dr. Andrews said. "But I will take care of her, tell Miss Dunbar to have nae fear." The coachman nodded and, after giving Harry a look, left the surgery.

"What has happened?" Alasdair found a cloth and handed it to her.

She just held the cloth in her hand.

"I don't know anyone else I could ask," she said.

"Aye, my lady?"

"I need you to take me to London."

Despite the doctor's gentle and sympathetic probing, Harry did not want to provide further explanation. She must not be hindered.

"Alasdair, it's important. It's a legal matter. I need you by my side."

And so Harry convinced the doctor, wise man that he was, that further protest would be fruitless. He managed to get them out of the house and into the village square as the mail coach came by. Harry and Dr. Andrews were lucky enough to find seats. They should be in London by mid to late afternoon.

She looked out the window of the coach. She was lucky to have Alasdair as a friend. He was a good man. It would be too bad to lose him along with everything else when she left Sommerleigh. Perhaps she could arrange for him to open a practice in London. That cheered her momentarily and then she realized she would be taking him away from Thomas. How would Thomas continue his studies of the calculus without the doctor?

No. She could not be that selfish. Alasdair would have to stay in Sommerleigh. Harry would have to find a way to do without him.

Forty-One

Thomas was quite pleased. He had gotten away early and had made good time to London. He had found the telescope ready for him at the small shop in the City, just as promised. He stepped out of the shop, the long, wooden box under his arm, excited to get back to the stable and take Octavius, himself, and the telescope all back to Sommerleigh. And to Harry.

He had made up the fiction of going to another county so she would not think he had gone to London to indulge in his old habits. He was not so deluded as to think that a visit to Madame Flora's would spark jealousy in Harry or hurt her, but he wanted the issue to be perfectly clear.

He was hers, and only hers, when and if she ever wanted him.

But after the telescope, this one surprise for her, in the future, he was going to avoid prevarication. He would be frank like Harry, herself. He would tell the truth.

He might even tell her his deepest desire.

The danger of that tore at his heart.

And then he thought of standing behind Harry as she

leaned over to look in the telescope, his lips by her ear, perhaps a hand on her waist, and he thought the danger might be worth the reward.

What the devil?

He saw curly brown hair, a long stride. Was he so bewitched that he saw his wife everywhere? No, no, that was the unmistakable figure of Harry. And a man with auburn hair—the doctor was with her. They were hurrying through the streets of London. Well, Harry was hurrying and Dr. Andrews was doing his best to catch up. Thomas shouted after them but they were too far away, the streets were too busy and noisy.

Then, his old fear set in.

The doctor.

Harry's admiration for him.

Their private walks and talks when Harry first came to Sommerleigh.

The doctor's fine mind. His dimples and green eyes and Scottish burr and the way half the women in the vicinity, including Thomas' own cook, doted on the still-unmarried young doctor. Thomas was sure Dr. Andrews made most of his fees in calling on lust-addled hypochondriacs.

Thomas set off after them.

He could not catch them. The box was quite heavy. Several times he was delayed by wagons in the street or a long string of carriages. He was still a good three hundred feet away when he saw Harry, followed by Dr. Andrews, mount the steps of St. Paul's and disappear.

"Lady Drake," the doctor said. "I am afraid ye are not being rational. I cannae imagine why I am here or why ye are here. I beg ye to tell me. I have been patient but ye must tell me why we are here to see the bishop."

They were in the anteroom for the bishop's private study. A young curate had intercepted Harry and assured her and Dr. Andrews that the bishop was not here. Harry had flung herself into a chair and announced to the young man, "I'll wait for him, then." The curate had crept away, after grimacing in such a way that indicated he was very glad that *he* was not the bishop.

Harry could feel her agitation rising. She was tapping her hands on her knees.

"I can't lose my nerve, Alasdair. It's for the best. I just have to do it."

The doctor crouched in front of her and stilled her hands with his own.

"What do ye have to do, Harry?"

"I have to get an annulment. That's why you're here. So you can tell the bishop that Thomas and I can have an annulment. That I am . . . whole."

"That's not how it works, Harry. Are ye unhappy with yer marriage then?"

"No, no, but I'm unhappy because I think Thomas wants an annulment but he feels sorry for me after what happened . . . in the stable. That Phillip beat me. But Phillip is dead so I think Thomas needs an heir now. And since I can't give that to him and someone else could, it would be for the best. He should have what he wants."

"Harry," the doctor shook his head, smiling for the first time since Harry had come into his surgery. "I think ye can have what ye want and Lord Drake can as well. I think ye want the same thing. Harry, Harry, Harry."

Thomas had gone into the cathedral, but he had no idea where Harry had gone. After running about a bit in the narthex and the nave and various chapels, Thomas had found the young curate who directed him to the anteroom of the bishop's study.

Thomas opened the door and saw Dr. Andrews crouching and holding Harry's hands. The two were staring at each other intently, the doctor smiling and saying Thomas' wife's name in a caressing manner.

Dr. Andrews did not seem startled or embarrassed by Thomas' sudden entrance. He gently let go of Harry's hands and got to his feet. He bowed. "My lord."

Harry, on the other hand, looked away from Thomas.

"I would like to know what you're doing here, Harry, Dr. Andrews," Thomas said. He put the wooden box containing the telescope down. He took out a handkerchief and wiped his forehead.

Neither said anything. Finally, Dr. Andrews spoke.

"My lady, ye must tell Lord Drake. I should not be the one—"

"I'm here to get an annulment!" The words burst out of Harry's mouth.

A deep, dark bitter horror spread over Thomas, starting in his chest and then going to his stomach and his head.

She was going to leave him.

The feeling spread to his legs.

She didn't want him. She had never wanted him.

He willed himself to stay standing, to keep breathing, to hold back his vomit.

Harry stood and began to pace. "You have to see the bishop of the place where you are married. So I came here. And I brought Alasdair."

Of course, she wanted to marry Alasdair. Of course, she did. He might have a hope of keeping up with Harry's mind. Thomas never would.

"You're a grown woman who knows her own mind. I want you to be happy. I am sorry to have to warn you that it would take me some years to return your dowry to you," Thomas said. He stared at his boots. And then, the hardest words he had ever had to say, "But I will not oppose you."

Harry stopped pacing then and stood still, facing a window. "You can have a son by next year."

Thomas took three quick steps toward Dr. Andrews and thrust his hand out to him, "I . . . wish you every happiness."

The doctor took his hand and shook it but looked confused. "I think—"

Thomas faced Harry and spoke stiffly. "There was no reason, Lady Drake, for you to come here secretly. We have been, if nothing else, forthright with each other. You should have told me your wish."

Harry whirled and exploded, "You should have told me yours!"

"My . . . wish?"

"Your wish, your wish to marry Hope Dunbar, to be rid of me, to have a son—"

"Harry—"

"—to have a normal wife and a normal life and all that entails! And you can have it—"

"Harry!" Thomas thundered.

She stopped. She looked at her feet now.

"Harry, look at me so I know you understand what I'm saying."

She raised her eyes to him. They were full of tears. He longed to go to her and crush her to his chest. But he did not. She wasn't his. She had never been his.

"Harry, I have no wish to marry Hope Dunbar."

"But she has agreed—" Harry started and stopped.

"What has Hope Dunbar agreed to?"

"I asked her if she would marry you if you were free and she said yes. I just thought I had better make sure before I got the annulment, that's all. It would be a shame to go through this and then she wouldn't have you."

"Harry, I am perfectly capable of making my own marriage proposals."

"I didn't think much of the one you made my stepmother, and, of course, it was *me* who proposed to *you*."

"Yes, well, it doesn't matter, because I am not going to marry Hope Dunbar."

"Why not?"

"Because . . . it doesn't matter. I will not oppose you, Harry. You can have your annulment. I want you to have what you want. I'm sure you and Alasdair will be very happy together."

Harry had a rare look of bewilderment on her face. "Alasdair?"

"Yes," Thomas said. He looked at Dr. Andrews, who looked very uncomfortable, indeed.

"Oh, Tommy." She sighed.

Why must she have finally reverted to using Tommy just as she was leaving him?

"Tommy, Alasdair is here as a doctor to say we can have an annulment because I'm intact. We are not consummated." She wiped her eyes.

"You're not going to get married?" Thomas turned to Dr. Andrews.

"I hope to marry someday, my lord," Dr. Andrews said carefully, "but I dinnae think Lady Drake's affections tend toward me."

Thomas turned toward Harry. "Why do you want an annulment?"

"So that you can marry Hope Dunbar."

"Which we have established I am not going to do."

"Yes. But so you can have a son and an heir."

"Right now, I have no care whatsoever for what happens

after I die. As far as I am concerned, the title, Sommerleigh, the Drake name—they can all go to the devil."

It was at this point that the bishop came into the anteroom.

Harry thought the bishop looked like a rather nice man. She hadn't recognized him because he was in a suit and looked so different from when she had met him before about the banns and when he had married her to Thomas. Then he had been wearing a surplice of some kind, she thought. But still, his eyes were kind.

He greeted them and asked their names.

"My lord, my lady, Doctor, please come into my study. I heard something about a devil as I came in so I suspect some theological wisdom may help the situation here." He chuckled.

Once seated in the study, Harry thought she should make the purpose of their visit clear.

"Lord Drake and I are seeking an annulment."

"I see." The bishop steepled his fingers. "Whose desire is this?"

"My lady's." "My lord's." They spoke in near unison.

"And your part in this, doctor?"

"Ah, aye," Dr. Andrews came forward. "Lady Drake is under the misapprehension that I might be of use in testifying to ye that she remains intact and unspoiled. I was very nearly about to explain—"

"What misapprehension?" Thomas stood. "Where is the misapprehension? Harry told me, she said, she said that Phillip did not, did not . . ." He turned to Harry then, "Did you say that just to spare me?"

"No, Tommy. I didn't lie to you. I'm still a virgin."

Thomas collapsed back into his chair. He put his face in his hands.

"The misapprehension, my lord," Dr. Andrews continued, "as the bishop will make clear presently, I am sure, is that the virginity of the bride alone is of consequence in an annulment."

"It's not of consequence?" Harry couldn't believe this. "It doesn't matter that I am, well, not untouched, I can't say that, but . . . unpenetrated?" She turned to the bishop.

"Yes," the bishop answered. "It is not enough that the woman is a virgin. On the other hand, impotence of the husband in addition to virginity of the wife can lead to an annulment. You must be married for three years and remain a virgin while sharing a bed with your husband."

"Three years. We've been married a year," Harry said, "so we will come back in two years?"

How was she going to manage to share a bed with Tommy for two years and not be tempted to touch him in all manner of ways? There, in the bishop's office, at the thought of Tommy's heat, his scent, his chest and thighs, his head on a pillow next to hers, his hands and mouth on her body, she felt herself begin to get wet between her legs. Traitorous pudenda.

"Of course," the bishop continued, "it leaves a horrible stain on the reputation of both parties. In addition, your husband must be proven to be unable to produce an erection with anyone, including highly trained courtesans."

"Can he be intoxicated at the time?"

The bishop darted a look of alarm at Dr. Andrews.

"Nae, Lady Drake," the doctor said.

Harry snorted. "I think we can forget about impotence as a reason for annulment."

"That leaves deception or fraud. Or madness," the bishop said and smiled. "And I think, all appearances to the contrary, that neither of you are mad. You are both of age and previously unmarried. You used the correct names on the register. There will be no annulment."

Thomas took his face out of his hands.

"I do wonder at the non-consummation of the marriage, Lord Drake, Lady Drake," the bishop said. "What is the reluctance?"

Harry looked at Thomas and then back at the bishop. "It was one of the terms of our marriage. I had an aversion to copulation then, only caring for the conjecture, and Tommy agreed to my condition that I remain a virgin so that he could use my dowry to save Sommerleigh." Her eyes started to fill with tears. She blinked rapidly. "So, it's my fault. Besides I am no beauty and I don't have red hair."

"Stop it." This came from Thomas as he stood. "I won't listen to that anymore. You are beautiful. And I don't know why you are fixated on—Harry, I have no attachment to red hair. And, of course, I would have bedded you long ago, if you were willing."

She was beautiful.

He didn't care for red hair.

He was willing.

But still.

"But what about," Harry gulped, "what about the never having children?"

Dr. Andrews cleared his throat. "I should have said something sooner. I hope ye will forgive me. Despite yer recent injuries, ye have been in such good health for so many months, Lady Drake, that I quite forgot the prohibition against child-bearing that we discussed when ye first came to Sommerleigh a year ago. At that time, ye may remember, ye were quite ill, malnourished, weak. I agreed then with the other doctors ye had seen here in London that a pregnancy at that time would have almost certainly killed ye. However, ye are a different woman now. Ye have gained almost three stone and just ran from the Old White Horse Cellar to St. Paul's, a distance of perhaps two miles, with breath to spare. I believe that yer risk in childbirth is now essentially the same as any other woman."

Harry looked at the ceiling of the study.

"Tommy. Do you really not care that much for red hair?"

"I hate it," Thomas said. "Meaning no insult to you, Dr. Andrews."

"I am not insulted, Lord Drake," Dr. Andrews said. "I dinnae like it myself."

Thomas came close to Harry's chair and tucked a tendril of Harry's hair back behind her ear, which made her shiver. "I like brown hair, Harry."

She shifted her gaze to his waistcoat buttons.

"And what about large breasts?" Harry asked.

Thomas leaned down and put his head directly next to hers. His warm breath tickled her ear. The lightest brush of his fingertips on her shoulder blade. He whispered, "Anything more than a handful is just wasteful extravagance. I like your breasts, Harry."

A knock then came on the door just as Harry was performing several strategic triangulations in her head that involved distances and speeds. And the exigencies of her situation.

"I am glad the matter has been resolved before my next appointment," the bishop said. "You will know my visitors, I think. How fortuitous. Of course, I am influenced by my calling, but I sense the hand of divinity in these events." And then he winked.

Harry thought the world was a very confusing place sometimes. Certainly, with the heat of her willing husband next to her and the triangulation calculations she was doing in her head and her own slippery arousal between her legs, she had reason to feel overwhelmed. And then the world became even more confusing. Her stepmother Catherine came through the door first, followed next by Arabella, her sister. Harry stood and suddenly found her left hand in Thomas' hand.

"Harry!" Catherine came forward and hugged and kissed her stepdaughter with none of the reserve she had used in the past with her. It was almost as if she knew Harry would permit it. Or she didn't care. But then she pulled back and her eyes ran over Harry.

"What are these bruises on your face, Harry? And you have hurt your hand?"

"Uh, an accident in the stables, Mama Katie. I'm fine, really."

"Well, you must take care, Harry. How wonderful that you and Thomas are here! Jamie—" she turned to the man who had followed her and Arabella into the study, "did you tell Thomas and Harry behind my back? I thought we agreed to go down to Sommerleigh on Friday to tell them?"

As Arabella also hugged her, Harry realized that the man who had come in was James, Thomas' friend, the one who had come for Christmas and then given them the Lacroix text. His hair was shorter than before.

Thomas was shaking hands with him and greeting Catherine and Arabella.

Harry remembered what she should say on occasions like these. "Mama Katie, this is Dr. Andrews."

"The famous doctor." Catherine curtsied. "We all owe so much to you for returning my lovely girl to health."

Dr. Andrews blushed. "Nae, 'twere all down to Lady Drake herself and Lord Drake, too, of course."

"This is my other daughter, Miss Arabella Lovelock, Dr. Andrews."

Dr. Andrews bent low over Arabella's hand.

Catherine went on, "And of course, His Grace, the Duke of Middlewich." But Dr. Andrews had not yet taken his eyes from Arabella's.

Thomas then voiced the question Harry would have asked if she had any thought to spare for anything besides what might happen when she and Thomas left the bishop's study. "How do you come to be here?"

Catherine looked at James.

James laughed and said, "We're here to arrange the banns."

"Congratulations, Jamie! We will be brothers!" Thomas clapped him on the back.

Dr. Andrews took a step away from Arabella.

Thomas went on, "And I wish you all happiness, Miss Lovelock." He bowed to Arabella.

There was silence, at first.

"No, no, no," Arabella said, blushing, looking at the doctor.

James and Catherine began laughing.

"No, no, Tom," James said. "I, uh, thought I might succeed where you had failed. I am very happy to say that Mrs. Catherine Lovelock will shortly become the Duchess of Middlewich." He grinned. "So, in a way, I will be your father-in-law."

Harry looked at Catherine. There was something in her face that Harry had not seen since her father died. Was it happiness? Were she and her stepmother feeling the same thing right now?

"Many happy returns, Mama Katie."

"Thank you, Harry. It is hard to believe that I have found love twice in a lifetime. I feel myself very fortunate, indeed."

Catherine then crossed to the bishop and began to talk about the banns and the wedding. Arabella and Dr. Andrews were discussing—was it the weather? Thomas leaned in close to James but Harry could hear what passed between them.

"Good man, Jamie. I am happy for you."

"Thank you. I knew you would be."

"A duke and a husband in the same year."

"And a father, too."

"It's a good joke but I think you're a bit young to consider yourself father to Arabella and Harry and me."

"No, I know."

Harry whipped her head around now to gaze at her stepmother. The fashion was for high-waisted dresses that flowed from beneath the breasts down to the floor. The gowns hid all manner of thick waists and large hips. But—was it possible? Did the tiny Catherine have a visible bump over her abdomen?

Thomas spoke again and smiled, "Let me not delay your banns then."

Everything was taking far too long. It was pleasant to see her family and she was glad for her stepmother but the delay was intolerable. Intolerable, as in she could not tolerate it a second longer. She had a most pressing need.

Harry spoke very loudly, "I must . . ."

The room stilled.

She went on, "I must go. There is a very significant corollary I have overlooked." She looked at Thomas. "I must go." She seized his arm. "And Tommy must come with me."

FORTY-TWO

Harry yanked Thomas down the steps of the cathedral. She let go of him only to get in the middle of the street to wave her arms and shout like a Bedlamite. Thomas had to pull her by her shoulders to get her out of the way of the hackney-coach that was trying to stop so they could get in. She shouted at the driver to take them to her house and named the street of the town house in Mayfair where Thomas had paid all those calls on her stepmother over a year ago.

Thomas' heart sank a bit that Harry still thought of the Lovelock house as her house. She did not consider Sommerleigh home, even after a year. Of course, with Mrs. Lovelock marrying James and becoming the Duchess of Middlewich, the Lovelock house would likely be sold. Or perhaps, it would be part of Harry's new inheritance, the one she would receive when her stepmother married. She might choose then to live in London, apart from him, since she could create the haven she wanted in her own house. No blundering husband hanging about, making demands on her time.

In the carriage, Harry avoided his eyes. She sat on her left hand and thrummed loudly and swayed to and fro. He had not seen her this agitated in a long time. For a moment, he was frightened because she reminded him of his sister Jane, on that last morning in Manchester. But then he calmed himself. Harry might have fallen into the habit of neglecting her body in the past but she would never abuse it. She merely was excited in some unaccountable way. She likely was trying to capture some fleeting but incandescent mathematical masterstroke.

She was not Jane. He was not Mr. Hugh Drake.

By the time Thomas had paid the driver, Harry had pounded her way up the front steps of the house and had burst past the butler Chelsom while he opened the rather grand front door.

"Hurry, Tommy!" Halfway up the main staircase, she turned around, scampered back down, grabbed his hand as he entered the house, and started up again.

Only now did he begin to have some sense of the reason for his wife's urgency. And why she had wanted him to come with her. He hoped that Harry could forgive her husband for how slow and dull-witted he was sometimes.

Thomas tried to nod politely at the maids they passed as they ran up stairs and down halls. And then Harry came to a halt abruptly in front of a door and dropped Thomas' hand.

Harry pulled the chain off her neck and took one of the keys and used her left hand to open the door. She pulled him in and slammed the door shut. She turned the key in the lock.

She hesitated a moment and then she shoved the chain and the keys into his hand.

"You can hold these." Her voice was gruff.

He looked down at his hand, at the two keys and the chain laying there, and then up to watch his wife walk away from him.

She hadn't far to go. It was not a bedchamber. It was a tall and narrow room, made even more narrow by shelves lining the walls, some empty, some containing scraps of paper and empty inkpots. On the shelf nearest Thomas, he saw a cup with long-dried dregs of coffee in the bottom. The room smelled of Harry, of course. It must be *her room* from before he had married her. Her London aerie.

Harry reached the table at the far end of the room, under the window, and with one sweep of her left arm, knocked all the papers there to the floor. She turned around and, using her left hand on the table for support, she jumped just a bit so that she was seated atop the table, her legs dangling down.

He was still breathing heavily, like she was, from their rapid traverse of the house.

"Tommy," she said.

She held his gaze with her eyes and lifted her skirts up all the way to her waist.

"Now, Tommy, now!"

She wanted him. She had to have him. Her husband. She had waited too long, and now she was about to burst. She wanted him close. She was starving, aching, and throbbing.

As Tommy came toward her, reaching for her, she felt certain he would kiss her mouth. She would not stop him from doing that if that was what he wanted. Right now, he could do anything he wanted. He could have anything he wanted from her.

But as he stepped between her legs, he seemed to remember just in time. His face swerved to her neck and his hot mouth was on her throat, his tongue swirling over her skin. His stubble scratched her pleasurably. She shuddered. She wanted to be scratched by his stubble and licked by his searing tongue. All over her body.

And then he put his hand between her legs where she had

lifted up her skirts. Oh, yes. Yes. His left hand was a vast improvement over her own.

"Oh, Tommy."

His fingers were probing at her wetness, and he had found what she called her member, and he was rubbing it.

She was wild now. Wild and uncontrolled in a totally new way. It felt dangerous. *She* felt dangerous. She heard a growl issue from her own throat. If he took his hand from her now, if he stepped away from her, she would pull this house down around their ears with her fury.

But there was no need for that. He was here, solid, radiating heat, smelling of cinnamon, leaning into her. One arm around her back. One hand between her legs. He had her.

She reached out with her good hand and felt the front of his trousers. There. That was what she had expected from sitting on his lap. Thick. Long. Rigid. She slid her hand up and down and heard him groan into her neck. She did it harder, quicker and his member grew even more under her hand. Bernoulli's principle in fluid dynamics clearly did not apply to erections. Or at least not to Tommy's.

She was having a very difficult time concentrating, but she managed to use the fingertips of her bandaged hand to help her good hand unbutton the fall of his trousers. And then his fall was undone and she could put her hand directly on his shaft, which was sticking straight out at her. Hard. Hot. Silky skin. Ready for her. What she had imagined. What she wanted.

"Please, Tommy."

She pulled her neck away from his lips and looked at him. Those blue eyes. That saw her. As no one had ever seen her.

She licked her lips. "Please."

"Lie back, Harry." His voice was hoarse.

She lay back on the desk but still she clutched his member. "Please," she whispered. "I want you, Tommy."

"Let go, Harry."

She let go. She didn't want to, but she did. She had to trust him.

He took himself in his own hand then and she felt the head of his cock in her wetness, rubbing at her.

She nearly came up off the table then with her thrill but he had one hand on her chest, holding her breast through her dress, holding her down.

"I'm going to try not to hurt you, Harry," he panted.

"I know but I don't care, I don't care." She wrapped her legs around him and locked her ankles. "Please. Please."

She could not remember when she had said please so many times.

Would he help her? He had helped her before. And he was her husband. He had to, surely.

And then she felt him breach her. And yes, it hurt. And yes, she didn't care. He was so close to her now. So close. And that hungry, empty place was full. Of him.

He leaned over her and she put both her hands, the bandaged one and the good one, on his face and held him there so she could look in his eyes. To make sure he understood her.

He did.

She saw he did.

And as he moved his sex in and out of her sex, like a beautifully undulating sine wave, she felt a sensation deep inside. A sensation besides fullness and pain. It was not the same excitement that she had felt when he had put his finger or his tongue on her. It was different. It was deeper.

But she kept her eyes on his eyes. A bead of sweat rolled off his forehead, between his brows. He was breathing very hard.

"Tommy," she crooned.

He grunted. He was moving faster now, stroking in and

out of her, the frequency of the sine wave increasing even as the period shortened.

There was a different look in his eye now. A lost look.

"I'm here, Tommy."

"Yes," he said, "yes."

The sine wave grew erratic.

"I love you, Harry."

And then there was another look in his eyes, something more than lost, something like the look she imagined Euler might have had when he had refined his number, the base of the natural logarithm, the e.

It was the look of ecstasy.

His body raised up off hers even as he kept his eyes on hers. He spasmed one, two, three, four times, clutching one of her shoulders, one of her breasts. He did not blink until the very end.

She had given him that ecstasy.

And then his face came very close to hers. And she lost sight of his eyes when he put his mouth on hers. How very soft his lips were. How very warm and sweet his breath was. She had not expected that.

He did not linger too long. When he took his mouth away, she said, "Can we do something else now?"

His lungs were burning, his heart pounding. He was sweating. He had just taken the virginity of his exceptional wife, after a year of marriage, on a wooden table. He had been so aroused, she had been so eager, the positioning had been so awkward that he had not performed as well as he would have wished.

And his legs were trembling even now. Because he was not so sure that what had passed between them had anything to do with pleasure.

She had held his face and looked in his eyes the entire time that he had penetrated her.

He thought there could be no greater act of intimacy, surely. Not for his Harry.

And when he had told her he loved her just before he had released inside her, she had not flinched, she had not looked away, she had said very simply, "Of course you do, Tommy," and gazed at him with her enormous hazel eyes.

Yes, of course, he loved her. Of course. His Harry. At this moment, he felt that she *was* his. Or he was hers. Yes, he was hers. She owned him. What a terrible power she had. He would do anything for her, his wife.

With that in mind, he pulled her up from the table to a sitting position and found the buttons on the back of her dress.

"I want you naked," he breathed.

"Yes," she said and reached for the buttons of his waistcoat. "Both of us."

"Let's get off this table."

"Yes."

He fumbled at her buttons, still shaking a bit. She was defter than he despite her bandaged hand. But eventually, they were lying on their discarded clothes over dusty floorboards and he could touch every part of her, every inch of her velvet skin.

Her breasts were heaving, raised up to him. Those beautiful, taut handfuls that he had watched develop over the last year. He had helped bring them into being, hadn't he? Didn't he deserve to enjoy them now? Especially when he knew that his mouth on her exquisite pink areolas would make her mewl.

And so he fell on them now with his mouth and his hands. And he was rewarded by her beautiful, softly scented flesh, the puckering of her nipples under his tongue, and the sounds of her arousal.

"Tommy," she moaned. Yes, her mewls had turned to moans. Her good hand was on his chest, his flank, his buttock, his back, his jaw. The bandaged hand stayed on top of his head, resting lightly.

Then, "Tommy." More forcefully.

He raised his head from one of her breasts. "Yes, Harry?"

"I know," her breath was ragged, "you like," she exhaled, "breasts. But can you also," she raised her pelvis up off the floor, "touch me somewhere else?"

He wanted to tease her. She was bound to him now, in a way she hadn't been before, and he felt he had earned that right without fear of losing her.

"Where do you want me to touch you, Harry?"

"On my cunt."

He should have known that he could not tease her that way. She would demand what she wanted. His plain-speaking yet complicated wife with her gutter tongue that she did not know was a gutter tongue.

And so he put his hand where she wanted and began to touch her wetness and she sighed and fluttered her lashes and wriggled under his hand.

It was quite the most girlish thing he had ever seen her do, and he could feel his cock begin to throb again.

And as his mouth roamed over her breasts and his finger stroked that button at the top of her cleft, he heard her sound her howl and felt her body shake under his.

"Oh, Tommy," she said. And then she was still. And then her good hand found his cock and she was telling him that maybe he should be the one to lie flat now.

Hours later, as they gathered their clothing off the floor in the dimming light, Harry explained that she had brought him here because *her room* was the closest place she could think of with a lock and a key. Thomas had a great deal of respect for Harry's thinking process but this was clearly suspect. He knew that there was something deeper at play here—but he was not a deep man. And, he promised himself, he would never, ever complain that his first bedding of Harry had taken place on a wooden table with uneven legs, in front of an unshuttered and uncurtained window high above a busy Mayfair street, surrounded by the dust and scraps of paper and empty inkpots. What care had he for the surroundings?

After all, she had entrusted him with her beloved keys. Even if nothing else had happened in *her room*, he knew he had her heart.

"Recognize your luck, Thomas Drake," he said aloud. He peeled off a piece of foolscap that was covering the side of one of Harry's breasts as she struggled to fasten her petticoat with only one good hand. The ink from the paper left some unreadable equation printed there like a sailor's tattoo.

"Luck." Harry snorted. The ensuing lecture on odds and probabilities only lasted as long as it took Thomas to pull her petticoat off again and to unbutton his trousers.

Only later did Thomas think to wonder—if Harry had still had good use of her right hand, would she have been so motivated to consummate their marriage?

Luck.

Some months later, at the end of a long, warm summer, on the horse blanket and under the stars, her head pillowed on what she had told him was her favorite thigh, he had a thought.

"And what of Fermat's conjecture?"

"What of it?"

"Have you forsaken it, Harry?"

"No, I'm still working on it. The ideas are coming. Slowly. And no one else has proven it yet. I may still win."

"Shall we start testing every number?"

She laughed. "That will take a rather long time, Tommy."

"Weren't you the one who told me that Aristotle said time was meaningless without change?"

"Yes."

"Well, let's never change and then time will cease to exist."

"A proposition marred by faulty logic. And I am rather interested in change, Tommy, or at least in a certain one that might be coming in about seven months."

And she took his hand and placed it over that still flat expanse between her navel and her maidenhair.

And then Harry asked if he didn't consider it good news and if he did, why was he weeping?

Epilogue

Long shafts of light through the west-facing window. A quiet humming of the last fly of summer.

Eyes closed, Thomas lay spread-eagled on the bed Harry had asked to be put in her aerie. It was *her* aerie but it was *their* bed, she said.

These were their afternoons now.

Harry curled next to him, her head on his shoulder, one of her legs over one of his, her fingers tracing the trail of hair from his chest down to his navel and then farther down and around his satisfied member and back up again. The splint and the bandages were off and Harry had spent the afternoon demonstrating to Thomas, among other things, just how dexterous her right hand was. He kept still, unsure even now if any sudden move might spook her from his side. He told himself that he must still think of her as the elf queen—not quite human, not quite of this world, a rare faerie creature who often needed her own interpreter.

He thought he might be able to be such an interpreter.

"Tommy," she said.

"Mmmm."

"Do you think we shall have a son?" she asked.

He permitted himself to wrap his right arm around her and bring her closer, so now her nose was nestled just under his jaw.

"Of course, odds are, sooner or later," he said.

"And shall we name him Richard?" she said, sitting up, which although it meant her body was no longer pressed to his, it also meant he could open his eyes and look at her face and her breasts.

"I thought your father's name was Edward?" He was confused.

"Yes."

"And you know *my* father's Christian name was Thomas, also?"

"Yes?" She sounded confused, too.

He had found that it was best to ask the direct question.

"Why do you want to name our son Richard?"

She rolled her eyes at his idiocy and hit his chest lightly with her scarred palm.

"So, that we might be Tom, Dick, and Harry, of course!"

The only answer to this was to tickle her for a good five minutes until she was so limp with laughing that he could cover her body with his, hand to hand, arm to arm, chest to chest, navel to navel, leg to leg, and kiss her.

After his kiss, she caught her breath.

"I'm still not sure about this mouth kissing."

"No?" he said, only slightly bruised.

"However, I am willing to keep trying it, until I *am* sure." And then she kissed him back really, truly for the first time, her own kiss, her mouth partly open, brushing his lips with her lips and tongue. It was brief and sweet and wild and made him inhale sharply, and he began to feel himself stiffen again.

"But only with you, Tommy," she said seriously. "Nobody else."

He rolled onto his back, bringing her with him, and she quite naturally sat astride him and lowered herself onto his hardening member. He felt her warm, tight, silky wetness and marveled at her, shading his eyes while squinting in the bright sunlight. He thought he might see some subtle rounding of her lower abdomen, but surely it was much too early for that.

"I think . . . that's just fine," he managed to say.

"I thought you might." And then she did the two things that made him tremble—she looked in his eyes and she smiled.

Her long torso rose above him like the slender trunk of a birch tree. The hair on her head sprang loose and free and curled thickly down to her waist. She moved forward and up and back and down in the ancient rhythm, and as she did so, she blocked the light from the sun and he could move his hand away from his eyes. He encircled her ankles with his thumbs and forefingers. He leaned forward to kiss her breasts. And, then, he laid back and rested in her shade.

AUTHOR AFTERWORD: MATHEMATICAL AND HISTORICAL DETAILS

Fermat's conjecture is now known as Fermat's Last Theorem. Fermat's Last Theorem is as follows: there are no three positive integers x, y, and z that satisfy the equation $x^n+y^n=z^n$ for any integer value of n greater than 2. You may remember from math class that integers are whole numbers (like 102 and -17 but not 1.4 or 5/3). The equation $x^n+y^n=z^n$ might look familiar if n is 2. After all, $x^2+y^2=z^2$ is the Pythagorean theorem, if x and y are the legs and z is the hypotenuse of a right triangle.

It is true that Fermat wrote in the margin of a book that he had his own proof for the theorem but that he couldn't write it down because the margin was too small.

His proof was never found.

Most people believe that any proof Fermat had was likely incomplete or faulty in some other way.

After 358 years, Fermat's Last Theorem was proven in 1994 by Andrew Wiles, who did his PhD work at Cambridge and was a fifty-one-year-old mathematics professor at Princeton at the time of his solution (helping put paid to the myth that the best thinking in mathematics happens only when someone is young). Wiles had dreamed of solving the theorem since he was age ten.

There is a fantastic and fascinating fifty-minute documentary by the BBC on Fermat's Last Theorem and Wiles' work on solving it. You might be able to find it on the internet. (I did. Just Google *Fermat's Last Theorem BBC documentary*.) Even if you have no stomach for mathematics, it is worth watching the documentary at the 41 minute 30 second mark. You get to bear witness to a rare event: a reserved and cerebral man grappling openly with the emotion that comes with intellectual breakthrough.

For me, it is inspiring, soul-lifting, and devastatingly beautiful—an unparalleled demonstration of the sheer gorgeousness of humanity in an unexpected setting.

The neurodivergent Harriet Lovelock is an invention of my brain, but she was inspired by a female mathematician alive at the same time as the events of this novel. Sophie Germain (1776–1831) was French and almost entirely self-taught (her parents did not approve of a girl receiving an education). She wrote letters to the great mathematical minds of the time, and initially used the name Monsieur Le-Blanc ("Mr. White") and pretended to be a man.

Carl Friedrich Gauss, believed by many to have been one of the most influential mathematicians in history, wrote back to Germain after he learned she was a woman: "when a woman, because of her sex, our customs and prejudices, encounters infinitely more obstacles than men, in familiarizing herself with (mathematics') knotty problems, yet overcomes these fetters and penetrates that which is most hidden, she doubtless has the most noble courage, extraordinary talent, and superior genius."

Germain is thought to have been the first mathematician to undertake a master plan for solving Fermat's conjecture. However, she did not succeed (see above regarding Andrew Wiles). She died of breast cancer at the age of fifty-five.

MORE

REGARDING THE LOVELOCKS OF LONDON AND FELICITY NIVEN'S NEWSLETTER

www.felicityniven.com

Sign up for author Felicity Niven's newsletter at www.felicityniven.com/lovelocks to get news about upcoming romance releases and free books and stories. A **free** prequel novella ebook for this series (*The Lovelocks of London)* is available exclusively to newsletter subscribers. The novella ***When Ardor Blooms*** tells the love story of Harry's older sister Mary and how she comes to meet and marry the arrogant Viscount Tregaron during her first Season.

The next two books in the series *The Lovelocks of London* are *Clandestine Passion* (Catherine's love story) and *A Perilous Flirtation* (Arabella's love story). There is a sneak peek of *Clandestine Passion* included in this book after the "About the Author" section.

Finally, reviews can make a big difference to the success of a new series and an independent author. It would be lovely if you were willing to share your reaction to *Convergence of Desire* on Amazon or Goodreads.

Acknowledgments

My deepest and most fervent thanks to Molly Gunn, Jace Anderson, Sharon Gunn, Heather McLeod-Grant, Lisa Jones. You are the most generous of friends and readers.

A great deal of gratitude is also owed to my editor, Grace Bradley, and to Hannah Givens, sensitivity reader.

However, all errors are mine, and mine alone. Especially the mathematical ones.

Finally, a big hug to my family. I love you all. Thank you for everything.

About the Author

Felicity Niven is a hopeful romantic. Writing Regency romance is her third career after two degrees from Harvard. And you know what they say about third things? Yep, it's a charm. She splits her time between the temperate South in the winter and the cool Great Lakes in the summer and thinks there can be no greater comforts than a pot of soup on the stove, a set of clean sheets on the bed, and a Jimmy Stewart film on a screen in the living room.

facebook.com/felicityniven

twitter.com/FelicityNiven

instagram.com/felicitynivenauthor

CLANDESTINE PASSION

SNEAK PEEK OF BOOK TWO OF THE
LOVELOCKS OF LONDON

**Age and rank divide them. She will not face her
weakness. He will not embrace his strength. Never have
two people needed each other more.**

Wealthy widow Catherine Lovelock thinks she will never love
again. And then she meets James Cavendish, Marquess of
Daventry. A handsome, gray-eyed souse of a rake—and seventeen years her junior. He couldn't possibly be interested in
bedding her . . . or could he?

James Cavendish, heir apparent to the Duke of Middlewich,
has found a way he can serve his country and his future king.
But to do so, he must create a web of lies and destroy his own
reputation. And then he meets the one woman who can
unmask him.

For too long, Catherine and James have both played roles. She,
the good wife and mother. He, the dissolute rake.

The truth will come out when the clothes come off.

Chapter 1

Those eyes. Catherine felt a glow ignite in her abdomen. She lost sight of the gray eyes in question as the gentleman bowed over her hand. He touched the very tips of her gloved fingers, and a thrill raced from her hand up her arm to her head.

James Cavendish, Marquess of Daventry. She knew his reputation. Was he drunk right now? He must be. Wasn't he rumored to be inebriated at all times? She had seen him across a ballroom once or twice, but had they ever been introduced? Of course not. She would have remembered.

More than a hint of the boyish still about him. Slim. A wide grin. A ready laugh. Waves and curls of golden-brown hair that she longed to run her fingers through. A jaw with such clean, almost translucent skin that either he could not yet sport a beard or his valet was the best barber in London.

And those gorgeous, soft-gray eyes that crinkled at the edges when he laughed. As he seemed to do frequently. The thrill that had traveled from her fingers to her head was coursing downward, through her chest, joining the glow in her belly and spreading lower to her nether regions.

Stop it, Kate. You're a mother, a widow. You're no mooning girl, willing to pull up your skirts for the first set of handsome eyes you see. For a young souse of a rake. That part of your life is over, thank goodness. No one will ever have that power over you, ever again.

Lord Daventry straightened from his bow and looked down at her again with those very seductive gray eyes.

"Mrs. Lovelock, such a pleasure. As usual, the radiant Lady Huxley only attracts the most beautiful ladies to her ball. Like moths—nay, butterflies—to a flame, what?"

His voice was a light tenor. Melodious.

Lady Huxley, the very woman who had made the introduction, playfully struck Lord Daventry on his shoulder with her fan and moved off to tend to other guests. Lord Daventry swayed a bit with the tap of Lady Huxley's fan, off-balance for a moment before he recovered himself, saying "Upsidaisy" under his breath. Catherine almost put a hand out to steady him but restrained herself just in time.

Catherine wondered if Lord Daventry—James—had asked Lady Huxley to meet her. Possibly. Over the last few years, many gentlemen had been interested in meeting the widow Catherine Lovelock, and she had no illusions about why these men were eager for an introduction. She was one of the wealthiest widows in England. And she had leveraged that wealth to position her daughters and herself into the periphery of London's *ton*.

But perhaps James had asked for the introduction because he was interested in one of her unmarried daughters, Harriet or Arabella? Catherine suddenly felt vexed. A dissipated rake like Daventry had no business going after her daughters.

Not when she wanted him for herself.

Then what you're feeling is actually jealousy, isn't it, Kate? Are you jealous of your own daughters? Are you unbalanced, unhinged, undone?

"I must agree with Lord Daventry that there is an astonishing array of beauty on display in the room tonight. But, Mrs. Lovelock, you put the debutantes here to shame." This was from James' friend who stood next to him. "Would you do me the honor of taking this next dance with me?"

What was his name again? Oh, yes, Thomas Drake, the Right Honorable Earl Drake. Very tall like James. But with broad shoulders and chest, a head of dark hair. Dark rings under blue eyes, belying some fatigue, some worry nagging at him.

"Thank you, my lord," Catherine said and curtsied. "I am very pleased to accept your invitation."

Oh, why did it have to be Lord Drake and not the beautiful James who took her arm and led her to the floor?

She already thought of Lord Daventry as James. Utter foolishness.

Catherine smiled and curtsied as the music began. She felt sure her disappointment in her partner was not apparent to any of the onlookers. Her years on stage at the Theatre-Royal, Drury Lane had made her a mistress of dissimulation. She appeared just as she should—a respectable widow, flattered but not overwhelmed by dancing with a handsome young lord.

As they began the first figure of the dance, Catherine smiled and spoke to Lord Drake about the weather, the company, the astonishing beauty of the Elgin marbles. Finally, near the end of the dance, she felt she could safely query the earl and not betray her very real curiosity.

"Have you and Lord Daventry been friends for a long time, my lord?" she asked lightly, as Thomas Drake took her hand to walk down the row of fellow dancers.

"Oh, yes, since we were boys. His father, the Duke of Middlewich, and my father were quite good friends, you see."

Catherine remembered now she had read in her *Debrett's* that James was heir to the Duke of Middlewich. With a bevy of sisters, he was the duke's only living son.

But the Earl Drake seemed much older to her than James.

"You are of an age then, my lord?" she asked as she passed under his arm.

Thomas thought. "Yes, I'm just thirty, so that must mean Jamie is twenty-eight."

Not James, but Jamie.

Jamie.

Twenty-eight. Older than she had thought but still far, far, far too young.

Far too young. Far too silly. Far too drunk.

And she was far, far, far too aroused by him. Already, she

could hear the alarums in her head.

The dance was over, and Sir Francis Ffoulkes was at her elbow, reminding her that she had promised to dance the quadrille with him. Thomas Drake thanked her for his dance and bowed.

As Catherine moved into a new place on the ballroom floor, guided by Sir Francis' arm, she told herself that it was revitalizing to have a fancy for a man. Even a frivolous fancy for a frivolous young man like James. She was still a woman, after all. She wasn't dead to feeling.

But neither fancy nor its more wicked cousin full-blown obsession had a place in guiding her behavior. She had made that mistake in the past and never would again. She was stronger now and had an unassailable grip on the leash of her lust demon.

Unassailable. As in, no one could ever make her let go of it, ever again. No one.

As she turned in a full circle, she caught a glimpse of James on the perimeter of the ballroom for a moment, tall and slim in his tailcoat and breeches, running his fingers through his curly hair, leaning against the wall with his insouciant slouch. He seemed to be looking directly at her.

Her knees weakened and she stumbled. Sir Francis had to steady her.

Bloody blazes. She was in serious trouble if James could elicit this kind of reaction. In a ballroom. Fully dressed.

Very. Serious. Trouble.

James studied Mrs. Catherine Lovelock as she danced with Thomas. And then he sighed and turned away to search the throngs along the walls of the ballroom. There was a man he was looking for, a man with whom he meant to ingratiate himself, and the man should be here. But his gaze kept coming back to the dainty blonde dancing with his friend.

James was the one who had recommended to Thomas that he court Mrs. Lovelock. Thomas was in need of funds, quickly, and James had thought marrying a wealthy widow might be the solution to Thomas' monetary problems.

But he would not have suggested Mrs. Lovelock to Thomas if he had known. Known what exactly? Well, known that he, James, would feel upon meeting her that he already *knew* her. That quick uplift of the chin. That intelligent gaze that roamed over him. That quirk of the brows. That sparkle.

She reminded him so much of . . . what?

It itched at him. Itched at the back of his brain even as he felt the front of his groin also take notice.

Because, of course, she was more than just familiar. She was perfection, breathtaking perfection. Literally. He had felt the air leave his lungs as he had bowed to her. And then a true pink blush had tinted her face and the top of her bosom. That bosom. Generous and round and lush. Even though her husband had died some time ago, Catherine still wore the lavender of half mourning. But the current fashion meant even a modest widow's ball gown displayed a good bit of the top of a woman's breasts, especially when a man stood above her. And Catherine was tiny, so all men stood taller than she did.

James clenched his fists at his sides at the thought of other men, including his friend Thomas, gazing down at Catherine's chest. A fury briefly burned and then faded. He unclenched his fists and forced himself to grin. He was surprised at himself. He was well-known for being of such good temper, easygoing. Amenable to everything. What was this possessive passion for a woman he had just met? He had never felt such a thing before. Was he going mad? Wasn't he the one who had told Thomas to woo Mrs. Lovelock?

He watched Catherine smile at some remark made by Thomas.

Some men had all the luck. There were the well-favored men like Thomas, who just seemed more masculine than the average fellow. Given how James' own sisters swooned and flirted with his broad-shouldered friend, Thomas was clearly desirable to women. And would likely be so to Mrs. Lovelock.

And other men had a different kind of luck. James thought of the fortunate second and third and fourth sons who had been allowed—nay, encouraged—to fight in the now-ended wars against Napoleon. Although his father could have easily bought him a hundred commissions, James had not been allowed to go to war. While others had gone on to adventure and glory, James had been safeguarded in the name of the bloodline of the Duchy of Middlewich.

The Marchioness of Painswick walked toward him, her hips swaying, her dark hair in an impressive arrangement on top of her head, her dress scooping low in the front. He leered as he bowed over her hand and asked for a dance later. She arched an eyebrow, appraised him from head to toe, sniffed, and acquiesced. He did not fail to see the frankly salacious smile behind her fan as she walked away. It mirrored his.

James accepted a glass of champagne from a footman's tray and tried to keep from gulping it. He must keep his wits about him, yet he must be seen drinking. Just a sip, then. And then a bit of a stagger as he leaned up against the wall for support. Ah, the dance was ending.

And there, the very man he had been looking for, walked up to Mrs. Lovelock and took her elbow. His quarry for tonight, Sir Francis Ffoulkes.

Chapter 2

The Marchioness of Painswick lay on her bed, propped up on pillows, her long, raven locks spread out, naked except for her glittering ear bobs, her bejeweled rings, and a surprisingly plain gold locket hanging between her high, jutting breasts.

She stroked those breasts with her own slender fingers, up the sides and across the nipples, which hardened in response to the flick of her nails.

When the marchioness had begun the flirtation, she had had no idea it would take so long for an intimate tryst to come to fruition. She had waited a considerable time, and now she was going to enjoy herself. Immensely.

She had a view of the long, lean, golden-brown back of the young Lord Daventry across the room. Her husband was away on a shooting trip, and after months of looks and whispers and gropes in alcoves, she had finally managed to convince the gray-eyed rogue James Cavendish, Marquess of Daventry, to come to her bedchamber to consummate their long-standing dalliance. James was an absolutely delicious young man and well-known to be one of the most devilish of the rakes. And so amusing.

But he was supposed to be stripping off his own clothes, and he was taking far too long.

"Lord Daventry," she called to him. "Come to bed. I'll give you a night you'll always remember."

James drained his glass of claret and absent shirt, cravat, waistcoat and tailcoat, staggered across the room, still in his tight breeches and boots. She caught a glimpse of his youthful and tightly muscled torso at the foot of the bed before he obligingly crawled onto the mattress and over her body and began kissing her navel.

"No, not with your breeches and boots still on. Silly boy." She grabbed two handfuls of his thick, curly, golden-brown hair and lifted his head up.

He glared at her with gray eyes and growled. "I'm . . . no . . . shilly . . . boy." He seized both her wrists and lunged upward to pin them on the pillow above her head, his face inches above hers. He breathed wine fumes in her face.

"And if I want to ravish you, Marshens," his tongue was

thick and he seemed to have to force himself to speak clearly, "Marchioness, with my boots and breeches on, I damn well will, what? And that will be," he hiccoughed here, "a night *you* will always rebember."

James kissed her then, fiercely sucking and biting at her lips, and she responded eagerly to his savage and messy kiss, straining up to meet him, pressing her breasts to his smooth chest, pushing her own sex into his. He broke off the kiss.

"Shtay still," James commanded her, his voice harsh and raw, no doubt from the alcohol and the late hour. She obeyed him, small high-pitched moans escaping from her mouth. This was just the kind of play she liked.

He gathered both her wrists into just one of his hands, still keeping them above her head. As he covered her mouth again with his, he began to range his other hand freely over her body, kneading her breasts, pinching her nipples, and down to her sex where he pushed her legs apart roughly, tightly trapping one of her thighs between his two legs. Her excitement increased as he pawed at her slit but it was a clumsy touch, never quite finding the place where her *petite mort* lived.

She was finding it harder to stay still. She wanted, she needed, she desired in no uncertain terms that he touch her in *the right place*. She had guided boorish young men before, positioning their fingers on her hooded pearl, teaching them the rhythm, the pressure of the finger or tongue that brought her the greatest pleasure. Tonight, she was surprised that so infamous a lothario as Lord Daventry might need her tutoring. It must be the drink. But her hands were pinned above her head and James had covered her mouth again with his so she could not even speak. Her trapped position—at first, so arousing, so dangerous—was becoming tedious.

His hand that fumbled over her sex began to move more and more slowly. His body, leaning on her side, became more and more heavy and more and more slack. His head and mouth fell away from hers and his hand on her wrists relaxed. His fumbling hand stopped moving completely. His eyes were closed and he took a deep breath in and he . . . snored.

Unbelievable. She lurched to get from under him and he moved his hand from her mound to around her waist, snugging her into him, tightly. He was quite strong for a drunken, dozing, useless young man. She tried to break free again, batting at him with her hands, and again he squeezed her in more tightly, nuzzling into her, covering her with his body. She could not call for help. The servants would tell her husband about the young man in her bed. She was trapped until James woke up.

Sounds in the house. A dog barking. Her husband's dog. Her husband had returned to London. Early. Her eyes flew open. She lay on her bed alone. Naked. She heard her bedchamber door begin to open. She scrabbled helplessly, trying to find a dressing gown, a shawl, anything to cover herself.

"My dear," the Marquess of Painswick said from the doorway, "I should think your maid would find it shocking that you sleep naked atop the covers. A really filthy habit that you should try to avoid. Would you agree?"

The marchioness found a dressing gown on a chair and threw it over her shoulders and covered herself. As she did, she felt bare skin between her breasts. She grabbed at her neck, and her hands came up empty. The locket was gone. She looked at her right hand. A large sapphire ring was gone as well.

Her husband strode to the bed and plucked off a piece of paper that had been pinned to the brocade canopy.

"A note, my dear, left by whom I wonder? *Just helping you rebember*—surely, remember, yes?—*that turnabout is fair play.* What's this nonsense?"

The marchioness snatched the paper from her husband.

The note was signed with the letter *J.*

Made in United States
Troutdale, OR
01/05/2025

27649452R00202